A PLUME BOOK

LIFE WITHOUT PAROLE

CLARE O'DONOHUE is a freelance television writer and producer. She has worked worldwide on a variety of shows for Food Network, the History Channel, and truTV, among others. She is also the author of the Someday Quilts Mystery series.

Praise for *Missing Persons*

"O'Donohue puts her real-life expertise as a freelance TV writer and producer to good use in this sharp first in a new series. An absorbing read."
—*Publishers Weekly* (starred review)

"This is going to be a great series. Fans of Sue Grafton and V. I. Warshawski, and even Nancy Pickard's Truth trilogy, should try *Missing Persons*."
—iloveamystery.com

"Kate is funny and sarcastic . . . which makes her good company. This reader would welcome another appearance by the all-too-real Kate."
—*The Cleveland Plain-Dealer*

"Well written, with fascinating characters, multifaceted story lines, and plenty of action. A heroine readers can embrace." —*Midwest Book Review*

"A rollicking good start. O'Donohue exhibits a masterful approach with her classic red herrings and carefully placed foreshadowing as she drags us through the muckraking of yellow journalism. This will be a series worth collecting." —*Suspense* magazine

"Kate makes a great and sympathetic detective. Here's hoping there's more to come from her." —*The Parkersburg News and Sentinel*

"[4.5 stars.] It didn't take long for me to develop a girl crush on Kate Conway. With a fresh, sophisticated plot, snappy dialogue, cleverly placed red herrings, and a brisk pace, there isn't a single sentence in this novel that isn't thoroughly enjoyable." —*RT Book Reviews* (top pick)

Also by Clare O'Donohue

Someday Quilts Mystery Series

The Lover's Knot

A Drunkard's Path

The Double Cross

The Devil's Puzzle

Kate Conway Mystery Series

Missing Persons

LIFE
WITHOUT
PAROLE

A KATE CONWAY MYSTERY

Clare O'Donohue

A PLUME BOOK

PLUME
Published by Penguin Group
Penguin Group (USA) Inc., 375 Hudson Street, New York, New York 10014, U.S.A. • Penguin Group (Canada), 90 Eglinton Avenue East, Suite 700, Toronto, Ontario, Canada M4P 2Y3 (a division of Pearson Penguin Canada Inc.) • Penguin Books Ltd., 80 Strand, London WC2R 0RL, England • Penguin Ireland, 25 St. Stephen's Green, Dublin 2, Ireland (a division of Penguin Books Ltd.) • Penguin Group (Australia), 250 Camberwell Road, Camberwell, Victoria 3124, Australia (a division of Pearson Australia Group Pty. Ltd.) • Penguin Books India Pvt. Ltd., 11 Community Centre, Panchsheel Park, New Delhi – 110 017, India • Penguin Books (NZ), 67 Apollo Drive, Rosedale, Auckland 0632, New Zealand (a division of Pearson New Zealand Ltd.) • Penguin Books (South Africa) (Pty.) Ltd., 24 Sturdee Avenue, Rosebank, Johannesburg 2196, South Africa

Penguin Books Ltd., Registered Offices: 80 Strand, London WC2R 0RL, England

First published by Plume, a member of Penguin Group (USA) Inc.

First Printing, May 2012
10 9 8 7 6 5 4 3 2 1

Ⓟ REGISTERED TRADEMARK—MARCA REGISTRADA

LIBRARY OF CONGRESS CATALOGING-IN-PUBLICATION DATA

O'Donohue, Clare.
    Life without parole : a Kate Conway mystery / Clare O'Donohue.
      p. cm.
    ISBN 978-0-452-29782-1 (pbk.)
    1. Women television producers and directors—Fiction. I. Title.
    PS3615.D665L54 2012
    813'.6—dc23

                                        2011045703

Printed in the United States of America
Set in Adobe Garamond Pro
Designed by Eve L. Kirch

BOOKS ARE AVAILABLE AT QUANTITY DISCOUNTS WHEN USED TO PROMOTE PRODUCTS OR SERVICES. FOR INFORMATION PLEASE WRITE TO PREMIUM MARKETING DIVISION, PENGUIN GROUP (USA) INC., 375 HUDSON STREET, NEW YORK, NEW YORK 10014.

To Jack O'Donohue,
a gentleman and a scholar—and a darn fine brother.
You still owe me a quarter for each of the thousands of shirts
I ironed for you when we were growing up.

ACKNOWLEDGMENTS

These last few years have been a whirlwind of new experiences and new friendships. I am truly grateful to all the people who have e-mailed me, come to book signings, and help spread the word about my books. I'm thankful, too, to all of the talented people in the Mystery Writers of America and Sisters in Crime, without whose friendship, advice, and support, I would have felt completely alone. A special thanks to crime writer Libby Fischer Hellmann, for her generosity and kindness. As always, this book owes its life to my agent, Sharon Bowers, and my editor, Becky Cole, both of whom have an uncommon faith in my writing, or are just crazy optimists. In either case, I thank them both for helping me move forward on the series. Also Mary Pomponio, who does everything but kill to get publicity for my books, I owe you. To Liz Keenan, and the marketing and publicity teams at Plume, thanks once again for the efforts on my behalf. To Karen Meier and Tom Carroll, both of whom saw this book in early stages, thank you for tasting the cake when it was half baked. To Maura Sweeney, who always reads the acknowledgments, I thought it was about time you saw your name. To Kevin, for knowing the truth about me and keeping it to himself. To my mom, for helping with the final stages of the manuscript. To V, and my family, for always being there. And to my aunt Mary, I miss you.

LIFE
WITHOUT
PAROLE

One

I stayed by the window, hidden from view. The street was quiet and dark, but I kept watch. I'd been in this house, this stranger's house, for hours, waiting for the man who owned the place to come home. I was doing what had to be done. If I hadn't agreed to it, someone else would have. No one would get hurt. That's what I kept saying. But inside I died a little every time I had to do what I was doing today.

I waited another twenty minutes. Finally, I saw it. A car was pulling up. I nodded toward Jim, who was standing outside between two vans so no one could see. He lifted his camera and waited.

I watched the man get out of his car and walk toward the house. This was it.

Within seconds the door opened and the man walked in.

"Oh my God." He looked around the living room. "This is amazing."

His wife ran toward him and squealed with delight. "Are you sure?"

"Yeah, it's great," he said. "It's really . . . different. I wasn't expecting it at all." His wife kissed him, then looked around, beaming. The man looked toward me. "Is that enough or do you want more?"

"It's perfect," I said. "But, if we could just do it one more time. And this time, if you could be a little more surprised. You come home after a golf weekend with your buddies to a whole new living room. Completely redecorated. Your wife brought in a design team and a television crew. They've remade the place to be exactly what you've dreamed of and you had no idea this was happening."

"So I shouldn't mention the photos she e-mailed me last night?"

"The audience doesn't know you've seen photos," I said. "They've spent the last twenty minutes watching the host of our show pick out furniture and paint the walls this nice, um, reddish color."

The room had the feel of a college apartment. Hand-me-down tables from the husband's parents had been painted off-white, and pressboard shelves had been hung on two of the walls. Their cream sofa had been sloppily reupholstered with a wild floral pattern. And by "reuphol-stered" I mean cheap fabric was tucked around the cushions and sta-pled at the corners. Then the couch had been repositioned on an angle, which for some reason was supposed to make the room better for entertaining.

When I looked through the camera lens, the place looked amaz-ing. But when I looked at it in real life, I was depressed. I knew it would be about twenty minutes before the shelves started falling off the walls and the staples on the couch came undone.

"Our viewers," I said, turning to the equally unimpressed husband, "will be sitting on the edge of their seats, worried that you might not like the new rug or the mural over the fireplace."

"I don't really like it."

"You can paint right over it the minute we're gone."

This was my seventh episode of *Budget Design*, the Home Net-work's latest hit, and each time, I gave the same pep talk to the home-owners, who either hated the remodel or couldn't work themselves into the rabid dog/game show enthusiasm that the network wanted.

"Can we just do it again?" I asked. "Big surprise. Big enthusiasm. Lots of specifics. You love the drapes, love the rug, love the"—I pointed toward a weird sculpture our host had found at the Salvation Army—"you love whatever that thing is."

"It's just not what I wanted," he said.

I gave him my best fake smile. "The thing is, the sooner I get what I need, the sooner we're out of your lives. You and your wife have a nice DVD of your moment on TV, and a funny story to go with it."

He looked at his wife. "Next time you want to be on TV, leave me out of it." He walked out the door.

I crossed my fingers. Five minutes later, and exactly on cue, he was back. This time he was completely surprised, overwhelmed by the beauty of his new living room, and madly in love with his wife.

"We're done," I said. "And now you can have your living room all to yourselves."

As the cameras were packed up, I watched him throw the sculpture in the trash.

Two

Despite the stop-and-go Chicago traffic and the snow falling steadily against my windshield, I nearly fell asleep on the drive home. I hadn't been sleeping well lately, but it wasn't just tiredness. I was bored. For almost five months, I'd been working on decorating shows and makeover shows. Ugly rooms with a new coat of paint or ugly people in new clothes. One was just like the other, and I didn't care about any of it.

I'd always loved being freelance. It meant I could work on a documentary about a presidential election for three months, followed by two weeks on a golf special. After more than twelve years as a television producer, I knew everything there was to know about the history of the cookie and how the Wild West had gone from lawlessness to statehood. It was fun because those topics—most topics—were interesting to me. How to turn a perfectly nice living room into a piece of crap was not interesting to me. And it was beginning to show.

\\\

When I got home, I halfheartedly began cleaning up the living room. Sometimes, when I was working as much as I had been lately, I'd leave clothes, newspapers, and half-finished cups of coffee scattered around the entire house. I didn't love living like this, but it wasn't an indication of depression, anxiety, iron deficiency, or any other condition that my sister, Ellen, routinely diagnosed me with.

These days there was a lot of talk about my hair. Mixed in with the dark red were a few whitish gray strands, which Ellen swore needed to be taken care of by her stylist, who'd seen a picture of me and declared me "savable." The price of saving me was a hundred and seventy bucks a visit. I may have needed a little sprucing up, but I wasn't interested in being mugged by a hairdresser with a God complex. In a moment of compromise, I'd bought a box of Nice 'n Easy. It sat unused on my bathroom counter.

I moved all the clutter from the living room into the dining room and looked around. Little had changed in the past year. It was the same couch, the same rug, the same plant that was nearly, but not quite, dead. The painting of the couple walking down Michigan Avenue still hung over the fireplace. The bookcases were still littered with a combination of mass market paperbacks and hardcovers, a no-no according to the decorator/host of *Budget Design*. And there were still empty spaces where framed photographs had once been displayed. Except for my parents' wedding photo and a picture of my oldest nephew's confirmation, the whole house was devoid of any photographic evidence of my life before.

Before. I hated that word.

Frank had been dead for almost seven months. I'd canceled his cell service, donated his clothes, written thank-you letters to everyone who'd sent flowers, and gotten back to living, just like I was supposed to. And, as it turns out, living sucks. It's bills, and laundry, and boring television. The closest I've come to sex in nearly a year is watching a Viagra commercial. I'd read a couple of books on grieving that well-meaning friends had given me. Well, I'd read the covers. But they hadn't helped me feel better. They'd just made me less inclined to mention how I was feeling so my well-meaning friends would stop dumping books on me.

\\\

At seven thirty, as usual, my phone rang, and as usual, I debated whether to answer it before finally giving in and picking up.

"How are you?" Ellen asked in that way she had that projected both alarm and pity.

"Fine, Ellen. I was fine yesterday, and the day before, and the week before. You can stop calling me every evening to check up on me."

"I'm just . . ." I could hear her searching for the words that Dr. Phil would use. "I'm just concerned that you're not dealing with your life as it is now. I think you're wrapped up in what you wanted your life to be instead of what it actually is."

Given that I hadn't disclosed anything more personal to Ellen than the damage an ice storm had done to my gutters, I wasn't sure what she was basing that on. No, scratch that—I was certain. She was deciding what I should want for myself, then feeling sorry for me that I didn't have it. What she wasn't doing was asking me what I wanted. If she had, I would have told her what I wanted was an evening without a call from her.

"Are you doing anything tonight?" she asked. "Besides working?"

"I'm going to a movie."

"Oh." The surprise was evident. "With who?"

It's tricky when you lie to your sister. Ellen knew most of my friends, and I knew that tomorrow she would call whomever I named to casually ask how the movie was and therefore check my alibi. So it was too risky to name someone she knew.

On the other hand, using the name of a total stranger would only make her assume I was lying, and that would lead to another round of uninvited analysis.

"Vera Bingham," I said, grabbing the name of someone who was neither a stranger nor a friend. As soon as the words exited my mouth I knew I'd made a huge mistake.

"What?" She managed to extend the word to three syllables. "How can you? I mean after everything she's done to you? I don't understand you, Kate. I really don't." She just kept talking, asking me why over and over without giving me a chance to answer. And then the coup de grâce: "Does Mom know?"

"I'm almost thirty-eight, Ellen. I don't need Mom's permission to go to the movies."

"But why her?"

"If I said I was staying home, lying on the couch and eating take-out, would you feel better?"

"Much."

Now she tells me. "Well, then I was lying about Vera. I'm ordering Indian food and watching TV."

\\\

After we hung up, I plopped on the couch, reached for my cell phone, and dialed the Taj Mahal. One order of chicken tikka, naan bread, and vegetable samosa, my usual Tuesday night fare, arrived thirty minutes later. As I ate, I flipped through the television channels, trying to avoid any shows I'd worked on, and settled on *The Dick Van Dyke Show*, the one in which Laura accidentally reveals to the world that Alan Brady is bald. Then I fell asleep, waking up with drool falling from my mouth onto a couch cushion. I dragged myself to bed, leaving my teeth and face dirty, in case washing them would wake me up. Once in bed, I drifted in and out of sleep until roughly three a.m., when I woke up and stared at the ceiling until the alarm went off.

For the next five days, I did exactly the same thing. Only the menu was different.

Three

On day six, the phone rang. Lauren, the executive producer of *Budget Design*, offered another episode.

"It's a really cool couple in St. Louis who are having a baby. Our designer wants to turn the screened-in back porch into a nursery," Lauren said. "They have a guest room we could use, but, you know, blah! We've done a dozen guest rooms into nurseries. We're upping the budget to five hundred for the makeover because this will be totally different."

And crazy, I was going to add. But I didn't. Good television always wins out over good sense, especially on makeover shows. Protecting an infant from the weather wasn't nearly as important as having something new to show the audience. Not my problem, I reminded myself. I took a deep breath and said what I'd been rehearsing for days.

"I hate saying it," I admitted, "but I'm at the point where I just don't think I can bring you the kind of work you deserve."

Normally, I'd swear with my dying breath that I loved working on whatever show I was hired to do. Money is money. But I liked Lauren, liked working for her company. I didn't want to end a bigger relationship by screwing up on something like *Budget Design*.

I could hear her sigh, which made me immediately regret my choice. Maybe it wasn't so bad, I suddenly decided.

"On the other hand—" I started to say.

"We've just gotten the okay on a new show for Real TV," Lauren interrupted, saving me from a pathetic attempt at backpedaling. "It's a documentary on men who've committed serious crimes and now have long prison sentences. We want to focus on how they handle the reality that they will die in prison. How they spend their days, do they keep in touch with the outside . . . that sort of thing. We're calling it *Life Without Parole*." She took a breath and continued. "We've got two ex–death row inmates in Illinois that you could handle. I'm setting up interviews now. Do you know Dugan?"

"Only by reputation."

"Well, they're both at Dugan. The public officer is a woman named Joanie Rheinbeck. She isn't too thrilled about us being there, but we have the okay. I've talked to both inmates on the phone and they understand what we're looking for. It might be more up your alley, but I have to warn you, Kate, these are some hard-core criminals."

I'd given up working on true crime shows seven months ago, tired of being privy to the many ways human beings can destroy one another. But as it turned out, nothing is more exhausting than a job you hate.

"Kate?" Lauren asked. "You in?"

I was in, and a little giddy about it. I said yes quickly, before she could change her mind. After we hung up, I made coffee and waited for the e-mail Lauren would send giving me information on the show. When it arrived, I took a deep, cleansing breath and read through the backgrounds of the two men I'd be interviewing. I don't watch the creepy reality shows about drunken twentysomethings or spaced-out housewives, but I understand their success. We all like to feel superior to someone. And while it's easy to feel superior to guys serving life in prison, I was just excited to talk to two people who wouldn't care about throw pillows or paint chips.

\\\

Dugan Correctional Center, a large facility about thirty-five miles southwest of Chicago, is a legend in the prison system. Since its construction in the 1920s some of Illinois's most famous criminals, from Leopold and Loeb to Richard Speck, have spent time there. It's maximum security, with about half its population in for murder and the other half hitting all the other big felonies, from rape to kidnapping.

I'd been to a few prisons over the years as I worked on various true crime shows, but Dugan was different. In Dante's *Inferno* there's a line, "Abandon all hope, ye who enter here." It was written about hell, but by all accounts it could have been written about Dugan.

Driving up to it, I almost missed the entrance. I don't know what I was expecting, but what I found was a magnificent driveway with trees planted on either side and a large sign in stone that read, DUGAN COR-

RECTIONAL CENTER. It had an almost welcoming feel, until you got to the barbed wire fence and the armed guards. I wondered what the newly convicted felt as they were riding up to it for the first time, getting their last look at trees for decades, if not for a lifetime.

I parked in the visitor's lot and looked around for my cameraman's van. It wasn't there. My car sputtered even after the key had been removed. Frank and I had bought it more than ten years ago. It had nearly a hundred and forty thousand miles on it, a crack in the rearview mirror, and gunk all over the backseat from too many spilled cans of pop. But it still worked, and I wanted at least another year before I let it go.

After a few minutes of waiting, I got out. I felt a tightness in my chest. Winter in the Midwest is brutal: snow, cold, dark days, and long, empty nights. With six days still left in January, we had nearly two months to go before the first warm day, and it was getting to me.

I left my purse in the trunk of my car, as I'd been told to do, along with my gloves, hat, and scarf. Taking only my identification, I walked toward the visitors entrance. I nearly froze during the short walk, but the look of the place didn't exactly make me want to head inside. It was a long, tall, gray concrete wall with a battered steel door in the middle, dwarfed by the size of the building it allowed access to. There was a long list of rules posted just to the right of the entrance. Among them: no weapons, no fighting, and no drugs allowed on the premises. I wasn't reassured.

I'd been in several prisons before, but despite my familiarity with the routine, I always tensed up when I approached the door. Not that I was afraid. The security is tight and the inmates themselves are, at least in my presence, fairly agreeable. But there is an otherness about prisons, a place to hold the forgotten and unwanted. When I'd toured Alcatraz, long after it had gone from a penitentiary to a tourist attraction, I heard a story about how, on New Year's Eve, the inmates could hear the music and laughter wafting across the bay. I don't know if the story is true, but just hearing it saddened me. It was out there—life, happiness, celebration—but it was forever unreachable.

I let go of whatever momentary sympathy I felt. I've spent many years working on true crime shows, and I've sat with the mothers, fathers, husbands, and wives of murder victims. I've combed through the happy family photo albums and seen it all shattered in hundreds of crime scene pictures. I've breathed in the secondhand smoke of grief and anger that comes from losing a loved one to violence. I've lain in bed in the darkest hours of the night and wondered about the last moments of people I've never met, wondered if they were scared, if they understood what was happening.

Whatever excuses these guys at Dugan could come up with, it wouldn't be enough. Whatever stories they told about bad childhoods or love gone wrong, I didn't care. People were dead and they were responsible. It was nice, for once, to exploit people and feel good about it.

Four

I walked into the main building at Dugan Correctional and stopped at the long, high counter that took up most of the room. Behind it was a second metal door, which separated the inmates from the outside world.

"I'm Kate Conway," I said. "I'm here to see Joanie Rheinbeck."

The guard, a black man of about thirty, called Joanie's extension. After a few moments of friendly chatting, he hung up the phone and smiled. "You're the TV lady."

"I am. I'm waiting for my crew. They should be here any moment."

"No problem. I just need some ID."

I handed over my license.

"We have TV folks here from time to time. Network shows, cable crime shows. We even had a religious show in here once. Everybody wants to peek inside." He laughed. "But nobody wants to stay."

A woman in her midfifties entered the visitors area from the prison side. "Kate?" she asked.

"You must be Joanie. I'm really grateful you're letting us shoot here."

She walked toward me and I could see her sizing me up. She had the boxy shape and sensible shoes of a woman who doesn't want to remind anyone of her gender.

"I'm not sure it's a good idea to let these guys have media exposure," she said. "It tends to go to their heads. But the warden seemed to think it would offer people insight, so . . ." She bit the inside of her mouth. "The two men that are being interviewed have low points, but that doesn't exactly make them good guys."

"Low points meaning they haven't broken any rules in prison?"

She nodded. "Not recently. But they both kicked up a fuss years ago. I guess they're getting used to the place now."

"I read in the background materials that they've been here for about twenty years."

"Not just here. They've been transferred a bunch of times for issues at other prisons, but I think they'll be our guests for a while, if they behave," she said. "They were both on death row at Pontiac until the whole Ryan thing."

The "whole Ryan thing" was ex–Illinois governor George Ryan, who in 2006 had been convicted of corruption in a bribery case that had inadvertently led to the deaths of six children. But that wasn't the only thing he was famous for. While he was in office, thirteen death row inmates were released from prison after evidence proved them innocent of the crimes. The rest of death row had their sentences reduced. Ryan was either a hero or a cynical politician looking to remake his image, depending on your point of view.

Either way, a hundred and sixty-four people who had been facing the death penalty were now living a lifetime in prison without any hope of parole, which for some of these men could mean as much as fifty years behind bars. Since Ryan's successor had abolished the death penalty in the state, there would be a steady stream of people joining them for the long haul.

"I haven't spoken to either of them myself," I admitted, "but from what I gather, at least these two don't bother with a lot of talk about how they're wrongly convicted."

The guard behind the counter laughed. "We have a lot of those guys. I'd say at least half the population claims to be in here as a result of police incompetence or witness errors."

"And the other half?"

"They're bragging about crimes they didn't commit, just to look tougher," he said. "It's an interesting crowd."

"Well, that's why we're here," I told him. "We want interesting."

Just as I was running out of small talk, my crew arrived. Andres Pena, my cameraman, and Victor Pilot, who did audio, burst through the door with a cart full of equipment and a rushed explanation of why they were late. I waved them off.

"Let's just get in there," I said. "We have to stick to the prison's schedule, so set up quickly."

After being buzzed through three security gates, we were led into a small cement room painted a sherbet green. There was a cheap oil painting on the wall, a ship at sea in the middle of a storm. To the left, quite high up, was a window. There was a thick pane of dirty glass in the window, with no way to open it and bars across it.

"This is one of the conference rooms we have for when the inmates have meetings with their lawyers," Joanie said. "I hope this works, because it's all we have available today."

"Then it works." I smiled. "Thanks so much."

"Anything you need . . ." Her voice trailed off as she left the room.

"This is going to be a bitch to get any kind of depth," Andres said. "It can't be more than ten feet."

"Do the best you can, Andres."

He grunted. Then he walked around the room talking to himself. Even at forty, Andres had a strong, athletic build. He wasn't tall—we stood eye to eye and I'm barely five feet seven—but he seemed larger than his height. He was also the best cameraman I'd worked with in more than ten years as a television producer.

He stopped at the painting of the ship and tapped the frame. "You want the painting in the background?"

"No. We want it to look like a prison, not a Motel 6."

Andres looked around. "I guess I could position the camera so we get the corner of the window, in the wide shot. Just a hint of bars. The window is dirty enough that it's not going to let in too much light." As he talked, he moved equipment around, nearly dropping a C-clamp on Victor's foot; Victor had to jump to get out of the way. "Grab that Arri 300, will ya, Victor? Or are you going to stand around all day?"

Victor looked at me, and I shrugged. He wanted me to come to his defense. Victor was in his midtwenties, with a ninety-eight-pound-weakling body, a part-time career as a drummer, and a whole host of neuroses. He was deeply sensitive to slights, both real and imagined, despite the heavy metal clothes, tattoos, and piercings. But he was a good sound man and a decent guy, and he didn't deserve to have Andres take his bad mood out on him. Under other circumstances I would happily have told Andres to lighten up. But I needed my cameraman to get the lights up and ready for taping in thirty-five minutes. If it meant I had to live with a sulking Victor all day, then so be it.

We had a killer waiting.

Five

The information I'd been sent on Joseph "Brick" Tyler was pretty limited. He was forty-one, African American, had grown up on Chicago's West Side, and had been in and out of the prison system since he was fifteen. He was now in for life for the murder of three people in 1990, and while he had been known for prison violence in the first ten years of his sentence, lately things had been quiet and his record was clean.

When Andres was ready with the lights, after a tense and silent thirty minutes of prep, I asked Joanie to bring Brick to the room. He arrived a few minutes later, his hands cuffed in front of him. With a nickname like Brick, I was expecting a large man, something in the three-hundred-pound range. And while he was tall and muscular, he was surprisingly slim. His head was shaved and he had tattoos peeking out from the rolled-up sleeves of his blue denim shirt. He didn't look threatening, exactly, but he didn't look like a man to cross.

"I'm Kate Conway," I said, sounding warm and casual in hopes he'd be the same.

Brick slowly lowered his eyes, taking a long look at me from head to toe and then back again, resting his gaze on my breasts. I was dressed like the world's most conservative librarian: tan dress slacks, green cashmere turtleneck with a matching cardigan, and my hair in a pony-tail. But the outfit wasn't deterring his interest.

"If you want to take a seat," I said, "Victor, our sound man, will put a mic on you and we'll make a few adjustments to the lights."

Brick glanced behind him at the chair. He looked to the guard, who nodded. Brick, apparently satisfied with the situation, sat down and stared at each of us as Victor put a mic on him and Andres turned off the room's fluorescents, leaving us in darkness, and turned on the lights we'd set up for the interview. Brick blinked a little at the sudden brightness aimed at him, but he sat quietly. When we were ready for the interview, he held out his wrists for the guard to uncuff. As soon as he was free of the restraints, he reached out a hand toward me, and we shook. I could feel his strength and was, probably as intended, intimidated by it. People always assume a killer looks different somehow, and that being in the same room must be a frightening experience for me, but the killers I've met are normal, or seem to be. That's the only part that scares me.

"I'm Joseph," he said. "You should probably call me Brick, since I don't really answer to Joseph no more."

"Even with your family?"

"I don't talk to family. Not ones outside. I got a cousin here. But he calls me Brick."

"Okay, Brick it is. And I'm Kate."

He ran his eyes up and down one more time. "Okay. Kate. You got a bad temper?"

"Excuse me?"

He pointed to my hair. "Don't redheads have tempers?"

I smiled. "I do, when I don't get my way. But you've probably seen worse."

Brick looked over to Victor, who attempted to make himself look bigger. And failed. "You need a real man to handle that temper of yours."

"I manage, thank you."

"You married, Kate?"

I looked over at Andres, who signaled that he was rolling tape. I didn't want to mention that fact to Brick, since he seemed wary enough of the situation already. "What about you? Are you married?" I asked.

"No way. I never got trapped into that. I like my freedom."

I couldn't help but raise an eyebrow. It took only a second for Brick to catch on.

"Yeah." He rolled his eyes. "I guess I would have been better off with an old lady than with this shit."

"So what put you here?"

"You know that, or you wouldn't be here."

"Tell me your version of events."

"I ain't got no version. What happened, happened."

"You killed two men, and a seven-year-old girl named Tara Quinn."

His eyes got narrow. He leaned forward slightly. Behind him the guard tensed. "We don't need to talk about any of that."

"Actually we do, Brick. That's why I'm here."

I glanced toward the guard, who moved a few steps closer. In an interview it's important to bond with the subject. I put aside all judgment, even with convicted murderers, and look for common ground. I want that person to trust me so he'll give me the sound bites I need for the story. But it was clear it had been a long time since Brick had trusted anyone. If I was going to get a good interview from him, I realized it wasn't his trust I needed. It was his respect. And I wasn't going to win that if I backed down.

"You killed two men in a car and there was a child in the backseat," I said. "She got shot in the head and died three days later."

His eyes narrowed. "That's why I'm here."

"For three murders."

"For her murder. The other two . . . that was business. I was working that neighborhood; they were trying to cut into my business. They knew what would happen, so fuck 'em," he said. "But the girl . . . she didn't deserve what she got. I didn't expect her to be there. Who the fuck brings a seven-year-old on a drug buy?"

"Do you think about her?"

There was a moment's hesitation, then he laughed. "Yeah, baby, I cry in my pillow every night."

Dead end. I tried again. "You're kind of a tough guy, aren't you?"

"That turn you on?"

"Not really."

"What you like, sensitive types? Guys who bring you roses and write you love poems?"

"Does it matter?"

"Don't tell me you play for the home team."

Brick was having fun and I was not in control of the interview. Getting his respect was a long shot, at least for the moment. I took a breath and was about to start looking for another way to bond when I dropped my pen. I leaned down to get it.

"Hey, Kate, while you're down there you can suck my dick."

I grabbed the pen and sat up, staring him down. "Sorry, Brick, I don't put anything in my mouth if I don't know where it's been."

He laughed. I'd found my way in. "You're a smart-ass," he said.

"You're not the first person to tell me that."

"We all got survival instincts. You're a slim little lady. I guess you need a big mouth to survive in the bad world."

"What's your way to survive?"

"I pay attention to what people say and do. I notice things." He stopped looking at my chest and finally looked me in the eyes. "You avoided my question. That interests me."

"What was your question?"

"You married?"

Without meaning to, I looked down at my left hand. No ring. I'd forget sometimes that I didn't wear a ring anymore and be surprised, as I was now, that there wasn't one there.

"Not anymore," I said.

"Divorced?"

"A widow. My husband died about seven months ago." It sounded so simple when I said it to a stranger. But, of course, it wasn't simple.

Brick shifted in his chair. "Sorry about that."

I nodded. "Maybe we should start at the beginning. Why don't you tell me about growing up?"

"I'm not going to do that 'my mama didn't love me' shit."

"Did she love you?"

He pursed his lips and thought for a moment. "She was good. She looked after me and my little brother. It broke her heart when I got put in here. She wanted something better for me, and I let her down."

"Does she visit you?"

"She's dead. Heart attack three years ago. I didn't get to go to her funeral."

"Did she visit you?"

"Yeah. And my brother came for a while. But he don't bother no more."

"Where is he?"

Brick shrugged. "We're not in touch. He don't want to know me. I think he would of liked it better if I'd gotten the needle."

"That can't be true."

"Doesn't matter, me being dead or alive. If you ain't got somebody in the world that cares about you, then you already dead."

He stared right into my eyes on that one, with a certainty in his voice that made me feel more exposed than when he had been looking at my breasts.

Six

All documentaries are about voyeurism. Whether the subject is treasure hunters, aspiring models, or convicted killers, the role of a producer is to give viewers an intimate look at the real world of the subject's life. But the real world is dull. So a producer's job is to juice it up by "casting" each subject the way you would for a movie—a hero, a villain, the plucky underdog. . . . Some shows tape for weeks, waiting for one normally placid person to have a meltdown. And that's what you see on the show—not the twenty-two days of acceptable behavior, but the twenty-two seconds of yelling. It may not be accurate, but it's entertaining. Most shows don't have the time or the budget to wait, so the "characters" are created by asking whatever questions will get the answers the producer needs.

As I interviewed Brick I tried to figure out his role. He talked about his adventures as a child thug, recounting crimes with the same nostalgia I might have for family vacations. If I played it right, asked the right questions, he could be my unrepentant sociopath, or with other questions, my nice kid gone wrong. I realized as I was studying him, though, that he was studying me.

"I did some small stuff when I was a kid. I ran some dope, just holding it for older kids. You know, no cop gonna worry about a ten-year-old. Then I did a little stuff with guns. Holdin' on to them. Then I started with drugs," Brick told me.

"Taking them?"

"I never did that. Not really. Mostly I just sold it."

"You were in a gang."

"Everybody I knew was in a gang."

"What was your first arrest?"

He thought for a moment. "It was a piece I had that had been used on somebody. I thought it was cool to have something that had, you know, put air into a guy's head."

"How old were you?"

"I was fourteen, maybe fifteen."

"When was the first time you used a gun?"

"On somebody?"

I nodded.

"I guess after I got out of juvie. Maybe sixteen."

"What did you do?"

He smiled and seemed a little embarrassed. "Some punk kid called me skinny. I always had a little trouble keeping on weight. I eat, but I guess fat just don't like me. Anyway, he calls me skinny, so I capped him."

"You shot him?"

"Yeah. It's an Irish thing. You know that?"

"Capping someone?"

"Yeah. The Irish bad guys—what you call 'em, the IRA—they used to shoot people in the kneecap. Everybody does that, but they really made it an art form. I read that somewhere." He wagged his finger as if he were scolding me. "You should know that, Kate Conway. Ain't you an Irish girl?"

"My family came over a few generations ago, and from a different part of Ireland," I said. "You like to read?"

"Knowledge is power."

"Francis Bacon."

He smiled widely. "Yeah. You know that dude? He was cool. He was all into sensory experience leading to knowledge. You know that?"

"A little. Has sensory experience led you to knowledge?"

"First time I entered a woman, I learned everything I needed to know. Every time after I've just been chasing that high."

I laughed.

"You think it's bullshit," he said, "but the truth is we all just animals. I don't mean just the fools in here. I mean you, them"—he pointed toward Andres and Victor—"all of us. We dress nice and we learn shit, what fork to use, whatever. But we all just animals. And we at our best and our worst when we drop all the rules and live like what we are."

"Isn't dropping all the rules what put you here?"

"No, man. Living by the rules is what put me here. I was trying to do what was expected of me. But I was wrong. Sex, hunger, fear, love. Those are our instincts. Everything we do, good or bad, comes from that. I learned that you want to survive, you got to forget the rules and go with your gut." He punched his stomach hard enough that I heard a light thud, though he didn't seem to react. "You ever go with your gut, Kate?"

I ignored the question. "Doesn't that philosophy get you in trouble in a place like this?"

He gave me a half smile. "This place is a fuckin' lab experiment of animal behavior."

"So sex, hunger, love, fear . . . what do you do to satisfy those instincts?"

He laughed, a strong, deep laugh. "I see where you goin' with that. But I don't go that way. Men, I mean. Nothing against it. A dude has to survive any way he can. But it's not my way."

"What about hunger? Love? Fear? Are you into any of that?"

"I'm into all of it. I'm an animal, just like you."

Brick's intensity was starting to scare me, so good television or not, I looked for a change of subject. "You must like to read if you've found Francis Bacon," I said.

"Shit yeah. I read everything."

"Like?"

"Sun Tsu's *Art of War*. *Ulysses*. Dr. Seuss. I read everything I can get my hands on."

"So if I brought you some books . . ."

"You bribing me to get a good interview?"

"Will it work?"

He held his hands up in mock surrender. "I'm defenseless to the charms of a beautiful woman." He leaned forward. As he did, the guard moved slightly closer, but Brick waved him back. "Can I give you a list?" Brick asked. "I'm really trying to get my hands on a few things we ain't got in the prison library."

I smiled. I could feel myself relaxing, the tightness in my chest lifting. Whenever I sat in the darkness, with the slight hum of the camera in my ear and an interview subject who needed me to like him, I felt better. I felt in control.

"Tell me what you want," I said, "and I'll get it for you."

Brick leaned back. "Man, it's been a long time since someone said that to me."

Seven

You get anything useful from that asshole?" Andres slammed the door on the van after the last of the equipment was inside.

"I thought he was great," I said. "All that stuff about his early days in the gang and how we have to live by our instincts . . . I think that will help explain who he is."

"I thought he was supposed to talk about life in prison." Victor was standing back, out of Andres's way, since Andres's mood hadn't improved while we were shooting.

"He will," I said. "We have a few more shoot days with him."

"And he can always call you for a late-night chat," Victor said.

"I have to give them a number, just in case. You know that."

"Don't answer the phone if you're alone," Andres said. "You want someone with you in case he says anything."

"Andres, I'm a big girl. Besides, it's a throwaway."

Most producers use temporary pay-as-you-go cell phones for shoots that involve gang members, mobsters, and inmates—pretty much anyone you wouldn't want to show up on your doorstep unannounced. It's comforting to know once the shoot has ended, you can toss the phone and lose touch completely.

"When do we see this guy again?" Andres asked.

"Next week," I said. "And hopefully the other guy will recover from whatever his problem was."

After the interview with Brick, Joanie had come in to tell us that Tim Campbell, the other inmate I was supposed to interview, was ill. If we wanted him, it would have to be another day.

Andres lit his cigarette and threw the match on the ground. "Don't you think it glamorizes these guys, turning them into a documentary? Some stupid kid is going to think this loser is hard-core."

"He hasn't gotten laid in twenty years," Victor said. "What kid is going to want to step into those shoes?"

"The way he was leering at Kate I thought he was about to break his dry spell." Andres looked at me. "Didn't that creep you out?"

I laughed. "I had you two and a guard in the room. What was he going to do?"

"Nothing there," Victor said. "But I can pretty much guarantee he'll take the image of you back to his cell for later tonight."

"And on that charming note, I think I'll say good night," I said. "We meet back here in eight days."

"My band is playing tomorrow night," Victor said. "We've got a new sound we're trying out. We're thinking maybe we'll take it on the road this summer if we can get the scratch together."

"I don't think I can make it." I'd been to see three of Victor's bands, all variations on heavy metal with punk or rap mixed in. Another evening of loud, indecipherable banging was out of the question, even for a friend.

"So until we get together for work next week," Victor asked, "how are you going to fill your time?"

"I'll figure out something."

"You're spending too much time alone."

"What is it with everyone?" I asked, but I didn't really want an answer. "I'm fine."

Andres dropped his cigarette on the ground next to the discarded match. "He's right, you know. It's not healthy."

"When you stop smoking, Andres, I'll start socializing."

"You could call Vera. She asks about you." Victor said it to be helpful, and like most helpful suggestions, it was the wrong thing to say.

"Eight days," I said again, and headed to my car.

\\\

By the time I got home it was just after five o'clock and already dark. I microwaved a chicken potpie, ate about half of it, and wrapped the rest up for the next day's lunch. I changed into sweats and a T-shirt and climbed into bed to watch TV. There was nothing on. I flipped past a reality show about a family with twenty kids in which all anyone did was scream, spent a few minutes watching a detective show, and then settled on CNN. Bad news everywhere. After twenty minutes I clicked off. It was only seven o'clock but I was seriously thinking about going to sleep.

Just as I was about to turn off the light, my phone rang. I assumed it was Ellen calling early, but it was a number I didn't recognize. "Yeah?"

"Kate Conway?" A man's voice.

"I'm not interested in buying anything—"

"I'm Ralph Johnson, the executive producer of a new show on the Business Channel," he said. "Sorry to call in the evening but I'm in L.A., so we're still on the clock. I'd like to talk to you about producing something for us."

"Okay." I was wary. Good-looking men, winning lottery tickets, and jobs don't just show up unannounced. "How did you get my name?"

"You come highly recommended."

"That's nice to hear. From who?"

"Actually, I've seen a lot of stuff you've done. And we're working on this show I know you would really like. It's a new business reality show. It's totally different. It's about the struggles of opening a restaurant. It's called *Opening Night*."

He was talking fast, but the whole "totally different" thing was nonsense. I'd seen half a dozen shows about opening a restaurant, and I doubted anything the staid and traditional Business Channel would air could ever be defined as different, but a potential new client wasn't something I could just throw away.

"When do you want to start shooting?" I asked.

"Next Wednesday."

There it was, the catch I'd been waiting for. Booking a producer this late meant Ralph and his production team were either disorganized, cheap, or a nightmare to work with.

"I'm actually booked on something right now," I said.

"With Ladies Productions." He sounded confident now. "I talked with Lauren. She loves you."

"It's mutual," I said. "So she told you I was working for her."

"But she said your next shoot was late next week. What we're doing is just a day here and there for the next three months. We can work around your schedule."

Tempting, but my gut was telling me to pass. "I appreciate the offer, but there are a lot of great producers out there."

"The investors are some of the top people in Chicago business. They're skittish about letting us in on the behind-the-scenes of their opening, so I really need someone who is completely professional," he said. "And, to be honest, they're also media savvy. Unless I have a pro in there, I'm just going to get back nothing but canned PR sound bites that will completely alienate my audience."

Working with "media savvy, top Chicago businesspeople" sounded like a total bore, giving me one more reason to walk away. "I appreciate the offer, but—"

"I'll pay your day rate plus twenty-five percent."

I blinked, taking more than a few seconds to let it sink in. A television production company was willing to pay me more than I was asking. I knew it was a mistake. Every ounce of my body, every day of more than a decade's worth of experience was telling me it was a mistake. But twenty-five percent more than my day rate was the urban myth of freelancing.

"Fine," I said. "But I invoice weekly and expect to be paid within fourteen days." That part was improvised. I usually invoiced at the end of the job and prayed I'd get a check before thirty days. Not an easy miracle, since several production companies seem to think that paying anytime before the next ice age is fine.

"Not a problem," he said without missing a beat. "I'll e-mail you the details." Then he hung up, without giving me a chance to change my mind.

\\\

"I don't actually know him," Lauren confessed the next morning when I reached her. "He's sort of a friend of a friend. He called me asking about you."

"Looking for a recommendation?" I asked.

"Not really." I could hear hesitation. "He seemed more interested in your schedule than your qualifications."

"So you didn't recommend me?"

"Oh, God, of course I did—"

"No, Lauren, what I mean is he said that he had heard great things about me, but he obviously heard them before he called you," I said. "So now I'm wondering who."

"You're great," she said. "I'm sure he heard it from lots of people."

"But you don't know anything about him?"

Silence, then: "I'm sure he's not a creep. The Business Channel wouldn't hire him if he were. You could do an Internet search if you're worried."

"That's a good idea."

It was such a good idea I'd done it already, about ten seconds after I'd spoken to him. Ralph Johnson had worked on shows for the Business Channel for about five years, had won several Emmys, and had previously worked at ABC News. That didn't help much.

All I knew was that someone had given me such a good recommendation that the Business Channel was willing to pay extra to get me. I should have been glad to hear I had a good reputation, but instead it made me nervous.

Eight

Five days later I walked into the abandoned bank that was being transformed into a high-end restaurant, and came face-to-face with my benefactor.

"Kate!" She rushed toward me with arms outstretched, putting them down only at the last minute. "Sorry, I forgot you don't like hugs."

"Vera?" I didn't even bother hiding my surprise. "What are you doing here?"

"I'm an investor in this restaurant we're opening," she said. "Didn't you know that?"

If I'd known that, I wouldn't have taken the job.

"No," I said. "I wasn't given a list of the investors."

"I want you to meet someone."

And with that she ran off in the opposite direction. I hadn't seen her in months, but she looked and acted exactly the same. She was still earth-mother enthusiastic, with her graying hair a little longer than it had been the last time we'd seen each other. She was wearing an expensive cashmere sweater, but with a "This old thing?" casualness that comes from growing up with money.

Over the past six months or so, she'd left me a few messages, which I'd ignored, and sent me a Christmas card, which I'd thrown out. I didn't dislike her, exactly. She was a nice person. But she was Vera. And I didn't want a playdate with her.

"Kate, this is Doug Zieman," Vera announced as she came hurrying back to me. "He's also one of the investors, and he's, well, my new boyfriend." She blushed. Forty-one years old and she blushed.

I extended my hand. "Good to meet you, Doug. I'll be interviewing you, and getting footage of your meetings and the construction, as you and your partners put together the restaurant."

He gave my hand a weak shake. Not a good start. He was closing in on fifty, I guessed, shy, a few extra pounds, with a dull, plump face and a slight twitch in his left eye. But he smiled at Vera with genuine affection. For reasons beyond my grasp, I was happy that he seemed to care about her.

"Vera really wanted you on this project," he said. "She said you're the best."

I glanced toward Vera. "She's very insistent."

"So, how do you guys know each other?" he asked.

Vera's blush was stronger now. "She's Frank's widow."

Doug's eyes widened. He coughed. "Oh," he said. "I . . ."

"Yes," I said, half to get through an awkward conversation, half to prolong it. "My husband of fifteen years left me for Vera, and then died four months later."

Doug turned to Vera. "I thought you were together for almost a year," he said.

"They were." I walked away, leaving him to work out the overlap. I went back out to the street and found Andres and Victor unloading the van. Vera had apparently insisted on them as well, although I was the only one being paid more than my rate. I guess she knew I'd be a harder sell. But, it bothered me to admit, she also knew I could be bought.

"Hey, Katie," Victor called out. "Beautiful morning, isn't it?"

"It's twenty-eight degrees. Wind chill off the lake puts the temperature at thirteen."

He smiled. "I love winter." He grabbed the equipment cart, and with a surprising strength for his skinny frame, lifted a large light box onto the cart with what looked like minimum effort.

I walked to Andres, who was fiddling with his camera settings at the front of the van. "What's with Victor?"

"He probably got laid," Andres said.

I laughed. Victor liked to fill us in on his conquests, while Andres and I quietly made side bets as to which were fictional and which were true. My guess was running about ninety percent fiction.

Vera came outside and she and Victor hugged. She waved to Andres, who waved back, then she and Victor went inside, arm in arm. It was dumb to feel jealous, because it wasn't as if Victor and Andres were going to leave me for Vera.

Andres's voice softened. "Sorry about the other day, by the way."

"No worries, Andres. We all have bad days," I said.

"It's Victor. He was late getting to my house. He did the same thing with another client. It makes me look bad, showing up late for jobs."

"Have you tried talking to him?"

"Have you ever known Victor to listen?"

"Not so far, but he's a good guy and he wouldn't want you to look bad, so maybe if you said something . . ."

"Maybe you should talk to him," Andres said. "You're the client."

"I don't think I want to get in the middle of this."

He shook his head, signaling an end to that conversation. "You up for this?" He pointed in the general direction of the restaurant.

"Vera? I suppose."

"She's a nice lady, really, once you get past the affair," Andres said. It was hard for him, I knew. Out of loyalty to me, he wanted to dislike her, but Vera was hard to dislike, even for me. Though I certainly tried.

In my heart I knew that Frank and I had screwed up the marriage long before Vera came into the picture. Maybe we could have found our way back to what had once been something wonderful, but instead he found her. It didn't matter anyway, I reminded myself for the hundredth time. He was dead. There was no point in indulging in what-ifs.

Since his death, Vera had somehow pushed her way into my life and into the lives of Andres and Victor. Not in a bad way, not intentionally. She was more like a Saint Bernard jumping on his owner because he's happy to see him. Without malice, but overwhelming and vaguely destructive nonetheless.

"I feel like I sort of inherited her from Frank," I said.

"She likes you," Andres said. "And I think she feels you have something in common, in that you both loved him."

"I'm aware of her thought process."

"At least this beats spending time with killers," he said.

"The jury's still out on that one."

\\\

An hour later, I was even less sure. Doug gave us an on-camera tour of the place. The bamboo floors were in and a large bar had been constructed at the side of the restaurant, but the walls needed painting, and there was no sense of what the finished product would be. Doug talked a lot about high-end fabrics and expensive finishings, but so far it was just big, nearly empty, and full of dust.

"This will be ready in three months?" I asked.

"Six weeks," Doug corrected me.

"But Ralph Johnson at the Business Channel said three months."

"That was our original plan, but we've decided to move up the opening. We want the place to start making money for us, and we think it will be ready."

I looked around. "There isn't anyone here working. No carpenters, electricians, plumbers. How are you going to be ready if you don't have construction going on?"

Doug glanced toward the ground and then back at me, a smile widening his dull face. "We called off the crew for today so as not to interrupt your work."

"That's very nice of you, but you don't need to do that. A big part of why we're here is to get footage of the construction. We want to see men working. We want to see progress. So next time—"

He waved me off. "Absolutely. We'll do whatever you need."

I pulled out a stack of forms I kept in my tote bag and handed them out to the investors. "That's great, because I do need something. Everyone needs to sign one of these. It's a release form allowing us to show you on camera."

Everyone signed quickly, except an investor named Roman Papadakis, who carefully read the document. "In all media, in perpetuity," he read. "Sounds ominous."

"It's just standard, covering all bases," I explained.

"Can I cross out some of these conditions?"

"No, it's what the channel wants," I said. "If I don't have your signature I can't use you on camera."

Roman grunted and made a show of how he would prefer that his lawyer see the document, but when I didn't budge, he signed. He may have muttered "bitch" under his breath, but I wasn't sure, and I didn't care.

Doug looked up. "For my address, can I write in the address of the restaurant?"

It didn't really matter. Release forms usually went to some dark box in a dark room, never to be seen again, except of course for the one in a billion chance that there was a question about whether someone had given permission. But just in case this was that one in a billion, an unfinished restaurant was a sketchy address. "I'd prefer you give your home address," I told him.

Doug nodded and complied without another word. I watched as Vera slipped her hand into Doug's. He looked around at the others, seemed to blush a little, but he didn't move away. In fact, the two started whispering to each other, smiling brightly with each exchange. It was sickening, but I was a little envious too. She seemed to stumble into happiness wherever she went.

\\\

After the tour, the investors gathered together with coffee and crois-sants to discuss their vision for the restaurant. Since the whole thing was being faked for our camera, the conversation was stilted and forced. After the fourth or fifth time someone mentioned how the res-taurant would be the "it" place for "hip" Chicagoans, I started to tune them out. Just like with my prison interviews, I was trying to cast this group. Reluctantly, I decided Vera would be the sweet one, but that was only because the others were all in the running for the villain. At least it didn't look like I'd have to wait long to get the bitchy, self-involved sound bites that make for good TV.

Ilena Papadakis, Roman's wife, positioned herself so that she was directly in front of the camera. "The important thing," she said, for at least the third time, "is that we're not the place for people from the suburbs celebrating their tenth wedding anniversary. We're for people who expect, who *get* the finest every day. That's who we are." She said the final sentence slowly, for emphasis.

I could see Victor rolling his eyes as he held the boom mic inches above her head, and I agreed with the sentiment entirely. But it seemed to me that we were in the minority. Only Vera looked embarrassed. There were three other investors—Doug, Roman, and Erik Price, the restaurant's manager—and they all nodded their heads at Ilena's statement.

Ilena continued her one-woman crusade to separate the "elite" from the rest of us. She was attractive, in a Botoxy kind of way. She was maybe fortysomething, pencil thin, with expensive-looking rings on three of her fingers and a pair of drop diamond earrings so large I wondered if they would tear her ears. Her husband was a perfect fit for her. Big in every way, older, tall, fat, larger-than-life personality, Roman interrupted her frequently with statements about how much everything would cost, how no expense would be spared.

"I've been to the top places in the world," he said at one point, running his hand over his bald head. "Rome, London, Tokyo, Sydney . . . I've seen the best. I want this place to top them all."

Once again the others nodded. Vera, though, kept glancing toward me as if I might disappear. She seemed to have figured out that, on a good day, I had a limited tolerance for rich people flaunting their wealth. And this wasn't shaping up to be a good day.

"The thing we have to keep in mind," Roman continued, "is that we have to *be* the image we want to project. When our customers see anyone connected with this restaurant, they have to see the embodiment of sophistication."

"Absolutely," his wife chimed in.

I looked at my watch. Two hours until lunch.

"Twenty-five percent over my rate," I muttered to myself, but even as I said it I decided Andres was wrong. I'd rather spend time with anyone, even killers, than this crowd.

Nine

In the afternoon, I sat next to Andres's camera while the restaurant manager was telling me about his years in New York and Paris, working in kitchens of restaurants I'd never heard of but clearly was supposed to be impressed by. "But you aren't a chef anymore," I said.

"I was never a chef," he said. "I was a line cook and for a small window of time, a sous chef. I realized my talents were front of house. I look better in Armani than in kitchen whites." He laughed, indicating it was meant to be a self-deprecating joke, but he lightly brushed the lapel of what I guessed was an Armani suit, dark gray.

Erik Price was, by my guess, about thirty-five, slightly thinning on top, with hair cut almost military short. He had a day's growth of beard, an affectation to suggest he worked too hard to care about his appearance, except he was meticulous in all other aspects of his grooming, down to his perfectly manicured nails.

When he saw me looking at his hands, he pointed to his watch. "You like the Rolex?"

"It's nice."

"Would you like one? I have a friend who sells only the finest pieces. You can use my name to get a discount."

"A little out of my price range, even with a discount," I said. "And I don't wear a watch anymore. I use my cell phone for the time."

He smiled. "You should allow yourself the finest things available, Kate. What else is life for?"

"People."

"True," he said. "And some of them deserve a watch like this one."

"Only some of them? You don't think everyone should have a few luxuries?"

He laughed. "That word has been watered down so much. Luxury used to be for kings and the royal court. Now you can get so-called luxury goods with designer labels at discount malls. It's unfortunate. Really, it is. I think that people who are, for lack of a better word, *superior* ought to have an exclusive access to the best."

"What makes you superior?" I asked. "Were you born to the royal court?"

He laughed. "I was born . . ." he hesitated. "I was born with vision and ambition, and I earned a place at the table."

"And the rest of the world?"

"There's always a need for waiters and coat check girls."

I smiled. It's so wonderful when people make asses of themselves on videotape. "So, tell me about this restaurant you're opening," I said. "What are you calling it?"

Erik paused, then made a sweeping gesture toward the construction site that would soon be a high-end eatery. "Club Car."

"Like in a train?"

He rolled his eyes. "Like in the elegant trains of yesteryear, when people dressed for dinner. Do you know who Lucy Rutherford was?"

"Franklin Roosevelt's mistress," I said. I'd like to say I knew it from my extensive personal reading, but as with everything else I know, I'd learned that fact from a show I'd worked on—a bio on the Roosevelts' marriage I'd done a few years before.

Nonetheless, he was impressed. "She said in a letter to a friend that when her stepson returned from World War Two, he came down for dinner in a shirt and casual slacks. She asked him to put on a tuxedo, because that's how they always dressed for dinner before the war. He told her the world had changed, and people no longer cared about such things." Erik shifted in his chair. "Well, I care about such things. I care about doing things properly. I want Chicago to care."

"How will you make them care?"

"We're not just going to serve food here. We're going to transport people to the nineteen thirties, to the Stork Club, or Chez Paree. More than a restaurant, a nightspot where elegance is the key," he said. "If we give people a stylish place to dine, to listen to music, to dance, I think they will care about bringing back some of the sophistication we've lost as a city, and as a country."

"We have elegant restaurants in Chicago," I pointed out. "We have world-class restaurants."

"Yes, we have great food here. I won't quibble with you about that. At best we can hope to compete with Charlie Trotter's and Tru in terms of the food, but what I'm talking about is something else entirely. Somewhere along the way it got very difficult to tell the adults from the kids. We all wear blue jeans and baseball caps. We all listen to our iPods and update our status on Facebook. Sixteen or sixty, we all sort of seem the same."

"And you don't like it?"

"Do you?"

"I haven't really thought about it."

He took a breath, closing in on the final sentences of an impassioned speech I sensed he'd made dozens of times. "I want a place that separates the everyday from a world of excitement and romance. Where everyone in the room is *somebody*, even if outside this restaurant they're just accountants, and lawyers, and . . . TV producers. At Club Car, everyone will be special, because they'll be part of something special."

"I'm sold," I admitted. At least that part of his vision sounded appetizing. "If you can create that—"

"I *am* creating that, Kate. I've been envisioning this for years and I know Chicago is ready for it."

"So it's your vision, but not your money?"

He leaned back. "That's not really how the business works. We're doing a restaurant that will cost more than two million to construct, and have operating costs in the hundreds of thousands a year. It requires the resources of a group of people who share the same goals, and have the patience to wait for a profit."

"Which takes how long?"

"Months . . . years . . . maybe never." He laughed. "That's why you have to love it."

\\\

Two hours later, the day was finally, thankfully, over. As we packed up the equipment, I spotted Erik in the corner chatting with Ilena, moving his mouth just inches from her lips. She giggled and swept her hair away from her neck. Clearly he found time for more than the restaurant. Not that Roman seemed to care. He'd cornered Doug and Vera and was talking loudly about money.

I waited until the last of the lighting equipment was loaded into Andres's van before heading to my car. It was almost a clean getaway, except just as I was opening my car door, Vera broke away from Roman and came to me.

"Come to my house for dinner tomorrow," she said. "Seven."

"I have plans."

"No you don't. Victor said you've been spending all your time alone."

"How would he know that?"

"He knows you. He's worried. So is Andres."

"And you're the cure?"

"I'm a friend, Kate," she said. "And I have to talk to you about something very important. I need your advice."

"I'm not really that good with advice," I said.

"Sure you are." She smiled a little, certain she had me. The same way Frank would smile on the rare occasions when I didn't have a comeback. It was a victory smile. Before I had a chance to think of a sarcastic remark, she walked away. "See you at seven tomorrow night," she said, as she disappeared into the restaurant.

Ten

Here's something about myself I don't understand. I have no problem lying to grieving widows to get a good interview, but at seven o'clock the next night, I parked my car in front of Vera's Gold Coast brownstone, even though I didn't want to, and headed up the front stairs, a bottle of wine in my hand. I could have called her and canceled. I could have not shown up. But here I was. I can be a real jerk when I want to be, but for some reason I don't like being impolite.

I knew at that very minute Ellen was calling my house and getting my voice mail, picturing me on the couch with an empty bottle of sleeping pills dropping out of my dead hand; she would be filled with panic and dread. So at least there was an upside to seeing Vera.

"Pinot noir, my favorite," Vera said when she answered the door. Her two greyhounds, rescued from a life of racing, nudged at me as I walked inside. She took the bottle from me and we walked back toward her kitchen. "I made pasta," she said. "I wanted to keep it casual."

"Is pasta casual?"

She laughed. "You don't let anything go without challenging it, do you?" She motioned for me to sit at the kitchen table. "I won't ask how you've been because you probably wouldn't tell me, but I hope you're okay and not, you know, missing Frank too much."

"I'm fine."

"Of course you are," she said. "You're so strong. You can handle anything."

It wasn't true, but with all the concern coming toward me lately, from Ellen, Andres, and Victor, it was good to hear. Even if I had to hear it from Vera. "You seem to have moved on nicely," I said.

"Doug sent me those." She pointed toward a vase on the kitchen table, with a dozen long-stem red roses displayed in it. They were nice. Cliché, but nice. Next to the vase was a card. Vera turned toward the stove and started plating the pasta, so I took a peek. It read, "I'm crossing out #42." I dropped the note back in its spot just as Vera turned around.

"He's so sweet," she said. "And we agree on just about everything."

"Is he single?" I asked.

She blushed. "Divorced."

"As long as you don't get yourself hurt." The words escaped my mouth before my brain had a chance to stop them.

Vera smiled a little, but she had the grace not to pounce on my temporary interest. She put the pasta, a large platter of mushroom ravioli, on the table. She'd laid out quite a spread. Aside from the ravioli, there was a salad, garlic bread, and a bottle of expensive-looking red wine. Vera moved that bottle off the table and replaced it with the one I'd brought, pouring each of us a large glass. I dug into the ravioli and searched for conversation that did not include a discussion of how I might be feeling these days.

"Did you make this?" I asked. "It's really good."

"Yeah, thanks." She brightened. "I took a pasta-making class about a month ago. I called you to see if you might be interested but . . ."

"I've been working a lot."

She picked up a piece of ravioli but let it sit on her fork. "It's all a little weird, us having dinner. I'd understand if you felt awkward."

"I don't feel awkward," I lied.

"Well, I know how hesitant you've been to stay in touch. In your position I would probably be the same, I guess. But I like you. I don't have a lot of friends, and I consider you a friend," she said. "If it hurts too much to be around me, though . . ."

This was my out. Anyone could understand why I wouldn't want to be the BFF of my dead husband's girlfriend. It was chatting with her over pasta that was a little hard to explain. And yet, instead of bolting for the door I took it as a challenge. My leaving would be tantamount to admitting Vera's role in Frank's life still bothered me. Which, of course, it did. But that was my business.

"I really think you're giving yourself a greater role in the demise of my marriage than you deserve," I said.

Vera sank a little in her chair and spent the next few minutes chewing quietly on her salad. "I just can't forgive myself for having hurt you."

I finished off my glass of pinot noir and poured myself another, nearly finishing off the bottle. "We seem to be running low on wine."

She jumped up and grabbed the expensive bottle, setting it on the table in front of me, just in case I needed it. Which I would. Soon. She was quiet again for a while, but when she did speak, thankfully she'd found a new subject. "Andres said you're working on something at Dugan Correctional. That's very brave of you."

"It's not like I'm spending the night there."

"But you have to listen to all those sad stories," she said. "And get to know people who've wasted their lives, hurt so many others. It's such a dreary place to spend your time."

"I've only met one of them and he's pretty hard-core, but I think he has an interesting story to tell."

"You enjoy talking to him?"

"Well, he doesn't have Armani suits, or Rolex watches, or cater to the in crowd."

She rolled her eyes. "That was awful. Erik's interview was just embarrassing. That's why I was so glad you were free to work on the show."

"I wasn't exactly free. You got those guys at the Business Channel to pay me more than my usual rate."

"The people at the network obviously felt you were worth it."

"After you convinced them that without me they couldn't get access to the top Chicago investors they wanted."

Vera's blush told me I was right.

"Why are you doing this, anyway?" I asked. "If you want to open a restaurant, you don't need a TV show to film it. We'll just exploit you. You do know that?"

"It was Ilena's idea. She talked with someone at the Business Channel, some friend of a friend, and they worked out a deal. She thought it would make the restaurant look really important, bring it tons of publicity and get things off to a good start. I didn't really want to be on TV, but once I knew it was going to happen, I insisted on you."

"And, of course, Doug went along, since he's so . . . agreeable."

She smiled. "I knew he would. And the others thought it might be helpful to have a friend doing the story."

"Why do they need a friend? It's just another high-end restaurant opening. It's a formula. First act, excited investors with big plans, putting everything on the line—their houses, their marriages, everything. But it's okay because they have confidence in their dream. Second act, problems start."

"Like?"

"Like the pastry chef quits, or the bathroom tile that had been special-ordered from Italy doesn't show up on time."

"Minor stuff."

"Yeah, but we play it up big, like it's going to ruin them. That gets us all the way through act three, with things getting worse and worse. Usually we get footage of the owners fighting, one of them walking out, looking as if he's on the verge of collapse."

"But you just said it's minor stuff. Why would he be on the verge of collapse?"

"We stage it," I said, wondering if anyone could be that naive. "Then after the last commercial break, when it looks as if the whole venture's about to collapse, everything works out. The restaurant opens. There are lots of satisfied customers, great food, tired but happy investors. And then we put a slate at the end to say whether the place is still in business. Any half-assed, doesn't-give-a-damn producer could do that show in his sleep. So I ask again, why do you and your investors need a friend?"

Vera bit the inside of her cheek as if to keep herself from saying something. When she did speak, it was careful and slow. "I'm worried we'll come off looking like a bunch of rich brats trying to keep nice people from our exclusive place."

"You will." Before she could protest, I went on. "And there's nothing I can do about that. But keep your people from saying the ridiculous things Ilena and Erik were saying this afternoon and you'll be fine."

"They don't have to make it into the final piece, do they?"

Though I still had half a glass of wine, Vera topped me off.

"Vera," I said, "I'm a hired hand. I don't have the final say in what gets on TV and what doesn't. I'm not the only one who sees the raw footage, so I'm not the only one who's going to know what happened. If you, or one of those snotty investor friends, say something stupid on tape, I can't protect you. Assuming I even want to." I got up to bring my plate to the sink, and as I did, I felt the effects of the wine. "I should probably get going."

"But—"

"Look, you've made your pitch about the show, and . . ." I sighed. "I'll do what I can, if you tell them to cut down on the elitist crap."

"No," she said. "You should do your job. It's not fair of me to ask you not to, and maybe it wouldn't be the worst thing in the world if Ilena and Erik and the others had to see themselves on television acting like that."

"At least you'll know to say all the right things."

I grabbed my purse and took a step out of the kitchen, but Vera didn't follow. She just sat in her chair, moving bread crumbs around the table and generally avoiding my eyes.

"Vera, is there something else?"

She didn't say anything.

"If you didn't want to talk to me about protecting your friends," I said, "then why am I here?"

She tapped her fingers across the bread crumbs for what felt like a long time before she looked up at me. "Someone has been threatening to kill me, and I thought you might know what to do."

Eleven

She said it so matter-of-factly I thought I'd misheard her.

"Threatening to do *what*?" I sat back down at the table. "Have you called the police?"

"No," she said. "I called you. You're so good at this stuff. You helped that family with the missing daughter. You figured out what happened with Frank."

"I got lucky. I'm not Sherlock Holmes." Vera looked on the verge of tears. Crap. I gave in. "Who is threatening you?"

"I'm not sure," she said. "I got involved in the restaurant after I met Doug. They were getting a little cash poor and they needed a new investor. Doug thought I might be interested."

"And you're a sucker for being needed."

She smiled. "He really believed in the place, and I . . . well, I thought it might be fun to do something together, so I invested two hundred and fifty."

"Thousand?"

"Yes. Two hundred and fifty thousand. Doug was really sweet about it. He's very protective of me. You should get to know him better—"

"When did you start getting threats?" I interrupted.

"A couple of weeks ago. Telling me that I would end up dead unless I stayed away from Doug."

"Man or woman?"

"It sounded like one of those computerized voices, like when you call customer service for just about anything and you have to press zero half a dozen times to get an operator."

"What did Doug say when you told him?"

"He said he had an ex-girlfriend who was still hung up on him and I shouldn't worry. She's just trying to make him miserable, but she's not really dangerous."

"But you don't believe him."

"I—" Something caught in her throat. "It's not that I don't believe him. It's just that he sounded like he was . . ."

"Lying," I finished for her. "Was it Doug who suggested you invest?"

"But he doesn't have anything to do with this."

"How did he know you had that kind of money? I assume you don't go around introducing yourself as the heiress to Knutson Foods, the biggest chain of grocery stores east of the Mississippi."

"Of course not, but I don't lie about it either."

"Did he know when he met you?" I asked.

"I know what you're thinking."

"It might explain why he's so agreeable. Con men usually are."

"If he were going to take my money, then why is he still around? Why is he still dating me? Wouldn't he drop me once the check cleared the bank?"

The answer was obvious. There were millions more where that came from. I had, for a time, even convinced myself that Frank had left me for Vera's money. But despite his many faults, Frank was too nice for that. And unfortunately, Vera was too nice for that to be his only reason for liking her. But Doug was another story.

I leaned back in my chair. I was stuffed from two helpings of the ravioli, a salad, and three slices of garlic bread. I'd lost track of the amount of wine I'd drunk. I needed coffee, a good night's sleep, and some distance from Vera. What I didn't need was to get any more involved. "I think you should call the police."

"And say what? I don't have any proof of anything."

"Where did the calls come from?"

"It was a blocked number."

"But you're sure it's someone from the restaurant?"

"The voice mentioned the name of the restaurant. Club Car. We haven't told that name to anyone."

"You haven't. Can you be sure Erik or one of the others hasn't said anything?"

"It supposed to be a big reveal," she said. "And besides, the caller said I should forget about the two hundred and fifty thousand. Only the other investors know the exact amount. Certainly Doug's ex-girlfriend wouldn't. Would she?" She looked to me for answers I didn't have.

"But they have your money, Vera. So why threaten you?"

"I started asking about the costs. I'm a silent investor, but I'm not a stupid one."

"You only started asking about the costs after you handed over the money. That doesn't exactly make you Warren Buffett."

She laughed, sounding almost relaxed. "Fair point. But the whole thing was weird right from the beginning. I wrote the check out to some venture capital group and when I tried to trace them, I couldn't find any of the partners."

"Did you ask Doug about that?"

"Yeah. He said that there were some IRS issues and that the group had formed offshore." She saw the alarm in my eyes. "You would be surprised how often businesses do things like that."

It sounded dicey to me, but then my idea of high finance was paying off the full balance on my credit card. Vera understood that world better than I did. "How much did Doug invest?" I asked.

"The same as me," she said. "He was originally hired to get investors for the place, and he liked it so much he decided to put his own money in. That convinced me it was a good risk."

"Except that's not why you did it, Vera. You did it to bond with a guy you barely know."

"I know him. I met him on a dating site. He used to work for some financial firm that went under, so he opened his own small company and now he mainly invests his money and the money of some clients."

"And the others?"

"Roman's got money in eight Chicago restaurants, and two in New York. As far as I can tell he's a legitimate businessman. He's a tough guy, but he's been around a long time and this is Chicago, so he's got connections."

"Meaning what? He's mobbed up?" I said it as a joke, but Vera didn't laugh.

"I think he knows people, but that doesn't mean anything. It's just . . ." She hesitated. "Getting a liquor license in Chicago is a complicated process. There's all these classes of licenses and you have to apply for the right category, like if you have outdoor seating, or want to stay open late. And then there's the background check. Anyone with as little as five percent interest in the restaurant has to be fingerprinted, get a criminal background check, submit information about their finances."

"Did everybody pass the inspection?"

"I don't know. All I know is that when I looked at the liquor license application, Roman's name wasn't on the list as one of the owners. And he's supposed to own fifty percent," she said.

"You think he has a criminal record or something?"

"Maybe, but then how did he get liquor licenses for all his other places?"

She had a point. "And, as you said, this is Chicago," I said. "It may not be the same 'vote early, vote often' Chicago of my youth, but you can still bribe a public official, can't you? We haven't gone that straight."

"That's my thinking. If he wanted to be on the ownership papers, he could find a way around the licensing board."

"Was Ilena on the application?"

"Yes. Ilena, Erik, me, Doug, and Walt Russo."

"Who is Walt Russo?"

"The chef. I don't think he's putting up any money, but he's a five percent owner because of who he is."

"The chef."

She looked at me, puzzled. "He's not just any chef, Kate. He's one of the hottest chefs in the city. You've heard of Maison Pierre, haven't you?"

"Was that the fancy place on Michigan Avenue that had a fire?"

"It was on State Street, but yes. There was a fire that absolutely gutted the place about three months ago. That's the only reason Walt was available."

"So you, Doug, Ilena, Erik, and Walt—all of you are on the application for a liquor license. Except Roman," I said. "Did you ask him about it?"

"I asked Doug."

I waited again, and again Vera hesitated. "And he said . . ."

"He told me that I should stop worrying," she said. "That I wasn't a businessperson. That I didn't understand how these things work. That he'd make sure I didn't lose my money."

"He told you to be a nice little girlfriend and stand by your man."

"Pretty much."

I felt a wine headache coming on. "Call your lawyer, get your money back, and walk away."

"I can't do that."

I leaned across the table and grabbed her arm for emphasis. "Vera, if you're going to tell me that you care about Doug—"

"If it is a scam, I don't think Doug's behind it. I think Doug's getting scammed too."

"For Christ's sake, Vera. Even if he is, so what? He's a grown man. Let him take care of himself. The best thing you can do is put some distance between you and those people."

"But I don't have to, now that you're involved. You have the perfect opportunity to ask everyone questions and find out what's going on."

"You want me to investigate them while I'm interviewing them?"

"Isn't it pretty much the same thing?"

I sat back. It was the same thing, kind of. "It would make the show more interesting."

"But you won't use this on the show," she said, suddenly alarmed. "I understand about the rest of it, Kate. I do. You can make us all look like rich jerks if you want, but this isn't for public consumption."

"But it's the most interesting part of the story," I said. "All I've got so far is a bunch of self-important people spending ridiculous amounts of money on a restaurant that the vast majority of Chicagoans would not be welcome in. The kind of people who will watch this show will not be welcome there. I would not be welcome there," I pointed out. "If I can show some real problems, it will give the audience a reason to tune in after the break."

"But you can't tell anyone. Not anyone. If anyone suspected you were looking into the threats, someone might actually follow through on them. You wouldn't want that to happen, would you?"

I took a deep breath. "Let me think about that."

Vera laughed.

Twelve

I was hungover when I parked my car in the Dugan Correctional parking lot the next morning. The good news about having had too much wine was that I finally had my first full night's sleep in more than a month. The bad news was that alcohol-induced sleep isn't particularly restorative, so I didn't feel any better because of it.

Tim Campbell, the second inmate in the prison story, was finally over the flu or whatever else had held him up the first time. I'd meant to go through his file after dinner with Vera and write questions for the interview, but I never got around to it.

Instead, I sat in my car and briefly reviewed his background. It wasn't as colorful as Brick's past. It was just sad. Nearly twenty years earlier, in a meth-induced rage, he apparently stabbed his wife eighteen times with a steak knife; she bled to death on the kitchen floor. She had been eight weeks pregnant at the time, though Campbell claimed he didn't know and doubted his wife, also a meth addict, did either.

Since then, he'd had three execution dates set, with each date getting pushed back because of appeals. When Governor Ryan commuted his sentence, Campbell wigged out, demanding the state put him to death. For the next three years he'd been on suicide watch, then briefly found Jesus, but he seemed to have put that behind him. What he would be like today was anyone's guess.

\\\

Andres and Victor had the same small room from Brick's interview lit and ready in just under thirty minutes, record time that turned out to be unnecessary, as there was a delay bringing Campbell from his cell.

When he did arrive, he was all smiles. He was about forty, white, skinny, not particularly tall, with dirty blond hair grown to his shoulders and a small scar on his left cheek.

"Hey, y'all," he said as he entered, waving his cuffed hands. "Sorry this whole thing got delayed, but I'm so glad we finally got it all worked out."

He sat, smiling, looking from Andres to Victor, talking about the Blackhawks game on Sunday and how this was shaping up to be a good year for the team. He barely looked at me.

Once he was uncuffed, he settled back in his chair and started pointing at the equipment. "Man, you got a lot of fancy shit. Lights, camera, action, I guess." He shook his head in disbelief. "There's a whole world of changes out there, I'll bet."

"I saw from the information I was sent that you're from Peoria," I said, mostly just to get his attention. I sat in a metal chair across from him, with my knees maybe two feet from his.

He looked over at me as if he'd just noticed I was there. "Yes ma'am. Born and raised. You ever been to Peoria?"

"No, I don't think I have."

"You'd remember. If you go, get some pizza bread at Avanti's. It's the best there is. I was kind of hoping I'd get it for my last meal, but now that ain't gonna happen."

"So good it's worth dying for?"

He laughed. "Well, ma'am, you try it and tell me." He laughed harder, licked his lips, and looked around the room. "Man, I shouldn't a said anything about it, 'cause now I'm going to take the memory of it back to my cell."

"You don't have to keep calling me ma'am," I said. "I'm Kate."

He blushed a little, but he finally looked me in the eye. "Hi, Kate. I'm Tim."

Once the camera was rolling, I settled into the interview. I couldn't help notice that once we were officially introduced, Tim's eyes never left mine.

"You must miss a lot of things about home," I said.

"I sure do when I let myself think on it, which I don't most of the time. I try to keep my focus here, you know, in this place, 'cause this is all I got now."

"At the risk of making you homesick, tell me about Peoria."

"It's a nice town. Pretty. Right on the river, with big houses on the hill that look down on the water."

"You live in one of those houses?"

"No, not me. My folks weren't poor, they weren't rich. They were just decent people, that's all."

"What was your childhood like?"

He shrugged. "It wasn't *The Brady Bunch*, you know. It was just . . . normal, I guess. My dad worked as an accountant at Caterpillar tractor company and my mom stayed home with me. I was an only child but I wasn't alone much. I hung out with my best friends, Dickie Waters and Joe Santori. We used to be in Little League together. None of us any good, but we thought we were." He grinned widely. "I think every American boy thinks he's gonna make the major leagues."

"So what happened?"

"Drugs. I smoked pot, drank beer . . . everybody did. But Dickie and Joe knew when to stop, and I guess I didn't."

"What drugs did you do?"

"It was the eighties, ma'am. What drugs *didn't* I do?" He stopped for a minute, seemed to be enjoying memories of a better time. "Coke, speed, 'shrooms, anything I could get . . . but it was meth that did me in."

"How young were you when you started?"

"Fourteen, I think. Started with simple things, but by the time I was supposed to graduate high school, I was pretty well gone."

"And your parents?"

"I gave 'em trouble they did not deserve."

After Brick's wariness, I wanted to be clear. "You're going to have to go into some detail about that trouble," I said.

He lost his smile. "Yes ma'am. That's why we're doing this, isn't it? So some kid out there with a drug problem doesn't end up wasting his life away in here."

\\\

Ten minutes in, some trouble with the mic caused us to take a break in the interview. Victor rushed around trying to fix it, Andres glared at him, and Tim sat back and watched.

"Sorry about this," I said.

"I ain't got nowhere better to be, Kate."

I looked up at the guard, and Tim saw me looking.

"He don't got nowhere better either. Do you, Russell?"

The guard laughed. "No, Tim, not until six o'clock."

"Russell here has three kids. Twelve, nine and . . ." Tim looked back toward the guard. "How old is Gail?"

"Four," Russell answered.

Tim nodded. "That's right. She just had a birthday."

"That she did," Russell said. "Tim has a great memory."

I looked from one to the other. "Must be hard to work in a place like this. On one hand wanting to relate to each other as people, and on the other hand having to keep order."

Russell shifted his weight and shrugged. "Tim here is no trouble. We have some bad guys here, but Tim isn't one of them." He stopped, seemed to consider his words. "It's different once people are inside. What they did . . . well, no one is in Dugan for parking tickets."

"You don't think about their crimes?" I asked.

"I don't," he said. "What they did doesn't bother me as much as what they're capable of doing."

Tim smiled. "And Russell knows I'm not interested in picking any fights."

"So what if someone picks a fight with you?" I asked.

Tim seemed to consider the question, before quietly answering. "I guess it'll last long enough for him to stick me in the belly."

Thirteen

T ell me about the night your wife died," I said once the mic had been fixed. I usually prefer to ease into a situation as delicate as that, but I was looking to throw Tim off his game and get him to stop staring at me. Unlike Brick's attempt at seduction, Tim's steady gaze had no sexual intent. At least none that I could see.

He shifted in his chair. "It was bad. Jenny, that was my wife, she and I had been talking to my neighbor Cody." He stopped. Cleared his throat. "He wasn't just our neighbor. He was also our dealer. Meth was pretty new in my circles back then. Been around a couple of years, but it was getting popular and we were into it. I can't exactly say what happened that night, or really why it happened, but when the police come to the door because of some neighbors who heard screams, I had a knife in my hand and Jenny was dead. Long streaks of her blood were on the linoleum, like she'd been crawling away and just didn't make it. It took me a while to realize why. My knife had blood on it. Her blood."

"You stabbed her eighteen times."

"That's what the police said, ma'am." He breathed deep. "Sorry. That's what the police said, Kate. She was stabbed eighteen times, all over her body. At my trial, Cody said that I was screaming at her and I picked up a knife off the kitchen counter and just started cutting into her. Six stab wounds in her stomach, eight in her chest, and the others were in her arms and face."

"Why did you do it?"

"I don't recall doing it."

"You murdered your wife and you don't remember it?"

He let out a long breath. "Have you ever done drugs, Kate?"

Before I could answer he shook his head.

"No, you probably haven't," he said. "You look like you got some sense. Drugs cloud things, make you remember things differently than they actually occurred. My actions led me here, so regardless, I'm responsible."

"Did Jenny say anything while this was going on?"

"Not that I recall. But after she tried to get away from me, Cody said I stabbed her a couple more times. The ones that did the most damage. She stopped moving and she ended up lying in the corner of the kitchen. That's where she died. But I do remember that she put her hand out like this." He reached an arm out toward me, and then let it drop to his lap.

"Was she trying to touch you or shield herself from you?"

His eyes got wet but he blinked away the tears before they could fall. "I've asked myself that many times. Either way, I failed her."

"But you loved her?"

"I met Jenny when we were kids, in the fourth grade, Mrs. Tressel's class. She had long brown hair and a real pretty smile. We didn't become friends or nothing for a while. She gave me my first cigarette when I was twelve." He smiled. "It was my first step on the slippery slope."

"So she dragged you down?"

His eyes flared for a moment, anger and then embarrassment. "No, Kate. I did not mean to imply that. Jenny was just a nice girl, dabbling like all kids do. It was me that dragged her down. I just wasn't happy with myself, I guess."

"Drugs made you feel better?"

"They made me feel better. They made me feel nothing. And then they ended me."

That was a nice line that would fit perfectly with the story I was concocting. Tim was my "life that was wasted because of drugs" character, an almost archetypical prison type. What I needed was for Tim to have a wasted talent or a plan he'd had to give up. Something grand enough to make his current situation all the more tragic.

"What were your dreams, Tim, before the drugs?"

"Aside from being a pitcher for the Cubs?" he asked. He looked down at his hands, breaking his gaze for the first time. "I used to like music. I played piano and violin and a little guitar."

"So you wanted to be a musician?"

When he looked back up, his expression had changed. He looked excited, almost like a kid. "Not a rock musician or anything like that.

I wanted to be in an orchestra. My mom and I used to watch the Boston Pops on TV every Fourth of July. You know, with the fireworks going off. I thought for a while I'd get good enough to play with them," he said. "You play an instrument, Kate?"

I shook my head. Tim was playing his part perfectly, so I needed to play mine. "I don't have any talent for it," I said. "But if I did, I think I would like to play the violin. It's so versatile."

"It is." His smile widened. "I like country about as much as I like the orchestra stuff. I used to play a little bluegrass too. I love the sound of the violin. It's mournful, you know, longing. And then as a fiddle it's all playful joy." He held his hands in the air and played an imaginary violin for a moment. "My folks bought me one when I was eleven. I used to carry it with me to parties. Jenny loved it. She'd dance around when I'd play that thing. Even when she was thirteen, and all skinny legs and long hair, she looked like a goddess." His voice lowered to a whisper, as if he were talking to himself. "It's a gift to meet the love of your life that young."

The obvious joy he felt at remembering his life before it got so messed up saddened me for a moment. Frank and I had met in high school, a thought I pushed away as quickly as it came.

"You must miss her."

He cocked his head to the side and considered the question for a long time. "I think it would be unfair to Jenny's family to say I missed her. To look for sympathy because the woman I loved is dead. It might make it seem like I'm not taking responsibility for why she isn't here anymore."

We were scheduled to be in the room for only an hour and we'd run out of time. Andres turned the camera off, and Russell put Tim's handcuffs back on. As Tim was led out of the room, he turned back to me.

"Kate."

"Yes, Tim."

"Just between you and me. Every goddamned day."

Fourteen

I'd brought the books Brick had asked for, so after Russell escorted Tim back to his cell, he brought me to the visitors area. I left Andres and Victor, who seemed not to be speaking beyond what was absolutely necessary, and followed Russell down a long hallway, through two sets of secured doors, and into a large room that had about twenty metal tables in it. The seats were bolted to the tables and the floor. About half the tables were occupied, inmates on one side and visitors on the other, with guards near almost every group. The room was loud, almost deafening. People were laughing, drinking cans of pop, and eating potato chips and other items that were for sale in a vending machine at the back.

Brick was sitting alone, staring at the floor. When I put my bag of books on the table, he looked up and smiled.

"I got word that you were bringing me my books," he said. "I didn't want to believe it."

He gestured for me to sit, and I did, though I think it would have been more comfortable to stand. The seats were small, round metal stools, cold and hard.

Brick immediately started looking through the bag. I'd brought his entire list, ten books, ranging from the latest Stephen King to a biography on Cleopatra. "Damn," he laughed. "You got me everything I asked for."

"Neighborhood bookstore."

"I can't pay you back, you know."

"Give me a good interview."

"Shit, I'll tell you anything you want to hear."

I laughed. "Nice to see I'm not the only one who can be bought."

"What?"

"Nothing. I'm working on another show, something I don't really want to work on, because they're paying me more than my daily rate."

"That don't sound so bad."

"It's rich people talking about how rich they are," I said, glad to have a place to vent. "It's going to be one of those ridiculously expensive restaurants. The way they talk about how exclusive it will be, it's like they're figuring out who gets a seat on Noah's Ark."

"You gotta do what you gotta do, Kate," he said. "It's got to be tough, life as a widow. You lose the man you love and have to make your own way in the world. I admire that."

I don't generally know what to say to compliments. And since my relationship with Frank hadn't exactly been a perfect love story, I didn't wear the title of "widow" too heavily around people who knew me. Sometimes I found myself opening up about my life with virtual strangers—the man at the grocery checkout, the woman who cleaned my teeth—because I could be sad without consequences.

"I miss him," I admitted. "We were together a long time, since I was teenager."

"Life's like that, isn't it? Something you do as a kid stays with you, defines who you are. It's not easy."

"We all have our burdens."

"You talk to Tim Campbell?" he asked.

"I did."

"You get what you needed?"

"The start of it. We still have two more sit-down interviews with you and Tim, and we've been approved to get footage of both of you in your cells, and at a couple of other spots in the prison."

"He tell you a good story?"

"Better than yours. He's more willing to talk about himself."

Brick's eyes narrowed. Not angry, but sizing me up. "Yeah, but all I want from you is books."

As he spoke, a shouting match broke out between two of the inmates. One had apparently brushed up against the other's fiancée. Guards moved between them, and the men were removed. Their visitors—an older couple who was visiting the man who had pushed his chair, and the fiancée and three-year-old daughter of the other man—were escorted out the visitors door.

"I drove three hours to get here," the fiancée was saying to the guard. "And I only got to spend ten minutes with him. Can't you just let things cool down and bring him back for a minute?"

"Not today," the guard said. "Next time tell your man to behave himself."

"If he could behave himself he wouldn't be here," she said.

The guard just kept moving her toward the door.

When I looked back at Brick, he was laughing. "Never a dull moment," he said.

\\\

Andres and Victor waited for me by the van.

"Everything go okay with that sociopath?" Andres asked as I approached.

"I was just giving him some books."

"You don't want to get too chummy with these guys. They prey on lonely women."

"We're back at the restaurant tomorrow," I said, ignoring him. "Eleven a.m. call. And Victor, I expect you to be on time, with everything in working order."

Victor frowned, but I could see Andres smiling.

"I'm sorry about the mic," Victor said. "It just—"

I waved him away. "Things happen; equipment breaks down. It's just that someone hires me, and I hire Andres, and he hires you. So, what you do reflects on me." Before he could protest, or break down in tears, I continued. "And usually that's a good thing, because you're the best sound guy in the business."

Andres took a step forward. "Not lately."

I cut in before things got worse. "I think we've made our point." I glanced at Andres, who didn't seem satisfied, but there was nothing else I could say. I leaned in and kissed Victor on the cheek. "If something's going on you want to talk about, I'm here."

"Thanks, Kate," he said in a stage whisper. "I'm good. But it's nice to have at least one friend I can count on."

Andres shook his head. "I tried talking to him, Kate. You know I tried. He's got his head up his ass about that band of his."

"What's that supposed to mean?" Victor shouted.

"Tomorrow. Eleven a.m." I walked toward my car and left the two men arguing by the truck.

Fifteen

The next day, I sat in a comfortable chair amid the still-halted construction of the Club Car restaurant, conducting interview after interview. It was hard to tell them apart. Ilena, Roman, and Doug all said the exact same thing, each using the words "hip" and "exclusive" with the same inflection, in that rehearsed, talking-points way of political pundits on Sunday morning talk shows.

Vera's interview was the only exception. She talked about the restaurant the way someone else might talk about a lover, with giggly enthusiasm and unbridled optimism. Only she seemed to see the place as something other than an extension of her ego. In that moment I hoped Doug had been telling the truth: The phone calls to Vera were from a crazy old girlfriend who hoped to break them up. Looking at Doug it was hard to imagine he inspired that kind of passion, but then I never knew what anyone saw in anyone.

After the sit-down interviews, we broke for lunch. Ilena had arranged for a buffet from some Greek fusion restaurant. She told me it was "the best Greek food you will taste in your life, outside of Santorini." I've never been to Greece, but based on how good the food was, my guess was she was right.

"This is such a treat for us, to have you here, telling our story," Ilena told me as we ate. "It was so unexpected that anyone would be interested in our little restaurant."

"I was under the impression you arranged it with a friend at the Business Channel."

"I made a call," she admitted. "But I didn't expect to be chosen."

"They must have thought the place would be something special," I said. No sense in becoming enemies this early in the shoot. There was plenty of time for that when I was in editing.

We ate in silence for a few minutes. I watched her watch Roman as he strutted around the place, arguing with Erik about what the waitstaff should wear. Erik had special-ordered uniforms—black pants and short-waisted white coats with black ties, something he'd seen in 1930s movies. Roman thought the white coats would be too hard to keep clean. He said it was a waste of money. A dull subject, but the two men were quite heated about it. At one point Roman grabbed Erik's shirt and pushed him against the wall.

I turned to Andres, but he was one step ahead of me. He'd picked up the camera and had it pointed toward the men. Victor was right behind him, holding the boom mic safely out of reach of the argument but close enough to get the words clearly on tape.

"Listen, you little fucker!" Roman screamed. "I decide what happens in this place, not some nobody."

"I am a partner too," Erik said. The smooth arrogance had been replaced by a stammer, but it was gutsy of him to stand up to someone twice his size. Though, in all fairness, he wasn't actually standing. He was sort of dangling, a few inches off the ground, held up by Roman's massive fist. Both Doug and Vera jumped up to intervene, eventually pulling the men apart. Roman stormed off and Doug went after him, while Vera comforted a shaken Erik. I nearly broke out in applause. I didn't even have to stage the tension in this place. Andres and I exchanged a quick nod, and he continued shooting Vera and Erik.

Ilena just sat and watched with a detached amusement, then turned to me as if our conversation had never been interrupted. "This place really is a dream of mine," she said, looking around. "I didn't have much growing up. My father worked in a butcher shop owned by his uncle. We ate well," she laughed, "but we never had any money."

"You must be proud of what you've accomplished."

"What have I accomplished?"

It was a good question. "Once this place is open, I imagine you'll be the talk of Chicago. A businesswoman every bit as successful as her husband. That's what you want, isn't it?"

She cocked her head toward me. "I was twenty-four when I married Roman. My bank account was overdrawn. I had to borrow the dress I got married in." She sighed. "I thought I'd found the answer to my prayers. Then, the day before the wedding, Roman had me sign a pre-nup that if we divorced we'd each keep what we'd earned in the marriage." She looked square at me, and for the first time I could see a force behind her pale brown eyes. "You know how much I've earned in the years Roman and I have been married?"

"I can guess."

"Nothing." She slapped the table. "Absolutely nothing. He's made sure of that. But this place will be mine. My success story. My money."

"And your ticket out of the marriage?" I couldn't help but wish she were saying this on camera, but it was interesting either way.

Ilena sat up very straight. "I can butcher a hog, do you know that, Kate?" I shook my head. "And do you know why?"

"Because your father was a butcher."

"Because my father taught me that you have to do what needs to be done, even if it's distasteful."

"Good lesson."

"Damn good lesson."

She turned back to her food. As she bit into some chicken, I watched her. The put-on elegance was gone. My guess was that she'd conjured that image early in her marriage, or maybe before. She'd thought it would add a certain sophisticated air to the story I was doing, which was why she'd gone on and on about how exclusive Club Car would be. But she'd obviously seen that it hadn't worked. Now she was doing the humble roots bit, hoping I'd prefer that side of her. She was right about that. And I appreciated that she was pragmatic enough to make the switch midstream. But it also made me wonder if Vera's questions about the finances stood in the way of her plans. Ilena was more than capable of putting a stop to them.

Sixteen

As lunch was wrapping up, the famed Walt Russo, legendary "it" chef, arrived to conduct a tasting for the investors, and of course, for the cameras. He was lanky, late thirties, with light brown skin and just-got-out-of-bed dark brown hair. He didn't use the words "exclusive" or "hip," so five minutes after I'd met him, he was my favorite one of the whole group.

Like the rest of the restaurant, the kitchen was a mess. The tile floor was installed and about half of the appliances were in, but the rest of the space was covered in drop cloths and filled with boxes.

"You're going to cook for the tasting in here?" I asked.

"I started out at a barbecue place in Evanston. We served mostly students, so the food was cheap and greasy." He laughed. "I don't want to even guess how many health codes we violated. But if it taught me anything, it was how to deal with whatever kitchen I was in, including this one."

Walt had brought knives, pans, and tableware with him, as well as two large boxes of ingredients, and it took him very little time to start chopping, sautéing, frying, and boiling—often all at the same time. Without even tasting his cooking I could see why Vera had been so awed. Andres went handheld with the camera, shooting from all angles as Walt worked, cooking a dozen or more different things, which he then plated in tiny portions on large white dishes.

"This portion is just for the tasting?" I asked.

"No, this is how we're going to serve it. Portion size has gotten totally out of control, and the mark of a great restaurant, I think, is to give you great taste, not bust the button on your pants."

He took a forkful of a rice dish and fed it to me. It was tender, with just enough bite and a mix of flavors I couldn't identify, both savory and sweet. When I swallowed I could see Walt was waiting for approval.

"It's good," I said. "But it just makes me want more."

"You can have as much as you like. You know the chef." He smiled. It was warm and sweet.

"I don't think I could get in this place once it opens," I said. "I keep hearing how it's for the cool people."

"You're cool."

"No, I'm not."

He laughed. "Sure you are."

Victor stepped in. "She's really not. She thinks a hot dog is gourmet food."

Walt shrugged. "If it's from Superdawg, it is."

"I love that place," I said. "I haven't been there in forever."

"I'll get you one with everything," Walt said, "or you can go with me, and we'll do the drive-in. Nothing tastes better than a hot dog brought to your car." He laughed. "A bribe so you'll make me look good on the show."

"You're already in the running to be cast as 'the nice one,'" I admitted.

He chuckled. "Not exactly a tough race. Except Vera. She's sweet. And Erik is cool. He may be a bit pretentious, but his heart's in the right place."

"What about Roman and Ilena?"

Walt glanced toward the camera. "I met Roman about three years ago. I starting working in a restaurant he liked, and he took a special interest in me. He's a good guy, certainly knows the restaurant scene. He wanted me to work for him then but I couldn't leave because of my contract."

"Until it burned down."

Walt raised an eyebrow. "Yeah," he said. "That kind of freed me up for this."

"How did that fire start?"

"I don't know. It was after hours."

"Was it arson?"

Walt's eyes widened. "Could have been. Could have been electrical, or started by something left on in the kitchen. Restaurants catch on fire. Roman had a place burn down years ago. It happens."

"I didn't know that. Do you know what caused that fire?"

"Nope. A guy went to Pontiac prison for it, so I guess arson, but I don't know the details."

"Maybe Roman did it. He's got quite a temper. We had a little demonstration of it earlier."

Walt tried to laugh it off, but he looked a little worried. "He's all talk." He was looking toward Andres, looking for an escape. I doubted I could get more from him while the cameras rolled. I changed tactics.

"Why are you going into business with these guys?" I asked. "You seem an odd bunch, if you ask me."

"Roman approached me with the promise of carte blanche in the kitchen," he said. "To create a restaurant from the ground up, I think that's every chef's dream. When you go into an established place, there are menus already in place, expectations from customers and critics. But this"—he looked around the kitchen—"is a blank canvas. This is mine, and I want to do something really special with it."

He looked around the room with a dreamy smile. It looked like a mess to me, but I could see that in his eyes, it was already perfect.

\\\

After the interview, the investors dusted off the bar and used it as a makeshift table. They huddled around it, taking a spoonful from each dish as Walt explained why it would fit into the place. Doug seemed a little lost, so I assumed he wasn't a food guy, and Roman kept checking his BlackBerry, but Ilena and Erik were really into the tasting. They asked questions with every dish and made annoying comments like, "it has a teasing quality" and "it's retro but with a modern feel."

Erik questioned each ingredient, clearly offering one too many suggestions. I could see Walt trying to be patient, until he finally snapped. "You're front of house, Erik. You worry about the ambience. I'll worry about the food."

Ilena jumped in to defend Erik, but then Walt offered his resignation if there was no faith in his ability. Roman finally put a stop to it with a quick, "He's the chef." The others quickly backed down. My hopes for another on-camera outburst went unfulfilled.

Vera just stood to the side and tried to look cheerful. At one point I saw her making a face at me, a "Have you found out anything?" face. I shook my head. I was still going over my conversation with Walt, but the more I thought about it, the less information I seemed to have. The fires, at Walt's restaurant and at Roman's years ago, might be important, or they could be a coincidence. Walt's nervousness about the subject might mean something, or it could just be a star chef wanting to say good things about his boss. This whole place might be a front for some underworld business of Roman's, I suddenly realized. That excited me for a moment. It would certainly be a more interesting episode if they were really a criminal enterprise, and more palatable if the annoying personalities were just put on to hide the truth.

But as I looked around the room, at this cluster of mismatched snobs, I decided I wouldn't get that lucky.

After the tasting was over, Roman started to walk out.

"You still have a mic on," I called after Roman. Victor was texting someone on his phone, paying no attention.

"Can I take this off?" Roman looked at me. "I have to make a call."

"We still have stuff to shoot," I told him. "But it's wireless, so Victor can turn it off for now."

Finally Victor snapped to attention, but then got flustered turning off the mic. Roman looked put out for the entire twenty seconds it took for Victor to finish. Then he left the restaurant, dialing as he walked out.

"Charming guy," I said to Vera.

"He's just stressed. He's got about a dozen deals going on at once."

We watched out the window as Roman paced up and down, having a quiet but obviously angry conversation with whomever was on the other end.

"You think he's the type to make threatening phone calls?" I asked.

"One of the first things he told me is that he doesn't like to lose," Vera said. "He said he'll do anything rather than let it happen."

I looked back at Ilena, chatting with Erik and Walt. "I wonder what he's afraid he'll lose?"

Seventeen

The investors had a meeting they didn't want on tape, so I reluctantly agreed to get lost for a half hour. Andres, Victor, and I shot some exteriors of the building, a crumbling art deco structure made all the more depressing by the brown of midwinter. Then, just to keep ourselves busy, we got some footage of the neighborhood, an area known as the South Loop. Once the city's vice district, it's an up-and-coming neighborhood that attracts young professionals but isn't, at least not yet, the center of fun for the high-end gossip pages crowd Club Car was aiming to get.

"I wonder why they chose here?" I said to Andres as we ducked into a local coffee shop.

"Who cares? These people are brats." He put the camera on the seat next to him and ordered black coffee for himself and green tea for Victor, who was outside checking his phone messages.

"Hot chocolate for me," I said to the waitress. "And three slices of apple pie." Once she left with our order, I turned to Andres. "We need something sweet to balance out what a grouch you've become."

"Not me. Him."

Just as Andres spoke, Victor walked in. "What did I do now?"

"Sit down," I told him. "And tell me what's going on, so you two can kiss and make up. It's hard enough spending time with those restaurant people. If I can't at least have fun with you two, this job will be unbearable."

"He's not paying enough attention to the equipment," Andres said. "He's not prepared for the job when he walks on site."

"He's just upset because I have more going on in my life than work," Victor said.

Andres did a coffee spit-take. "I have a wife and three kids. And a dog. And a bowling team getting ready for the semifinals."

"You guys are like an old married couple," I said. "Maybe you're just taking each other for granted and need to work a little harder to get in sync."

"He needs to work harder," Andres muttered.

Before Victor could turn a small insult into a reason to sulk all afternoon, I took his hand. "I think Andres is just worried about you. You seem a bit preoccupied lately."

"That's funny," Victor said. "All Andres talks about is how he's worried about you."

I turned to Andres, whose gruffness had been replaced by an embarrassed half smile.

"Why are you worried about me?" I asked.

"A crew looks out for each other," he stammered. "We've got your back, making sure you get the shots you need, even the ones you forget to ask for, and you've got our backs, dealing with the clients, covering for us if we fuck up."

"Have I been forgetting shots?" I felt suddenly defensive, even though, at least as far as I could remember, I'd been getting everything we needed.

"That's not why we're worried," Victor jumped in. "It's because you're spending so much time alone. And you're letting your usual hotness factor slip a few notches with all the ponytails and shapeless turtlenecks."

"It's winter," I pointed out. "I'm dressing for warmth. Everybody does that."

"That's not really what we're talking about either," Andres said gently, but the damage was done. I swept a stray lock of hair behind my ear and clenched my jaw.

"This isn't one of those 'nobody on their deathbed says I wish I'd spent more time at work' speeches, is it?" I asked.

"No," the men answered together. They both looked a little nervous. Men always look a little nervous when a woman is about to get mad at them.

"But nobody writes songs about work either," Victor said quietly. "You ever notice that? People write love songs, not 'I really love my career' songs."

"What's your point?" I asked. "I have to make a living. And anyway, I'm not about to become one of those ridiculous characters in a romantic comedy who thinks my entire existence is defined by whether I have a man in my life."

"You don't seem to have *anything* in your life," Andres said. "What do you do when you're not working?"

"I watch television." A pathetic defense, but it was all I had. "And I . . ." I let the sentence trail off because my voice was starting to quiver.

"Sorry, Kate," Victor said. "It's just that you're losing your"—he looked over at Andres—"you know, your edge."

Andres half nodded, half shook his head. "You let those inmates flirt with you, you brought one of them books—"

"That was a bribe."

"And you were batting your eyelashes at that chef," Victor added.

"I was not. I was talking about hot dogs." I felt a little flushed. "And what difference does it make? I'm allowed to flirt if I want to. I've gotten some of my best interviews that way."

"This is different. It's not tactical," Andres said. "It's . . ." He looked to Victor for help.

"You're not being nearly as tough on these rich assholes as you would have been a year ago," Victor said.

"So now I'm not as good a producer as I used to be?" My voice took on a hardness that I didn't entirely intend. It must be an evolutionary thing that any attack, even a verbal one—even a *mild* verbal one—causes a person's defense mechanisms to go into hyper mode.

"That's not what we're saying," Andres said. "It's just if you're sad about Frank, it's only been seven months."

"I'm not sad."

"But if you were," he pressed. "If you're lonely . . ."

"I thought we were talking about Victor," I said.

"I'm fine," Victor said a little loudly, his defense mechanisms rising to meet mine. "The point is, Kate, you have friends. You have me, and Andres and Vera, if you let her."

"She has enough problems of her own," I said as I gulped the last of my hot chocolate, dribbling a little on what had been my favorite shapeless blue turtleneck.

"What problems?" Victor asked. "Doug's hanging with the wrong crowd but he seems okay."

I snorted dramatically. I'd promised to keep my mouth shut, but this was Victor and Andres. Vera was a regular whenever Victor's band played, and she had somehow become an alternate on Andres's bowling team. I told them about my dinner at Vera's and the death threats. I started feeling better immediately, the way I always did when it was someone else's life getting dissected. I'd have to remember this next time Ellen went on a tear about my lackluster complexion.

"But you can't say anything," I said when I finished. The favorite words of all gossips everywhere.

"She has to get away from those people," Andres said.

"She's worried about Doug. She thinks maybe someone is trying to hurt him by going after her. It's Vera logic, so it doesn't make any sense, but she's not going to just walk away," I explained.

Andres and Victor exchanged looks.

"We weren't going to say anything," Victor started.

"Because it doesn't necessarily mean anything," Andres finished the thought for him. "But when I was checking the tape after the tasting, you know, just to make sure we had it, I saw something." He paused and looked at Victor, who nodded. "I didn't notice it when we were shooting because I was focused on the main action and this was in the background, but I saw Ilena pass Doug something. It looked like a note. And their fingers lingered just a little too long, if you know what I mean."

"But I thought she was having an affair with Erik," I said. "I saw them giggling like schoolkids."

Victor leaned his elbows on the table. "Maybe she giggles with all the boys."

Eighteen

Andres propped his camera on the table, pressed "rewind," and let me watch through the viewfinder. The picture was tiny and it was in the background, but I could definitely see Ilena passing Doug something as Walt served up dishes for the tasting. What she had handed to Doug, however, wasn't clear.

"See how she kind of tickles his fingers with hers?" Victor pointed out. It was silly and childish, but it was spot on. Something was going on between Ilena and Doug. But it wasn't the fingers touching that made me sure; it was Doug's quick glance at Vera as the exchange was made. As if he were making sure she hadn't seen anything.

"Damn it," I said. "We have to show this to her."

"But it's going to hurt her," Victor said.

"Yeah, well, life hurts." Both of the guys looked shocked, but I shrugged. "See? I haven't lost my edge."

\\\

We'd stayed away just over the half hour that had been requested, and when we got back it looked at first as if we'd missed all the fun. Ilena was on the phone making dinner reservations, Walt and Roman were joking about the menu, and Doug was doing a crossword puzzle.

"I'm stuck on this one," he said as I approached. "A five-letter word. Michael J's breakout role."

"Alex P," I told him. "As in Alex P. Keaton, Michael J. Fox's character on *Family Ties*."

"I don't know that show," he said. "I don't watch a lot of TV."

Another strike against him. And not just because I work in television. I don't trust people who say they don't watch TV. Either they're lying, which is usually the case, or they're filling their time with productive endeavors—helping the poor, or running marathons, or something, which just makes me feel lazy and inferior. Since Doug didn't seem the marathon type, he must have been a liar.

"How are you enjoying all of this?" I asked. "Opening a restaurant must be quite a challenge."

"It was on my bucket list," he said. "You know what that is?"

"It's a list of things you want to accomplish before you die."

"I had seventy-three things on it. A lot of them are dumb, like surviving a zombie attack, but I've got some good ones too. Like this one. Though it's a lot harder than I thought it would be."

I let the zombie attack comment slide. It was just the sort of thing to make me dismiss him as a harmless nerd, and I'd worked up a pretty good case against him as a con artist asshole. "How is it harder?" I asked.

He tapped his pen against the crossword. "It just seems like things are slower than they're supposed to be. And there's a lot more hands out looking for a little incentive to get things done, if you catch my drift."

"Yes," I said. "It must be frustrating for all of you. Has Ilena ever mentioned anything about how she's feeling?"

"I don't deal with Ilena too much," he said, a sharpness in his voice. "Roman's really the one in charge."

"Yes, he seems very . . ." I searched for a phrase. "Certain of his power." Doug nodded but seemed disinclined to add anything, so I switched topics. "Do you know where Vera is?"

"The kitchen, I think. She and Erik were talking about tablecloths."

"She's really throwing herself into this. It must make you happy that she's taken such an interest in your business."

He looked confused. "I guess. I didn't really want her involved in this. Too much of a risk, but she practically insisted."

I smiled. Either Vera or Doug was lying, and my money was on Doug. "I guess I should go find her," I said. "I have something to show her."

\\\

As I walked toward the kitchen, I'd lost whatever small doubts I had about showing her the video. I might have wanted to sound tough around the boys, but I took no pleasure in the idea that Vera would be hurt. If showing her the tape got her to leave this crowd behind, though, it would be worth it. She would be safe, and I could go back to the uncomplicated pleasure I got from not being friends with my late husband's girlfriend.

I looked around the kitchen, in the pantry, and even in the office area. But Vera wasn't there. I walked back out into the main dining area and saw the others huddled together staring out the window. When I looked to see what the action was, it was quite a show. Vera and Erik were standing on the street outside the restaurant, circling each other like boxers in the ring, Erik throwing his hands up in frustration and Vera shaking her head insistently. I had a front row seat on the action. Only problem was, through the double-paned windows, I couldn't hear what they were saying.

Andres looked toward me, holding the camera up for my approval, but I shook him off. No sense in making Vera look bad on camera when I'd already cast her as the nice one. Annoyingly, I realized there was more to it: I didn't want Vera to look bad. I felt uncomfortably protective, so I tried to focus on the argument outside.

After about a minute, Erik threw up his hands a final time and stomped away, getting into a black BMW and tearing down the street.

Roman shrugged his shoulders. "Lovers' quarrel," he said, then wandered toward the kitchen. I caught Walt's amused look, but neither Ilena nor Doug seemed to find anything funny in the situation.

Doug walked out of the restaurant toward Vera, and she practically fell into his arms. He kissed her head, and she looked up at him. They kissed on the lips, a long, sweet kiss. I shouldn't have watched, but I felt stuck in place. If they wanted privacy, they shouldn't be having a private moment on a public street. After a few minutes, Doug kissed Vera's cheek and went walking up the street in the same direction as Erik's car.

I walked outside. "You okay?"

Vera sniffed a little, but quickly composed herself. "Fine, thanks."

"Where did Doug go?"

"He had a meeting. He didn't want to leave me after what happened with Erik, but . . ."

"That was quite a scene."

She shrugged. "I'm not very confrontational."

"You seemed to be holding your own. What was it about?"

"Nothing. Just a difference of opinion on how to market the restaurant. I don't want to be part of something that seems shallow."

"And Erik took that characterization a little too personally?"

"I guess."

Andres and Victor walked out of the restaurant and stopped a few feet away from us. "Everything okay?" Victor asked.

"Yes. But I think we're going to call it a day," I said. "There's no construction, and we've done all the interviews about this stage in the process. They need to get a little further before we can continue."

"So I should put the camera away?" Andres asked, each word enunciated, his eyes widening and his head tilted. If he'd been any less subtle, a dead man would have picked up on the cues.

"Yes, Andres, put the camera away." I wanted to add, *Vera is in no mood for videotape of her cheating boyfriend*, but she was two feet away, so *my* widened eyes and tilted head had to be enough of a clue that I knew what he'd meant.

Besides, my phone rang.

I glanced at the caller ID. "Ellen," I said as I answered. "Not the time."

"This is important. Mom called. She wants us to come over to her house Saturday to decide what we want when she dies."

"Mom's dying?"

"No. You're such a drama queen. She wants us to decide now what we each want so there's no fighting when she does die, years from now."

"I don't know if I'm free Saturday," I said.

"Of course you're free. We have to decide what time. I think we should take Mom to lunch after, so it should be about ten at her house. That way we can relax after we go through her stuff. It will be nice for all of us to get together."

I had a feeling my mom and Ellen had cooked up this morbid scheme as an excuse to get me out of my house. "What about Dad?" I asked. "Doesn't he want to join in the fun?"

"He figures he'll die before Mom, so he doesn't really care to get involved."

I sighed. I could hold off Ellen, but combined with the extra-strength guilt power of my mother, I didn't even bother to resist. "Okay. Ten a.m., Saturday." As I spoke, I saw Vera answer her phone. Her face went pale, and she looked at me, panic in her eyes. "Ellen, I have to go."

"Kate," I could hear Ellen saying, "We have to talk about Andrew's game. He's second string but you're his aunt and you—"

I hung up. I walked to Vera and she handed me her phone. A computerized voice was saying, "You're the next to be slashed," over and over. I handed it to Andres, who also listened. Victor, the last to hear, was the only one of us who had the sense to record the voice, with a pocket digital recorder he kept handy.

"That recorder was genius. I could kiss you," I said.

Victor leaned in.

I laughed. "I said I could kiss you, not that I would. Why do you have that with you, anyway?"

"I'm a songwriter. If I get inspired I got to put it somewhere until I have time to work on it."

He glanced toward Andres, expecting, as I did, some remark about focusing on work instead of writing songs on a client's dime. But Andres just smiled. "Smart move," he said. "Now we can take this to the police and find out who's been harassing Vera."

Vera looked at Andres, then at me.

"I told them," I admitted. "I was just—"

"It's fine," she said. "It's good that you did." She rested her head on Victor's shoulder, and he put his arm around her. "But this call turns everything upside down."

"Why?"

"They're all here," she said. "They're all inside. So who made the phone call?"

Victor shook his head. "That doesn't necessarily mean anything. Someone taped that, then used voice-changing software to disguise their identity. They might have programmed their computer to make the call at a predetermined time. The person who did it could be standing right next to you when you get the call."

"Or he could be around the corner. Maybe drove off pretending to be upset so he could send the message," I pointed out. "Erik does seem to take his vision for the place very seriously. If Vera were looking to change his plans, he might be upset. Except he doesn't strike me as a techie type."

"Any ten-year-old could do this," Victor said. "You download the software off the Internet. You can even compose the call, like a draft e-mail, and then when you're ready, tap into your account from a smartphone, and press 'send.'"

I looked back at the restaurant. I could see Doug and Walt through the window, but Roman and Ilena weren't in view. "So pretty much anyone with a cell phone and a computer?"

Victor nodded. "Pretty much."

That wasn't our only problem. "What did the caller mean by saying Vera was 'next to be slashed'?" I asked.

"That he's going to hurt her," Andres said.

"But he said 'next.' Who was first?"

"Everyone's fine, right?" Victor said. "All the investors are alive and healthy? So maybe it's something else."

"What about my car?" Vera asked. "Tires get slashed. Maybe that's what he meant."

The four of us ran the four blocks to where Vera had found the only available parking space in a three-mile radius. By the time we reached it, we were coughing from the below-zero air filling our lungs, and I was feeling a sharp pain in my chest, the kind you get from the lack of a consistent exercise program that would help you build the stamina to run four lousy blocks.

Each of the four tires on Vera's Mercedes was as good as new.

"God, I was really worried there for a minute," Vera said.

"I think you should keep worrying," I told her. "If it's not your tires the caller was talking about, then what was it?"

Nineteen

I curled up on my couch and did a sudoku puzzle online. I started with the hardest one, and after I failed at that I went to medium, and finally gave up and chose an easy one. I got an amazing sense of accomplishment when I typed the final number into the box and an electronic fireworks display indicated that I had solved it.

After that minor intellectual stretch, I opened up a Word document and started to make a list of all the things I had to do around the house. Things like go through my closet and weed out the clothes I didn't wear, and throw out the long-past-their-expiration-date spices in my kitchen cabinet. As I typed I knew I wouldn't do any of it. Even writing the list seemed like too much work. I deleted it and instead made a list of all the reasons someone would go to the trouble of computerizing their voice just to scare Vera.

There was Doug's reason: an old girlfriend who wanted Vera out of Doug's life. But that made sense only if you didn't think about it too much. Wouldn't threats make the two of them closer? If Doug really believed it was someone from his past, it would make him less likely to rekindle that romance and more likely to feel protective of Vera. Of course, that didn't mean an old girlfriend would think logically, but it just seemed far-fetched, particularly that the ex would go to so much trouble to disguise her identity. If she wanted Doug back, why not just tell Vera who she was? I deleted that option.

Then there was Vera's reason: She'd been asking about financials. Something fishy was going on and somehow Vera had managed to stumble across something. Maybe she'd seen a document or overheard a conversation but hadn't known what it meant. It might be a threat to any of them. They all had a strong reason for wanting the place to be a success, and if Vera put a stop to it, a threat would seem plausible. I put that possibility in bold.

Third was what Roman had said, a lovers' quarrel. That's how he'd described the fight between Vera and Erik. It seemed less likely, but I couldn't rule it out. It wouldn't be Vera's first love triangle. Maybe Doug was using the threats as a punishment. He seemed like a man who avoided direct confrontation and might prefer the anonymity of a computer-altered voice. Plus it would allow him to still play the concerned boyfriend. That option stayed too.

And if there was something going on between her and Erik, then Ilena, a self-described hog butcher, would certainly be upset about it. It was a maybe. Ilena seemed more likely to be blunt about her feelings. Unless she was concerned that a direct confrontation would open up divorce proceedings.

Finally there was what Walt had said about Roman. Walt became available for Club Car when the restaurant he'd been working at burned down. Just like an earlier restaurant of Roman's. I went back online and looked up Roman Papadakis. There were several entries, mainly about restaurants he had invested in, places that opened with great fanfare, many of which had since closed. According to the background material I'd gotten from the Business Channel, about half of all restaurants close in the first three years. As much as I wanted to see a pattern of bad business practices in Roman's track record, it could easily be chalked up to the realities of the restaurant business and the fickleness of the elite crowd that Roman always went after.

But the fire wasn't so easily explained. Especially since Walt had been wrong. That first fire hadn't been in Roman's restaurant, but in the home of his business partner, his cousin. I found a few articles detailing a 1989 fire that killed the cousin, Michael Papadakis. In one, I read that the victim's throat had been cut, then the house set on fire. The first article said that Michael was "embroiled in a legal battle with his cousin and co-owner, Roman Papadakis," and stopped just short of calling Roman a suspect.

But every subsequent account listed a man named John Fletcher as the person responsible. Fletcher had burned down some garages to cover up thefts and had done time in Stateville, a prison near Dugan with an even fiercer reputation. According to one article, after prison Fletcher had found work at the Papadakis restaurant as a busboy, but was fired after three weeks and wanted revenge. Within days of the fire, Fletcher was arrested and then, almost as quickly, convicted of murder and arson. Case closed. Any concerns about the legal battle between Roman and his cousin were gone after the conviction.

There's no statute of limitations on murder, so if Roman or one of his associates did kill his cousin, he might be nervous Vera had found something damaging. But that also seemed far-fetched. Roman was a smart guy. As a matter of practicality he surely knew that with one man already in prison for the murder, the police were unlikely to reopen the case without extremely compelling evidence. Assuming Vera hadn't found a videotape of Roman setting the fire, which I'm guessing she would have mentioned to me, he was safe from prosecution.

Just to cover my bases, I looked up the Illinois prison database for a John Fletcher, but there was no record of him in Pontiac, which Walt had mentioned, or in any prison in the system. Without John Fletcher to question, that was just another dead end.

I closed the computer and thought about watching TV, but I'd been doing too much of that lately. Annoyed as I was to admit it, Andres and Victor were right. I had been spending too much time locked in my house, and it was beginning to feel quiet and lonely and stale.

"Shoes." I startled myself with the sound of my own voice, and jumped off the couch in search of shoes. Once I found them, and a coat, gloves, hat, and scarf, I was pretty well exhausted. No wonder no one goes out in the Midwest in the winter. It takes too long to get dressed. But since I was all wrapped up, I grabbed my car keys and closed the door behind me, letting the cold air hit my face and wake me up.

That's where my plan hit a snag. I had nowhere to go. I didn't feel like seeing a movie or going to the mall. Most of my friends for the past fifteen years had, it turned out, really been Frank's friends. After he died there were a few concerned phone calls and promises of lunch, but they drifted away. It meant that unless I wanted to find out if Victor's band was playing somewhere, there was Ellen and Vera. Neither option appealed to me.

So I drove. I went toward the lake, zigzagging my way southeast, until I got to the Water Tower, the only building in the area to have survived the Chicago fire. At night it was lit up and had a beautiful eeriness to it that made me want to stare for a long while. I stopped the car at a bus stop, but when I saw a cop walking toward me, ticket book in hand, I moved on.

I drove nowhere in particular, taking a meandering route that was supposed to lead me home. Instead, I went in the opposite direction. Maybe it was because the threats toward Vera were connected to Club Car that I found myself on the street where the restaurant was to be built. I assumed I'd pass a dark building and, with nothing else to do, I'd drive northwest toward my Bucktown neighborhood. Maybe get a pizza.

But the restaurant wasn't dark. The dining area was lit by candles and there were people inside. I parked the car and walked toward the window. I saw a tall, lanky figure sitting at the bar, a tablecloth draped over it, an elaborate candelabra and two glasses of wine on the cloth. The figure, I quickly realized, was Walt. At first he seemed to be alone, but I saw movement from behind the bar. Ilena was holding a bottle of wine in her hand. She was laughing at something Walt had said.

"She gets around," I said to the cold, winter air. This put her at three men and a husband—a bit greedy, even for someone with Ilena's sense of entitlement.

A light came from the kitchen. I saw the door swing open and watched as Ilena and Walt turned their heads to greet the third person. I couldn't see who it was. I waited, hoping for whomever it was to walk toward the candlelight, but he just stood there. Ilena said something. Walt nodded. No one seemed angry or surprised. I moved a little closer to the window. If any of them had looked my way they would have seen a bundle of winter clothes staring into the window. They would probably assume I was a homeless person and ignore me. A sad reality of city life, but one I was counting on.

I could see the third figure move, taking steps toward the candle-light. I did my best to will him into view. And then, he stopped.

"Damn it," I whispered. "Two more steps."

As if he heard me, he moved two more steps. Roman. It was Roman.

It wasn't a romantic tryst between Walt and Ilena, or if it was, it included Roman, and that was a little more excitement than I was prepared to witness. Ilena poured her husband a glass of wine, which he sipped. He took a bundle of papers out of his coat pocket and handed them to Walt. I could see Walt looking at them. Then Walt signed them and gave them back. Roman patted him on the back, and Walt got up from his stool and put on a coat.

What business transaction takes place in a candlelit room under construction at night with only three of the partners present? I saw Walt walking toward the front door, so I jumped back from the window. There was no time to get to my car, so I went as quickly as I could around the corner and hoped for the best. I watched Walt come out into the cold air, his breath swirling around him. He stuffed his hands in his pockets and walked past me toward Canal Street.

I didn't know what Walt had been doing, and I reminded myself I didn't really know him. But he'd been the one I liked, the one who seemed different from the rest of them. But he wasn't different. From where I stood, shivering in the cold, Walt was just one more greedy guy making backroom deals.

This was why I liked to stay home, I realized. People are not easy sudokus.

Twenty

It was ten a.m. when I drove into the parking lot at Dugan. Right on time, but I still felt like I was behind schedule. I liked being busy, liked having two shows to focus on, but I didn't like feeling responsible for anyone other than myself. And this mess with Vera was somehow becoming my problem too.

Vera had called me the night before, frantic with news of another threat. It had been three days since the "slashed" call, so it seemed to me the caller was on a deadline to get rid of her one way or another. This time the computerized voice suggested she update her will.

I'd been just about to fall asleep, but I stayed up, trying to calm her down and keep her focused on finding out who was behind the calls. I told her about what I'd seen at the restaurant as a potential conspiracy of investors looking to oust her. Perhaps they were all involved in the threat, I suggested. But Vera didn't buy it. She'd grown up in the world of power and money and saw the meeting with Walt as just another way the Romans of the world conducted business. Vera said that the day after I'd spotted the three in the restaurant, it was announced that Walt now owned eight percent of the restaurant, with his additional share coming off Ilena's ownership of nearly a third. It must have been what they were meeting about, but it didn't explain why Walt was rewarded with a larger share of the profits, or why it had come out of Ilena's percentage. Knowing how badly she wanted to make money, I knew Ilena couldn't have given up those points easily.

I gave Vera one more speech about calling the police or a lawyer, but now it wasn't just Doug who was keeping her involved in Club Car. Vera was determined not to be pushed around, a quality I would have admired if it weren't costing me sleep. I told her to stay at a hotel, but she felt her dogs would protect her. I didn't want to send her to bed with the thought that anyone willing to kill her would probably be willing to kill two past-their-prime greyhounds, so instead I told her to triple-lock the doors and go to bed.

The rest of the night, and on the hour-long drive to Dugan, I waited for another call from her, but none came. When my cell phone did ring, just as I was getting out of my car, it was Ellen.

"Where have you been?" It was her way of saying hello.

"I'm working."

"Honestly, Kate, do you expect me to believe that you're working so much you can't return a phone call?"

"I don't know what I expect you to believe, Ellen." I yawned. "I can't talk now."

"You hung up on me the other day. I was trying to tell you about Andrew's basketball game. He has a uniform and everything. It's adorable," she said. "I'll get you a ticket."

I wanted to ask why I would want to see a fourth-grade basketball game, but I didn't bother. "I have to work that day."

"You don't even know when it is." She grunted. "I'm just trying to help you get out more."

Sadly, I knew that was true. "I don't need help."

"I've made an appointment for you with my stylist. Friday, eleven a.m. My treat. It'll be better if Mom doesn't see you looking all . . . tired. It's a spa, so while you're there, you should really consider getting a facial. It will do wonders for those little lines around your eyes." Without giving me a chance to respond, she hung up.

I looked in the rearview mirror at the little lines around my eyes. First Andres and Victor, and now Ellen. How bad did I look? Lucky for me, unlike in the fairy tales, this mirror didn't answer.

Twenty-one

We got the first shot of the day off at eleven: Tim, Brick, and about sixty other inmates eating lunch in the cafeteria. My image of a prison cafeteria was hundreds of guys lined up at long, rectangular metal tables, clanking their forks and demanding better food. But at Dugan the cafeteria was small, only ten circular tables with six seats each. Like in the visitors room, the metal stools were connected to the tables, which were bolted to the floor.

But unlike the visitors room, which had guards near each of the tables, in the cafeteria the guards stood back, near the entrance and at the chow line. It took me a minute to realize that security hadn't suddenly gone lax. On either side of the room, about eight feet off the ground, were two small windows covered with mesh. Behind each was an armed guard, his rifle pointed toward the inmates.

I stood to the side and watched Andres move around the room, his camera on his shoulder, getting shots of the men eating lunch. Some of the inmates hammed it up, but others stuck their faces close to their plates and did their best to ignore us. Victor followed Andres around with the boom mic, trying to capture ambient noise and snippets of conversation. He didn't look happy about it. Even for someone used to heavy metal music and the constant sound of a drumbeat, the noise was overwhelming.

The food didn't look particularly appetizing either—two bologna sandwiches on white bread, potato chips, and a small mound of iceberg lettuce with one cherry tomato. I knew that the food at Club Car would be better, but it wouldn't be more exclusive. You had to do a lot more than make a reservation to get a place at these tables.

I pointed to the bolted-down table. "I guess no one is going to throw one of the tables over if they don't like the food."

Dugan's public officer, Joanie Rheinbeck, didn't even break a smile. She'd joined us for the shoot to see if she could help us, but it was my guess she was really there to make sure we didn't get in anyone's way.

"That's not a problem," she said. "We do meals in shifts. It keeps the number of inmates out of their cells to a minimum and that keeps the risk to a minimum."

"Inmates against the guards?"

"That," she said, "and inmates hurting each other. They can turn a soup ladle into a deadly weapon. And believe me, they will if they feel even the slightest insult."

"But those guys are watching." I pointed toward the men behind the mesh-covered windows.

"A lot of these inmates are getting backdoor paroles, so they have nothing to lose."

I grew up in the suburbs, married young, and have lived in the same house in the arty Bucktown neighborhood of Chicago for the past ten years. I haven't gotten so much as a parking ticket since I was in my twenties. But because of my work on true crime shows, I knew enough prison slang to understand what a backdoor parole was—dying inside these walls. And knowing that made me feel kind of badass in my Ann Taylor business-casual and Aerosoles pumps.

"The food meets nutritional standards," Joanie continued a little defensively. "We have a very small budget, but no inmates go hungry. They have three meals from us, and they can buy food from the commissary."

"They can buy their own food?"

"Sure," she said. "Most of them do, and they can get hot pots, typewriters, toiletries."

"A lot of call for typewriters?"

"Once in a while. The most popular items are coffee and cigarettes."

"Where do they get the money?"

"Family, usually. Or jobs around the prison," she said. "Tim works at the library. That's how he earns."

"And Brick?"

"He's not working at the moment. He must get his money from family."

"He doesn't have any family, at least any who care enough to visit him," I said. "He told me he's estranged from his brother, so I doubt he's getting money that way."

Joanie shrugged. "Well, he's getting it somewhere. He always reaches the two-hundred dollar limit for the account. So does Tim, between his earnings and the money he gets from his parents."

"Have you met Tim's parents?"

"No, but he's still very close to both of them."

"You know that much about his life?"

"Everyone knows Tim. He's friendly with the staff," she said. "I think he's trying to convince himself he's not a bad guy."

"Is he?"

"The court system thought so."

Andres and Victor walked toward us. "We have them lining up for food, eating, and talking," Andres said, his camera at his side. "What else do you need in here?"

I looked over at Brick, holding court with five other men. He was doing most of the talking, while the others seemed to hang on his every word. When Brick laughed, the others laughed, and he looked to be enjoying both the attention he was getting from the men and the fact that I was watching.

Several tables away, Tim sat in silence. His table was full too, and the other men were quietly chatting, but Tim wasn't included. He seemed lost in his thoughts, or bored, or tired. In any case, he was making no special effort to notice Andres, Victor, or me.

My job was to make prison seem bleak. People have expectations about prison, about it being a place of punishment and isolation. While it's always interesting to tweak those expectations a little, no one, especially Crime TV, would want some viewer to change the channel because he was pissed off about a bunch of killers sharing a laugh over lunch.

"I guess that's it for this scene," I said to Andres, then I turned to Joanie. "What do you think of these guys?"

"All of them or just your two?"

"My two."

"They're okay. That one"—she pointed to Tim—"is quiet enough these days, but he raised some hell for a while. When he was at Pontiac, he was suspected of beating up on a guy for calling him a liar."

"What had he lied about?"

She cocked an eyebrow at me. "Who knows? Who cares? These guys will kill each other over anything."

"Nothing redeemable?"

"That's not really my department."

"And Brick?"

"They call him the professor. He goes around quoting Shakespeare and Freud, and anything he can. He seems to know what he's talking about, but most of these guys didn't make it through the tenth grade, so if he's full of shit, they wouldn't know anyway."

"Seems pretty harmless now," I said. "Even if he is full of shit."

She shrugged. "As long as he doesn't cause any trouble, I really don't care. Sort of like you."

"Me?"

"We have TV crews here from time to time, and all the producers say the same thing prison guards do: You can like them as people, but you can't get so caught up in their lives that you don't do your job, right?"

I looked over at Brick and Tim. "Right," I said.

Twenty-two

The inmates had fifteen minutes for lunch, including the walk from their cells to the cafeteria and back. Joanie had allowed us an additional ten to make sure we got what we needed, but she made it clear what an inconvenience it was to both the kitchen staff and the other inmates.

Even more of an inconvenience was shooting Tim and Brick in their cells. It meant locking down their section so none of their neighbors could cause us any trouble. Both of the men were housed in the same block, a long row of nothing but cement walls and iron bars. Tim was on the far end of the second floor, near the staircase to the cafeteria. Brick was in the middle of the row, so we went to his cell first.

While Andres readied the camera, Joanie and I waited outside the cell. We were only allowed to open the door once we were ready to shoot and had a guard in place to make sure things were calm.

"How big is this cell?" I asked Joanie while we waited for the guard.

"Six by eight. Brick is in his alone, but Tim shares." Before I could ask, she answered, "Brick's old cell mate is in protective custody at the moment because of an incident with another inmate."

Brick laughed. "He tried to get to know a new guy better than he wanted to be known. And the new guy apparently had a few friends that my cellie wasn't aware of."

I looked through the bars at Brick, sitting on his cot. The place was small, just enough room for bunk beds, a sink, a toilet, and a small shelf crowded with a dozen or so items. Among them were a small TV, a bag of coffee, a hot pot, vanilla wafers, and some instant soup. The cell was packed, but it would have been almost livable except for the piles of books Brick had stacked on nearly every inch of floor space.

"You know you're going to get a write-up for that," Joanie said to him. "You've got to return them to the library."

"These are mine," he said. "Kate even got some of 'em for me."

I looked at Joanie. "I didn't think it was against the rules."

"It's not," she said. "But he has to keep them away from the cell door. It makes it hard for guards to get in if they need to, and if one of these firebugs gets an idea and lights this paper walking past his cell, the whole place is in chaos."

Brick immediately began moving the books under his bed, stacking them in neat rows after separating them into piles.

"You must get sick of this," I said, once Andres had the camera rolling and the guard had arrived and unlocked the door to Brick's cell. "All of these rules."

"It is what it is, Kate. I would prefer to decide for myself what time I got up in the morning, or when I ate dinner, but that's not the life I have," he said. "I sometimes think heaven is walking out into the sunshine with the day ahead of me and no idea what would happen." He smiled. "I'd probably spend most of it in the library, so I guess it don't matter if the sun shines or not."

"Are you sure you wouldn't end up back with your gang?"

"They got no use for an old man like me," he said. "Shit. They got no respect for me either. I see these young punks come in here with their attitude, thinking they can do twenty standing on their heads. They don't get what it's like."

"What's it like?"

He waved his arm around. "It's this. Day in, day out. Year after year."

"It must get to you."

"It did. A long time ago. I got tired, trying to be tough all the time, trying to show I had it under control. Being on death row, it was all lawyers and appeals, and one guy after another being taken for his walk and never coming back. I got just in-my-bones tired."

"Did you think you deserved the death penalty?"

He shrugged. "I think an eye for an eye, you know? But then I got blood on my hands. I don't pretend to be a good man. I don't pretend to believe in mercy or forgiveness, or all that God shit. But those judges do. The juries do. So them wanting to kill someone, that I never understood."

"Is this better? Knowing you won't be executed?"

"Yeah, it's Shangri-La." He laughed.

I laughed with him. "How do you cope, Brick? How do you get through the day knowing it's always going to be the same, always going to be lonely, always going to be out of your control?"

He pointed to the books under his bed. "That's how I cope. I escape into my imagination."

\\\

Fifteen minutes later Tim was giving a different explanation for his serenity, in a very different environment. Tim's cell was almost monastic in appearance. His cell mate, who declined to be on camera, was waiting out the interview in the warden's office. But it was clear which bunk was Tim's. While the top bunk had dozens of photos of naked and half-naked women taped to the wall, the rest of the cell, including Tim's bunk, was stark. The fixtures were the same as in Brick's cell—toilet, sink, shelf—but there was no clutter, no food, no TV, no books.

Tim stood in the middle of his cell, giving us a tour as if he were showing us around his home. Which, I had to remind myself, he was.

"I thought maybe you would have a picture of Jenny," I said.

He pursed his lips. "Don't think I could look at her face. I don't think I have that right," he said. "Or the stomach for it. It's hard enough with just my memories."

"Prison must be lonely."

"It is, Kate," he said. "I guess anywhere can be lonely. Being in a crowd where you don't belong, that's a kind of loneliness, or being with someone that don't suit you. But it's lonely here. You ever get lonely, Kate?"

I ignored the question. "You seem to make friends with the guards," I said. "But I noticed you weren't friendly at lunch with the other inmates."

"They talk about things that don't interest me. I just try to be a good person. I think that if Jenny can see me, and I'm doing everything I can to be a good man, then maybe it will help her rest in peace. That's all I want."

"That's all? You don't miss women?"

He smiled. "You mean sex? Yeah, I miss sex. It's been so long I can barely remember what it's like to run my hand down the soft curves of a woman's skin, or to feel her face against my neck." He seemed to get lost in the thought for a moment, but then he raised an eyebrow. "And maybe this ain't the moment for rememberin'."

He rested his arm on his cell mate's bed and took a deep breath, turning his eyes on mine and staring into them. "But to your question, Kate, I do miss women. And not just for sex. Women keep men sane. You give us a place to be scared, to be gentle, to be forgiven. In here, among all these men, we have to be hard all the time. There's no place to rest."

"What does that do to you, years of living like this?"

He smiled faintly. "I . . ." He paused; just a hint of water in his eyes that he quickly blinked away. He set his jaw firmly. "Some men fall into a dark hole, get angry and bitter. Some men build a new life here, new family, as if the world outside doesn't exist." He hadn't answered my question, not directly, but there was a catch in his throat. There was something vulnerable, some part of himself he was trying to hide, but he wasn't doing a good job. He saw some reaction in my eyes, which in truth was part sadness for Tim and part concern that Andres was getting the right angle for the shot. Whatever Tim reacted to, he put his vulnerability away, the way I might toss a pair of socks in a drawer, closed away and hidden from view. It took only a second before the smile was back.

"Brick says he finds his escape in books," I said.

"I don't try to escape. I stay right here. Today. I don't think about tomorrow. I don't think about years of this. I've resigned myself to it. I admit I do sometimes think about the past. And I do remember with regrets, but I try not to indulge. I try to stay focused on the situation as it exists and get through it as best I can."

"And that works?"

"So far."

I smiled. He had a casual charm to him, so I knew he would come across well on camera. I could picture the women watching the show, the prison groupie types, who would line up to be Tim's place to rest. Murdered wife notwithstanding. Which brought me to an interesting point.

"Do you have a girlfriend, Tim?"

"You applying?"

"No. Just wondering. I know a lot of men cope with their loneliness by forming relationships with women on the outside."

He shook his head. "No, I don't. I tried that once, about ten years ago. I met a nice lady through the Internet. There's sites up for guys inside to meet women." He blushed a little. "It's sad, really. Guys post things about how they like to send flowers and take long walks on the beach. Guys doing fifty years."

"But some women fall for it."

"They do. And some of it's sincere. Wishful thinkin'. You know, 'Maybe I'll get out and take that long walk on the beach with this nice lady who cares enough about me to drop money in my commissary account and visit me on alternate Saturdays.'" He smiled a shy smile. "I did, for a while. I was just off death row and somehow I had this idea that maybe I would get out someday. I half-convinced this lady it would happen. But it wasn't fair to her, so I stopped things cold."

"Why did you think you'd get out?"

He paused, was quiet for a long time, then finally said, "I thought differently then." He moved a little farther back in the cell, prompting Andres, Victor, and me to move as well so we could keep him in the shot.

"You want coffee, Kate?" Tim asked. "I keep a small stash."

"That's okay," I said. I could see Joanie checking her watch out of the corner of my eye, and I knew her patience was running thin. "We're going to have to wrap up for today."

"Well, next time, then," Tim said. "And be careful driving home. There's going to be a terrible storm tonight."

"Really? I hadn't heard that."

"Weather is a bit of a hobby of mine; always has been," he said. "And I was listenin' to the radio earlier, heard that Chicago is in for a terrible pile of snow."

"Chicago is thirty-five miles from here," I pointed out.

"But that's where you live, isn't it?"

I smiled. "Thanks for the warning, Tim."

Twenty-three

I do not drink hard liquor. It takes a certain kind of woman to walk into a bar and slam Jim Beam. I am not that woman. Which, in certain circumstances, is a character trait I regret.

I walked into my house and put down my tote bag. I had maybe five seconds of peace and quiet before the phone rang. The caller ID, the world's greatest invention for passive-aggressives, showed that it was Vera, so I didn't pick up. I figured she'd gotten another threatening call, and though I felt bad about it, there wasn't anything I could do to help. What Vera needed to do was get as far away from Doug and the others as possible. Advice I'd already given her several times. If she wasn't going to follow it, there was no sense in repeating myself when I was tired and hungry.

I wandered into the kitchen, heard my cell phone ringing, ignored it, and looked for some food. I didn't have anything in the fridge except a stick of butter and some wilted lettuce.

"I need to get my act together."

I grabbed the two dozen delivery menus I kept stored in a drawer by the sink. I was getting a little too familiar with the selection, and the delivery guys were getting too familiar with me. At my favorite Chinese restaurant, the nice, if nosy, woman who answered the phone always asked if I was ordering "just one entrée" again. Saying yes, and hearing her sigh in response, made me feel like I'd failed somehow. On occasion I'd order two entrées just to cheer her up.

Leaving out Chinese as an option, I spread out the menus on my kitchen counter like a deck of cards, closed my eyes, and pointed.

"Bucktown Burgers," I said. "Mediocre food with button-popping portions. Sorry, Walt, but that's just my style."

I picked up my home phone to dial Bucktown Burgers, but as I did, it rang.

"Kate?"

Damn it. "Vera. I just got home. I'm really hungry and about to order dinner."

"There's a problem."

"Can it wait?"

"No."

"Where are you?"

"At the restaurant," she said. "You have to come. Something has happened."

"What?"

"I don't think I should say over the phone."

I put the menu on the kitchen counter and thought about not going for a minute, but there was that rudeness thing again. Plus she did sound like something was wrong. And I was curious. Maybe mostly I was curious. If she'd told me over the phone what had happened, I might not have been so quick to put my coat back on.

I stopped at Bucktown Burgers's pick-up window on the way to the restaurant and did my best to cram the half-pounder into my mouth while still more or less staying in my lane as I drove downtown.

Tim had been right about the storm. Just as I walked to my car the snow began falling, and not the pretty, fluffy, Hollywood snow, the kind you can brush playfully off a cheek. This was furious clumps of snow mixed with sleet, pelting anyone stupid enough to be out in it. Just the kind of weather that makes everyone wonder why Chicagoans live in Chicago.

The snow wasn't the worst of it. The wind was crazy. Snow was blowing everywhere, and even with the windshield wipers at full speed I could barely see past the hood of my car. I had to slam my brakes to avoid some idiot who was crossing the street against the light, sending my fries flying all over the floor of the passenger seat. And despite having sacrificed half my dinner to keep from hitting him, the guy gave me the finger. Nice.

By the time I pulled up in front of Club Car, I was wet, annoyed, and holding a soggy, half-eaten hamburger.

"Whatever it is, it better be life changing," I said to Vera, who greeted me at the door of the restaurant with a pale expression and grateful smile.

"It is."

She led me back to the restaurant's kitchen. No work had been done on the place since I'd been there a few days before. It was dusty, and with no heat on, very cold. The cookware and other items Walt had brought in for the tasting were sitting on the counter untouched since then.

"So what is it?" I asked.

She didn't answer. But as I got to the stove, I saw what had been so important. Blood was coagulating on the floor. Blood that had come from more than a few gaping holes in Erik Price's body.

From past shows I'd worked on, I'd seen crime scene photos. I'd looked at pictures in which people had been shot, strangled, bludg-eoned, stabbed, or drowned. I'd sorted through images of half-naked women left dead on the street, and bloated, long-dead corpses found in trash cans. I'd always thought seeing it in person could be no worse than seeing it in a photo. I'd been wrong.

"I think he's dead," Vera said as she stepped just inches behind me.

His eyes were open but blank, his face slightly swollen, as if he'd been punched in the eye. I tapped my foot against his calf. It was stiff. I felt acid coming up into my throat. I bit my lip and swallowed hard. "He's dead."

Vera took a step closer to the body, but I put my arm up to stop her. "Where are the police?"

"I haven't called them yet."

I spun around. "You haven't called them?"

"I wanted to get your advice first."

I grabbed her shoulders and pushed her slowly out of the room. I didn't want to be near the body anymore, and I sure as hell didn't want to accidentally leave evidence of my being at the crime scene.

Once we were in the main dining area, I felt the acid leave my throat and panic replace it. "We have to get out of here," I said. "The killer—"

"There's no one else here," she said. "I checked while I was waiting for you."

"You checked?" I stared at her. She was either much braver than I'd thought or much, much dumber. "Look, I'm going to ask this, because it has to be asked," I started.

"I didn't kill him."

"Then what the hell are you doing here?"

"Doug called me. He told me to meet him here."

"In the middle of a snowstorm?"

"The storm hadn't started yet." She said it so matter-of-factly, as if meeting her boyfriend on a cold night at an unfinished restaurant was a normal thing to do. I wanted to strangle her, but I could only handle one dead body at a time.

"So where's Doug?"

"I don't know. The door was open when I got here. I heard something in the kitchen. I walked in and saw Erik on the ground. I didn't know what to do. If Doug . . ." She didn't finish the sentence. "I called you."

"You heard something? What did you hear?"

"Noise. I don't know." She looked at me; finally fear was registering. "Do you think I heard the murder?"

"Did you call me right after you found Erik?"

"Yes. Within five minutes."

"Then you didn't hear the murder. He's been dead at least a couple of hours. Rigor mortis has set in," I said. "But you may have heard the murderer. He was probably hanging around long enough to make sure he'd set you up for killing Erik."

"Who could it be?"

"Really, Vera? You can't take a guess?"

"Doug would never do something like that."

"Did he call you from his home or his cell?"

"I didn't recognize the number. It must have been a new office number or something," she said. "I don't see why that matters right now."

"It doesn't," I admitted. "There's a dead man in the other room. We have to focus on that."

"So what should we do?"

I took a deep breath. "Call the police." I grabbed my cell phone and stared blankly for a moment, trying to remember the number for 911, before the panic lifted and I realized *that* was the number.

"Kate," Vera said. "Wait."

"Why?"

"I have to ask you something."

"What?"

"Do you think he was shot?"

"I don't know. He has holes in him. He could have been shot. Or he could have been stabbed, I guess. He didn't die of natural causes, that's for damn sure."

"Then I have to tell you something else."

I was almost afraid to ask. "Vera, if this is going to turn into one of those B-movie thrillers where the nicest person in the world is revealed as a sadistic killer, then I want you to know that my last meal will have been a soggy Bucktown burger, and frankly that's just not acceptable. So whatever you're about to tell me better not end with the words 'serial killer.'"

"My gun is missing."

I had to replay her last sentence in my head just to be sure. "You own a gun? You, who once scolded me for killing a bug because all living creatures share an equal place on the planet?" I snapped at her. "You own a gun?"

"Doug and I bought it yesterday. I told him about the message. The one you and the guys heard. He said it sounded dangerous. He said he didn't think his ex-girlfriend would know any of that voice-altering stuff Victor talked about, so it must be someone from the restaurant. He wanted me to have protection."

"Did he buy the gun?"

She shook her head. "Technically, I did. We bought from a private dealer in the western suburbs and afterwards, just so we were doing everything properly, I insisted we drive straight to the police station near my house, so I could get an application to register it."

"So the police know you own a gun, which is now missing and possibly the murder weapon."

"Yes."

"Tell me you're kidding."

She shook her head. "This looks bad, doesn't it? That's why I wanted to call you first, because I figured it would look really bad."

"I've worked on a dozen true crime shows where people were convicted with less evidence."

"But aside from the gun—"

"You invested a heap of money in a restaurant that's basically a construction site, without any construction going on. You started asking questions. Maybe you wanted your money back. Maybe you and Erik got into it about that. You did have words the other day."

"That wasn't about anything. I didn't think we should keep emphasizing how elite the restaurant would be. What he said in his interview with you made the place look really bad," she said. "But it wasn't enough to kill anyone over."

"That's what *you* say it was about. The only person who could corroborate your story is permanently unavailable for comment," I pointed out. "You say Doug called you. But if he didn't call from a number traceable to him, then all we have is your word that he called. What if he doesn't back you up? Then it looks like you came to the restaurant to meet Erik, got into a fight, and killed him with a gun you bought yesterday, just a few days after your argument."

"But if we think it through, if you tell me what to say, it can all be explained, don't you think?"

I stared at her. She believed somehow I knew what she should say, that I could protect her. That I'd want to. "Vera, when you found the body you called *me*. Not the police. They generally frown on people who stumble across a murder and neglect to mention it."

"I just delayed calling. We're going to call."

This was getting worse by the minute. "Sometimes once the police latch onto a suspect . . ." I started to say, then tried to figure out the nicest way to tell her. "I've done my fair share of shows about people who were wrongly convicted because once the police found the person who seemed like the killer, they stopped looking for anyone else."

"I know I look guilty," she conceded. "We have to figure something out. But not just because I look bad. It's also because of Doug."

The fact that she could be insulted at my assumption that Doug had set her up for murder and yet be convinced that he himself was a reasonable suspect in the crime was baffling to me. I told her as much.

"*I* don't think he did it," she protested. "I think the police will think he did it and I don't want him to get in trouble. There's got to be a way we can tell the police what happened that doesn't make him look like he set me up for Erik's murder. I just need you to help me figure out what that is."

"That's why you called me? To protect Doug?"

She didn't answer. I looked at this gullible, silly, middle-aged woman who was more interested in protecting a man she barely knew than in protecting herself. I knew she'd been lonely these past few months, but is being alone really so bad?

Of course, I was the idiot who kept ordering shrimp fried rice for two at the China Palace.

Twenty-four

D id you touch anything?" I asked.

"Like what? I mean, I touched the doorknob and stuff like that."

"Anything that wasn't here earlier today?"

"No."

"Because the police are going to find your fingerprints, but that's okay. They can't determine when you touched these things," I said. "Since you have access to the restaurant, your fingerprints all over the crime scene don't mean anything. Unless you touched something that wasn't here before."

"I don't think so."

"Think, Vera. Think carefully. I did a show once where this guy killed his roommate. They got into a fight over Wii bowling." I stopped myself from giving the long version of the story and just tried to focus on the point. "Anyway, when he was first questioned, the killer said he'd left the apartment at four in the afternoon and had been out all night. When he got home the next morning, the police were already at the apartment; they'd already found his roommate dead. The killer's fingerprints were all over the place, but why wouldn't they be? He lived there." I took a breath and tried to calm myself. "Only there was this pizza box. The roommate had ordered pizza at eight o'clock that night. The receipt was time-stamped and the restaurant could verify when the pizza was delivered. The killer's prints were on the pizza box. If he hadn't been there after four o'clock, then how did his fingerprints get on the box?"

"He was lying about it?"

"Yes, Vera. And he's in prison for twenty-five years because he forgot he touched the damn pizza box," I said. "So think. Did you touch anything that wasn't here this afternoon? Anything that could have been delivered this evening? Or Erik's blood. Or maybe the knives."

"What knives?"

"I noticed Walt left his knives in the kitchen. Have you ever touched them?"

She scratched at her neck, thinking. She started to pace. "Maybe. After the recipe tasting I helped Walt clean up."

"Walt was with you?"

"Yes."

"Then if one of those knives is the murder weapon and your print is on it, that's how it got there." I took a breath, tried to come up with a plan. "We're going to my car. We're going to call the police and give them more or less the true story. Your biggest problem is the time. But maybe we can fix that. We're going to say you called me on your way to meet Doug because he sounded weird, and I was worried about you. . . ."

"That's nice of you to worry."

I sighed. "I wasn't actually worried, Vera. I'm just going to say I was worried and that's why I came."

"Why did you come if you weren't worried about me?"

"Curiosity. Stupidity. I don't really know."

She smiled a little. "I'm sorry, Kate. I don't mean to be so much trouble. It's just that I knew I could count on you."

"What did I ever do to give you that idea?"

\\\

The operator told us it would take the police nearly an hour to arrive. In a snowstorm, dead bodies don't rate as high as nearly dead ones, and it seemed there were plenty of those—people whose cars had stalled on the highway, those with little or no heat who were using ovens to keep warm, and fools having heart attacks from trying to shovel their driveways as the snow pelted down and inches piled around us.

Vera and I were nearly two more victims of the storm, sitting in my car, alternating between bursts of heat and turning the engine off so as not to use up all the gas.

"Why don't we just wait inside?" she asked after about forty minutes.

"Because it's a crime scene. Besides, there's no heat in there," I said. "We're better off here. At least we can occasionally get warm."

"Maybe we could see if any of the other places are open?" Vera pointed out the restaurants and bars that lined the street.

"Closed," I said. In the best of weather, a lot of places in the South Loop close after dinner, when the businesspeople have all gone home. Tonight, it looked like every one of them had had the good sense to leave before the snow started falling.

She sat quiet for a moment. "Doug called me and said he was worried about something at the restaurant, and needed me to take a look."

"But he didn't tell you what?"

"No."

"And he's not answering his cell?"

She shook her head. "Do you think the killer went after Doug? Maybe he got to the restaurant just when Erik was being murdered. Maybe he saw the whole thing."

"If Doug were dead, why wouldn't the killer just leave his body next to Erik's?"

"So you think he's alive?" A small amount of relief crept into Vera's voice.

"I think he's the killer."

Just as Vera was about to debate me, a squad car and a second car, a dark sedan, pulled up behind me. I watched as two patrol officers and two men in plain clothes got out of the cars and started for the restaurant.

"Remember, Vera," I said, "you called me on your way to the restaurant. I came to meet you here. You were almost at the restaurant when you called. A block away at the most. You understand?"

"Why wouldn't I have called you from home?"

"Vera. We have one chance to tell this story; that's it. And what we say has to fit the facts. So tell me you understand."

She nodded. "A block away. At most."

"Let's just go over this one more time," I said. "You called me, parked your car, then waited in your car for a few minutes, looking for Doug's car. When he didn't arrive, you went to the restaurant, you went inside, waited in the dining room. Eventually, maybe ten or fifteen minutes after you called me, you walked in the kitchen looking for Doug. You found Erik. You were scared, freaked out. You ran out of the restaurant, went to your car. Then I arrived. We went back into the restaurant and then called 911."

"What if he asks me something I can't answer?"

"Just say you were flustered, you don't remember. Be upset. Be frightened."

"I won't have to fake that."

"Good. Homicide detectives have pretty fine-tuned bullshit detectors, so stay as close to the truth as you can. The only thing you lie about is when you found the body."

We got out of the car and headed toward the police.

"I'm Kate Conway," I said to one of the patrol officers. "I called this in."

One of the plainclothes officers walked toward me. "I'm Detective Makina," he said. "Can you tell me what happened?"

"This is Vera Bingham." I indicated Vera, who stood so close to me we were practically holding hands. "We found the body."

"What were you ladies doing here tonight?"

"Vera got a call from her boyfriend, Doug Zieman. He asked her to meet him here, so she started to drive over, but then she got worried that something was off. She called me. I don't like Doug, so I met her here just to make sure everything was okay."

I could feel Vera pinch my hand, but I ignored it. I'd already decided if someone was going to be thrown under the bus it was going to be Doug. If he wanted to prove he was innocent then he could answer his damn phone.

"When I got here," I continued, "Vera was hysterical. She'd found Erik Price lying dead. I checked for myself, just to be sure. I thought maybe he was just injured or something. But he was dead." I took a breath and realized it was the first one I'd taken since I'd started my story. As I exhaled I watched my breath float toward Detective Makina's face. "We came outside, called you guys, and waited in my car." I was hoping it didn't sound as rehearsed as it was.

The detective, balding, square-jawed, maybe sixty, looked at me. He waited, but I didn't add to my story. He turned to Vera.

"Either of you ever been in this place before?" he asked.

"Yes," Vera said. "I'm an investor in the restaurant, and Kate is a TV producer doing a story on us. We've both been inside several times."

He nodded. "And Doug Zieman?"

"He's also an investor," I said.

"And he's missing," Vera added.

Detective Makina raised an eyebrow. "You've been trying to reach him?"

Vera started to talk, so I grabbed her arm and twisted it a little. That shut her up. "He hasn't shown up," I said. "He was supposed to be here over an hour ago, and he's not here."

"Did either of you touch anything?" Makina asked.

"We could see he was dead," I said. I tried to keep my answer vague, just in case we had touched something we shouldn't have. "And obviously we didn't know if the killer was still inside, so we wanted to get out as quickly as possible. But I don't remember if I touched anything, if either of us did. It was pretty frightening."

"Ms. Bingham, when did you call Ms. Conway?"

"I was almost here," she told him. "Less than a block away."

"And how long did it take you to drive over, Ms. Conway?" He turned back to me.

"Ten minutes or so," I said. "Hard to say exactly in this weather."

These were small lies, tiny little lies. And actually, they were helpful lies, I told myself, because instead of focusing on Vera, the police would go after the real killer.

"Okay," Detective Makina said. "Wait here. No, wait in your car. You stand out here, you'll freeze your balls off." Even in the flickering light from the streetlamp, I could see him blush. "Sorry about that, ladies. I meant you'll be really cold."

I grabbed Vera's elbow and led her back toward my car. Once we'd closed and locked the doors, I turned the heat to high, and took a deep breath.

"He seemed to believe us," she said.

"Why wouldn't he believe us? We were telling the truth. More or less."

Twenty-five

After another twenty minutes, Detective Makina took our names and addresses and sent us home. We'd been there long enough to watch a stream of crime scene investigators arrive and begin carrying out evidence. But Erik's body was still inside, dead, along with his dreams of running the reincarnation of a 1930s nightclub.

I told Vera to leave her car at the scene and come home with me. I wanted to make sure we had our stories straight for the inevitable follow-up we'd get from Makina, but there was another reason.

"If someone was trying to set you up, they may have realized that won't work. Plan B could be to kill you," I told her on the drive to my house.

"Do we tell the police about the threats?" she asked.

I thought for a moment. "Yes, I guess we should. Maybe if they check the phone records of the other investors they'll figure out who's been calling you, and whoever that is is probably Erik's killer."

"And we have to find out if Doug is okay."

"Oh, for heaven's sake, Vera!" I snapped. "Stop believing in people, will you?"

\\\

We walked into my living room around eleven. The storm was still going, and I was shaking from the cold and the murder. But I was grateful to be home. I left Vera in the living room and went to put on the kettle.

As I stood in the kitchen waiting for the water to boil, it hit me. I was an idiot. I should have just called the police, told the truth, and let the chips fall where they may. If Vera ended up in a six-by-eight cell, eating bologna sandwiches, what business was that of mine? Even if she was innocent, I could hardly be faulted for stepping out of it.

But I knew why I hadn't. It was stupid, and no one would understand if I tried to explain it. I didn't even understand. I was helping Vera because Frank would have wanted me to. Because, as Tim said about Jenny, if Frank could see me trying to be a good person, maybe it would help him rest in peace.

"I don't have anything to eat," I said to Vera as I brought two mugs of tea into the living room.

"That's okay. I'm not hungry." She was standing in front of the fireplace, looking at the painting Frank had done of the couple walking down Michigan Avenue. She took her mug, had a sip, but her eyes never left the painting. "He was a really talented artist, wasn't he?"

"He was," I said, nudging her toward the couch.

"I'm glad you have his paintings up." She hesitated. "But no photographs of him. Why not?"

"I took them down when he left the house. To move in with you, if I recall. I just never felt like putting them back up."

"I have one photo of us, Frank and me, that I kept in my bedroom. I put it away when I met Doug."

"Vera, this will be easier for both of us if we leave Frank out of it, don't you think?" I said. "Our little . . . friendship, for lack of a better word, may have begun when Frank died, but we really have to focus on the situation as it exists and get through it as best we can."

"That's good thinking," she said.

As she spoke, I realized I was taking Tim's advice for the second time in just a few minutes.

"Poor Erik," she said. "I don't even know if he was from Chicago or where he lived or if he had a girlfriend, do you know that, Kate? I never really talked to him about his life, about anything aside from the restaurant."

"Too late now." I tried to shake the image of the blood from my mind. "Vera, I have to know everything if we're going to get through this."

"I'm not holding anything back."

I wasn't sure I believed her, but I was stuck in this mess now, so I had no choice but to hope she was telling the truth. "We're going to have a problem once the police check the phone records."

"I was just thinking that. I called you at seven fifteen, but it was almost eight when we called the police. They're going to ask why we didn't call them sooner," she said. "But I'll just say I waited for you outside the restaurant."

"In the middle of a snowstorm? They'll wonder why you didn't go inside looking for Doug. Unless you say you were afraid of being alone with him and only went inside minutes before I arrived."

"But that will make him look guilty."

"It's better than making you look guilty."

"I want to stay out of trouble but not at the expense of an innocent person," she said. "I might be willing to believe that Doug liked me at least partially because of my money, but I don't believe he killed Erik."

"Okay, so just tell the police what we do know about Doug. The lies about not wanting you to invest and insisting you buy a gun," I said. "If he looks guilty to them you can always pay for his lawyer."

"You said yourself that people get wrongly convicted just because they're the first suspect the police have."

"Be sensible."

She shook her head. "Next option."

"Okay." I sat and stared at my ceiling. It needed a fresh coat of paint. I closed my eyes and tried to think. "The battery in your phone died. You called me when you were almost at the restaurant . . ."

"A block away," she said. "Why was that so important?"

"Cell phones ping off towers. The police can locate where you made a call by triangulating the call from nearby cell towers. They won't be able to tell if you were in the restaurant or a block away, but if you said you called from your house, or even twenty blocks from the restaurant, they'd know you were lying."

"You're very clever."

"My misspent youth of television producing," I said. "But we still have the problem of time. Assuming you called me, drove another block, parked the car . . . Where did you park your car, by the way?"

"Around the corner."

"Why down the street? The place was deserted. You could have parked in front of the restaurant."

"Doug told me to," she said, then quickly added, "and nothing about that request makes him guilty of setting me up to take the fall for Erik's murder. He just didn't want me in front of the restaurant. He said that the block was too dark, and my car could get vandalized. I parked around the corner because there's more traffic. Doug thought it would be safer." There was a little doubt in her voice, which was the first reassuring sign of self-preservation I'd heard from her all evening.

"Fine." I sipped my tea. "After you called me, a block from Club Car, it might have taken you ten minutes with the snow coming down to park and walk to the restaurant. You went inside, called Doug's name a few times—"

"I did call his name."

"Good, then so far it's maybe fifteen minutes since you called me. You wait. You try to call Doug but realize your battery is dead. You hear a noise. You think it's Doug. You go into the kitchen. No Doug. You walk a little farther in. You see Erik's body on the floor. You run to the front door, try and call 911—"

"But my phone doesn't work."

"Exactly," I said. "That whole thing could easily take twenty-five minutes. I arrive. You tell me what you saw. I check it out for myself because I'm that sort of person."

"You are. You never let anything go unchallenged." She seemed almost proud of me.

"So I go in and see that Erik is dead. We go back outside, we're flustered. I'm shaking. We go to my car, where I use my cell phone to call the police."

I sank back on the couch, relieved. The story fit the facts, was true in every way except that Vera's cell phone hadn't died, which the police would not be able to verify. . . .

"Damn it." I snapped back up. "You called Doug. You called him and called him."

"So . . ." I could see Vera slowly figure it out. "I called Doug with a cell phone that had a dead battery." She wrinkled her mouth. "I could say I used the cell phone charger you have in your car."

"I don't have one."

"Okay, so I got the cell phone charger from my car. And I charged my phone in your car. And that's where I called Doug."

"Do you have a cell phone charger in your car?"

She shook her head. "I could buy one. They're so handy. I've been meaning to get one anyway."

"Stores have video cameras," I said. "If you bought one now, and they somehow found the tape of it, it would look like you were trying to create an alibi."

"They're not going to look for videotape of me at stores. They'll just believe me."

"Vera, prisons are filled with people who thought the police would believe them," I said. "Besides, if you called Doug in the time between when you called me and when I called the police—"

"So let's just tell them that I called you, went in and found the body, and waited until you arrived," she said. "There was a lot of blood, right?"

"It looked like it to me."

"So wouldn't there be blood on me if I'd killed him? Doesn't blood spray?"

"Spatter."

"Whatever." She was excited, figured she had found a way out. "Wouldn't I have blood on me?"

"You could have changed your clothes in the time between calling me and calling them."

Vera's shoulders slumped. She sat quietly for a minute, then looked at me. "I'm in trouble, aren't I?"

"No, Vera," I corrected her. "We're in trouble."

Twenty-six

The next morning, I met Andres and Victor outside Dugan and told them the same story Vera and I had planned for the police—about Vera's calling me before she found Erik's body. We'd decided to ditch the dead cell phone story and just say she was flustered, uncertain what to do next. Anyone who knew Vera would vouch for that. Of course, I didn't think the police would find forty-five minutes a reasonable length of time to be flustered. Even Victor and Andres seemed surprised that Vera wouldn't have thought of calling 911, but since it was me telling the story, they bought it. I hated to lie to them, but I couldn't get any more people involved in my stupidity.

"That's weird, though," Victor said. "The caller said Vera was next to be slashed. But it turned out Erik was next."

"So either the caller sent the threat to the wrong person," Andres started.

"Or he sent the call to Vera a few days early," I finished.

Victor's fingers started tapping out a beat on the light case. "So the interesting question is, was Erik also getting threats? Or was our Vera the only person receiving them?"

"That's two questions," Andres said. "And it's beside the point. We have the recording of the threat Vera got. We'll turn it over to the detective on the case, and he'll be able to figure it out."

Victor wasn't so willing to let it go. "So what happened when Doug turned up?"

"He hasn't," I told him. "At least as of an hour ago. Vera's been calling him since she found the body. She's probably left a hundred messages at his home, his office, and on his cell. No Doug."

"So he could be dead somewhere," Andres said.

"Or he could be on a plane to Belize with Vera's money and whatever he took off Erik's dead body," Victor said. "I got a bad vibe from the guy."

Victor gets a bad vibe from nearly everyone, so mostly I don't take it seriously, but this time I was interested. "Why?"

"He told me he didn't listen to music."

"That's weird," I said. "He told me he didn't watch TV."

"So what does he do with his time?" Victor asked, then answered his own question. "I'll tell you what he does. He rips people off, and then slashes them."

"Then the police will catch up with him." Andres wrapped an arm around my shoulders. "Where's Vera now?"

"She went home," I said. "She was worried about her dogs. She promised to be careful, and, you know, she's a grown woman. She can more or less take care of herself, so . . ."

As I said it, I felt worried. Worried about her, about the whole scheme. I've lived a dull life, in which I've done very few really risky things. Time after time friends have said I need to stir things up, make some trouble once in a while. Now I had, and it made me queasy.

"You and Vera were really stupid, you know?" Andres said.

My face turned red. "Why am I stupid?"

"The killer, whoever it is, could have still been there. He could have taken you and Vera out," he said. "Thank God you're safe."

I leaned into his thick, muscular shoulder. But I didn't feel safe. "Let's just get this over with, shall we?" I said. "And then beers. My treat."

\\\

"You okay, Kate?" Tim asked. "You seem kind of distracted today."

Andres and Victor were doing the last-minute adjustments on the lights, leaving Tim and me to the usual preinterview chat. Under normal circumstances these few minutes provide a crucial opportunity for the subject to relax in front of the camera and to feel comfortable with me. But I wasn't really up for bonding with a convicted killer at the moment.

"I'm fine. Just tired," I told him. "I was worried my car would be under ten feet of snow today."

"Digging out a car. I remember that. I guess not having to do that anymore is one of the perks of my situation." He frowned. "It's got to be hard to be a widow."

"What makes you say I'm a widow?"

"Brick mentioned it."

"Are you two friends?"

"No."

"But you've been chatting about me."

Just at the moment I didn't want Andres to turn the camera on, he signaled to me that he was rolling. Now my being the subject of prison gossip would be on tape. In a few weeks, when the show was being put together, an editor and a postproduction supervisor would hear all about it. Not that it mattered, I reminded myself. I had bigger problems than exposing my private life to strangers.

Tim squinted a little, turned his head to the side, as if he were trying to figure me out. "That worry you? Brick and me talking about you? 'Cause we didn't mean anything by it," he said. "Brick and me were next to each other at the chow line last night for dinner. I mentioned how well the filming was going. He said you were a nice lady with a tough job. Said your husband had died. That's it. Explained some stuff, though."

"About me?"

"No. About Brick. He's very protective of vulnerable women. We had a guard in here, a lady guard. She was a bitch." He bit his lip. "Pardon me. She was a tough old bird. Got in the face of a Mexican crew on our cellblock. Took away a bunch of privileges. They were not pleased, let me just say that." He laughed. "Anyway, one day Brick found out somehow that she had cancer. That was it. He never seemed to notice the lady before, but then he made it clear. She was off-limits. The Mexicans left her alone. Everyone left her alone."

"Brick has that kind of power?"

He nodded slowly. "He's respected. People do him favors. They pay him for stuff."

"And you?"

He laughed. "You know how in high school there are the leaders, the nerds, the jocks, the druggies . . . and this whole group of kids, the largest group, that isn't really anythin' in particular? They're just sort of there. Ignored by all the other groups, just getting through high school, day by day."

"I was one of those kids."

"Well, it's like that in prison too. We got all those same groups. Maybe organized a little differently, but it turns out the same. Brick's a leader. I'm just one of the ignored."

"What I remember from high school is that flying under the radar has its advantages," I said. "You can sometimes get away with stuff because no one is looking."

"I'd keep that in mind, but I'm not looking to get away with anything," Tim said.

"You know most of the time I think you're being straight with me, but when you say stuff like that, it makes me think you're full of shit," I blurted out.

His expression went from shock to amusement. "I guess I am full of shit."

"So what do you try to get away with?"

He glanced over at Russell, who was once again the guard on duty for the interview. "I've smoked a little weed in my younger days."

"You're talking about in prison, I assume."

"Yeah."

"How'd you get it?"

"I know you don't do weed," he said, instead of answering my question. "But what about other things—fast cars, picking up sailors, dropping money on the ponies?"

I laughed. "Yeah, I'm heavy into gambling, Tim. Just the other day I went to the grocery store with expired coupons. I was betting the clerk wouldn't notice, which he didn't, so it was a big payday for me."

"Don't you do anything bad, Kate?"

I took a breath. "Not usually," I said. I like giving my interview subjects carefully edited insights into my life because in general it makes them more open about their own, and that leads to better interviews, but today I was off my game. Tim had been asking more questions than he'd been answering, and that had to stop. "Back to you, Tim. Where did you get drugs in prison?"

Tim sat up straight, considered it for a moment, then said, "We have dealers, guys who find a way to get it in and then they sell it at a markup, same as the outside."

"How do they get it in?"

"Girlfriends hiding it in their underthings, bribed guards, things like that." He turned again to Russell. "I'm not shocking you with this, am I?"

"You want to give me some names, Tim?" Russell asked.

"What do I get if I do?" Tim laughed. The guard laughed.

"What else do you get away with, Tim?" I asked.

"I used to make some homemade hooch, once in a while, but I don't bother with that no more. I'd prefer to make coffee. I even gave up cigarettes," he said. "I sound kind of boring, don't I?"

"Boring is good, Tim."

He smiled, looking like he thought he'd won my approval.

Twenty-seven

Tim was led back to his cell, and Russell told me it would be twenty minutes before he could bring Brick to the interview room. Security had tightened due to some fights between prisoners, so it would take that long, he explained, to get a man secured for the walk. Even though Brick and Tim lived only about a hundred yards away from the room I was in, they had to be searched, handcuffed, and led through a security check.

I didn't mind the wait. I was anxious to check my cell phone and see if there were any calls from Vera. I hadn't been allowed to bring my phone with me into the prison, so I went back to my car, got my purse out of the trunk, and checked my messages.

Vera had called, but only to say that her dogs were fine, and it didn't look like anyone had broken into her house in the middle of the night. Ellen had called, something about remembering my hair appointment tomorrow. And Detective Makina had called.

"Mrs. Conway," he said on the voice mail. "I just wanted to follow up on the incident last night and get a formal statement. When you have the opportunity, if you could give me a call back and we'll set up a time, I'd appreciate it."

A normal, ordinary follow-up to last night's incident. That's what he'd called it, an incident. A man lying dead with half a dozen gaping wounds. I'd been so focused on keeping Vera out of trouble that I hadn't fully taken in how awful it had been to see Erik like that. Not that I had the time for it now, or the inclination. Erik Price was an annoying, self-important prick. And I'd barely known him. His death didn't need to bother me, I told myself. Except it did. No one, not even self-important pricks, deserved to finish life in a pool of blood.

I called Makina back, leaving a message that I was working and would be able to give my statement anytime tomorrow. I put my cell phone in my purse, put my purse in the trunk, and walked back toward the prison door, relieved by Makina's call and sickened by the images of Erik that were now floating in my mind.

\\\

Brick was getting his handcuffs removed when I returned. "Hey there," he said. "I thought you were tired of me."

I looked up at him and smiled a little. "No. Not yet, anyway." I tried to sound light, happy. I sat in my chair and gestured for him to sit opposite me.

Brick looked at me, puzzled, but he said nothing. He sat and waited while Victor put his mic on. Then he smiled at me. "How's that other shoot goin'? The one with all them rich people."

I glanced up at Andres, then back at Brick. "Same old thing. They're still talking about how amazing they are and how amazing their restaurant will be."

"What's the name of it? Chez somethin'? They all got names like that."

"Club Car."

He thought for a moment. "Isn't that the place where a dude got offed last night?"

"How do you know that?"

"I watch the Channel Nine news first thing every day," he said. "Shit, Kate, you mixed up in that?"

"Not mixed up, Brick. I happened to be doing a story there."

"We all were," Andres chimed in, ignoring the fact that the camera was rolling. "And from what I saw, a couple of them were pretty shady. Any one of them could have done it."

"That sort of shit you want to stay clear of," Brick said, with the gravity of a man who knew what he was talking about.

"I'll do that," I said. "But we're here to talk about you."

The rest of the interview was routine, with Brick going into surprising detail about the many ways an inmate can get into trouble in prison, from infractions that lead to solitary confinement to making the wrong friends.

"When there's somethin' that needs discussin' everyone's got their favorite place," he said. "Mine is the stairway at the north end of the block. It's quiet and the camera in there keeps gettin' broke."

"What do you do when you're discussing something?" I asked.

"I discuss. And that's all I do, Kate. A man has to know his limitations." He smiled.

Like Tim, Brick was sensing that I wasn't completely focused, and he was playing with me. Losing control of an interview is bad. It's not as if I can pretend to the client that I did everything I could to get the best answers. My best, and worst, work is preserved on videotape. Today wasn't going to be my best day, no matter what questions I asked. I thought about faking it, but I didn't have the energy even for that, so I just dropped my producer hat and asked what I was curious about.

"Why are you doing this interview, Brick? I mean, what do you get out of it?"

That confused him. "What you want me to say?" His voice was a little unsteady. "You want me to tell you I'm doing this for the kids out there who might be thinking of takin' the wrong path?"

"But you're not."

He looked into my eyes. I wondered if he could see the fear, the stress, the tiredness. He smiled a little, a sad smile, and I realized he could. "I don't get to talk to people from the outside much," he said. "The guards, I guess, but they don't count. I don't get outside my cell except to eat or exercise. This is like a vacation for me." He sat back. "And I got books out of it. Which was the first kind thing I've seen in a while."

"But doesn't it ever bother you that you're going to die here?"

"You have to die somewhere," he said. "Like that friend of yours, the one at the restaurant. He had everything, right? He had fancy clothes and a big car. All that shit."

"He did."

"And he's dead on the floor."

"He is." It wasn't just Erik's body on my mind; it was the image of me lying to the police about Erik's body that was suddenly front and center. I was hot and cold all at the same time. "I guess you're right,

Brick," I said. "No matter how careful you think you are, you make one bad choice and it can all go to hell."

Brick stared at me, and looked for a minute like he was thinking of reaching out to me. But he folded his hands in his lap. "You got nothin' to worry about, Kate. You got friends. You got your boys over there." He nodded toward Victor and Andres. "And you got me."

"We're friends, Brick?"

"We ain't enemies."

I looked into his dark walnut eyes. There was a kindness there. "Then I guess we're friends."

He was the first new friend I'd made since Frank died. Except, of course, for Vera. And look how that was working out.

Twenty-eight

It was bumper-to-bumper on I-55 going back into the city. Normally this much traffic would drive me nuts, but I wasn't anxious to go home. I just sat in my car, switching between NPR and the alternative-rock station, trying to untie the knot in my stomach that had formed the minute I'd seen Erik's body.

One of the great privileges of my profession is the opportunity to meet people from all walks of life, spend time in their world and ask whatever questions pop into my head—and whatever questions get the kinds of answers my clients want.

As I stared at the SUV in front of me, I ticked through a mental list of cool experiences my job had given me: trying on Mike Ditka's Super Bowl ring, attending an Oscar party (I was treated as a nuisance, but it was still an Oscar party), touring FBI headquarters, eating fried chicken with a presidential candidate. It made me feel almost lucky. Almost, because without my job, I wouldn't be feeling sorry for two killers or have nearly tripped over Erik's dead body. There are some experiences in life that you don't want to have, and I seemed to be cramming them all into one week.

This was the sort of day when I really missed being married. In the early years Frank would have listened, given me a foot rub, and ordered mushroom and spinach pizza from my favorite Italian restaurant, a place that had long since closed. Like so many other things, it just hadn't lasted.

Before I could talk myself out of it, I grabbed my cell phone and dialed. I figured it couldn't be breaking the law if my car wasn't actually moving. I waited a few rings for Ellen to answer the phone, but when voice mail picked up, I didn't know what to say, so I hung up.

Ellen would kill me for not leaving a message. She was always on my case about something, always quick to let me know the many ways my life could stand a little of her brand of improvement. It was odd, but there was something kind of reassuring in that. Ellen was the most normal part of my life at the moment, maybe the most normal part of my life always.

I hit the "redial" button and waited for the voice mail.

"Hi, we're the Becketts." The outgoing message was a recording of Ellen using her most cheerful voice. "No one is here right now to take your call, so leave a message for Ellen, Tony, the kids, or the dog, and we'll get back to you."

"Hey, Ellen, it's Kate," I said. "Sorry, work is crazy. Just wanted to touch base. Talk to you soon."

I felt better. I spent too much time hiding from people. I didn't give others a chance to care about me, or show their best selves. I was too cynical. That's what I decided until the car behind me honked long and loud because I'd delayed three seconds in pulling forward the thirty feet that had suddenly opened up.

\\\

"Detective Makina came to my house." Vera called me just as I was settling down to a quiet dinner of microwave pizza. It had taken me nearly two hours to get home, and I was starving and tired. It was as if Vera had a sixth sense about when I was least interested in talking, and that's when she chose to call.

"What did you tell him?" I asked.

"Don't be mad."

Not just my heart, but all of my internal organs fell, collapsing to the ground and leaving a mere skeleton of me standing at the phone, waiting. "What did you say?"

"He checked the phone records and saw the time gap, just like we thought he would. I told him what we decided I would say, that I was flustered. Which, really, I was. But he didn't think a person would be flustered for forty-five minutes."

"So please tell me you told him you were protecting Doug, and that's why you didn't call the police."

"Not exactly." She hesitated. "I told him the story about the phone being dead. I couldn't think of what to say."

"But that won't fit the facts, Vera."

"I know. But I didn't know what to say. I'm sorry, Kate. I got very scared. I kept thinking about what you said, about people getting convicted with less evidence than what they have on me." Vera was crying on the other end of the phone. "But I'm going to call Detective Makina and explain to him what really happened, and put an end to this nonsense right now. I know it's going to make me look guilty, but it's better than dragging you into this mess any further."

"Don't," I said. "Not yet. Let me think."

"Are you sure?"

"No." I took a breath, but I couldn't seem to take enough air in. My lungs sputtered, like a car running out of gas. "Have you heard from Doug?"

"No. Nothing. What do you think happened to him?"

"I don't know," I said, not wanting to play that game with her again. "Keep your doors locked. Call me if Doug, or anyone, calls you, and let me think before you call Makina, okay?"

"Okay."

But I didn't have time to think. Ten minutes after I hung up with Vera I got another call—this time from a number I didn't recognize. If I'd been clearheaded, I would have let voice mail pick it up, but like an idiot, I answered.

"Mrs. Conway?" A deep male voice was on the other end. "This is Detective Makina. I need to speak to you."

"Sure." I tried to sound calm. "I got your message. I can come by the police station tomorrow."

"I'm actually in your neighborhood. Why don't I stop by your house in, say, fifteen minutes?"

"I was just on my way out."

"It's really important I speak to you now, Mrs. Conway," he said, his voice getting even deeper. "Besides, it shouldn't take long. See you in fifteen."

I probably should have straightened up the house, which was beginning to look like it had been ransacked, but instead I used the fifteen minutes to do some research on exactly how much trouble I was in.

According to various websites, obstructing justice carries a one- to three-year sentence in Illinois, and about the same for an accessory-after-the-fact charge. Maybe I could get a suspended sentence and pay a hefty fine. I could take a second mortgage out on the house, I decided. Maybe community service. It's not as if I'd lived a life of crime—I came to the aid of a friend and tried to help. It was stupid, that's all. The police would believe me. I popped open a can of Pepsi and tried to tell myself it wasn't going to be that bad.

Of course, if it was determined that Vera had murdered Erik, and I'd helped cover it up, I could kiss the next twenty years of my life good-bye.

When the doorbell rang, I nearly jumped. I closed the computer and went to answer the door, wondering if spending the night in prison was just as unpleasant as spending the day there.

Twenty-nine

Ms. Bingham said she'd been getting threatening phone calls."
Detective Makina was standing in my kitchen, sipping from the glass of water he'd asked for the moment he'd arrived at the house.

"Probably from someone connected to the restaurant," I said. "We were looking into it, just in the course of doing the show, and found out that Roman Papadakis had been involved in some shady business dealings. He may have been a suspect in the murder of his cousin, who was his business partner in a failing venture. Kind of like what's happened here." I was tying a bow around a great big present of a murder suspect, but Makina didn't seem interested.

"Did you hear any of these calls that Ms. Bingham said she received?"

"Yes, I did. In fact, one of our friends taped it on his digital recorder. And he figured out that it was disguised with some sort of software you can download. He also said that a computer can be programmed to delay sending the message."

"That can be done," Makina agreed.

"Pretty amazing stuff."

"What's his name? Your friend who knew all about the threatening message?" Makina grabbed a small notebook from his coat pocket and turned to an empty page.

"Victor Pilot," I said.

"Pilot? Is that his real last name?"

"No. It's sort of a stage name." I remembered Victor telling me that several years ago, when we first met.

"What's his real name?"

I bit my lip. "I don't remember. He never uses it. I have his cell number, though."

"Where does he live?"

"Victor kind of moves around a lot. Crashes with friends, that sort of thing. He's not that responsible about paying his rent." It sounded bad, so I tried to explain. "He's a musician."

"Victor Pilot," Makina said. He flipped through the pages of his notebook and smiled. "He might be the kind of guy who could use a few bucks."

I couldn't figure out what Makina was getting at. "Victor would have no reason to threaten Vera."

"But if Ms. Bingham paid him to set up the messages and send them to her so it would look like she was getting threatened . . ."

"Why would she do that?"

"I don't know. You tell me."

I stood for a moment, debating whether I should just explain what had actually happened, but I realized my doing that now would just make Vera look more guilty. "I think you're getting the wrong idea about Vera. She wouldn't hurt anyone."

"She hurt you, didn't she?"

"Excuse me?"

"Your husband, Mrs. Conway."

"How do you know about that?"

"I asked Ms. Bingham."

I smiled a little, tried to relax. "Well, there, you see? Vera came right out and told you something that makes her look bad. That's how little she has to hide."

"Or she knew I would find out anyway."

He somehow managed to twist everything I said. It would have been an interview skill worth studying if I hadn't been on the receiving end. "She didn't kill Erik," I said. "I was with her, remember?"

"She called you at seven fifteen. The call was made from her cell to your home phone."

"I'd just gotten home. Hadn't even taken off my coat, so I turned around immediately and drove to meet her."

"You drove straight there?"

I'd stopped for a burger. What were the odds they would check that? What were the odds he already knew?

"I went through the drive-in at Bucktown Burgers," I admitted.

He nodded, relaxed his stance a little. He'd already known about the drive-through. I'd passed his little test. Things were looking better for me, but much worse for Vera.

"When did you arrive at Club Car?" he asked.

"I don't know, exactly."

"Twenty minutes later? Thirty? It was a pretty bad night for driving. You must have had to go slow, and on a good day, with no traffic, it's still got to be a twenty-minute drive."

"Maybe twenty minutes. I didn't look at the time. When I got there Vera was waiting for me outside by the door. She was scared. We went back to the kitchen. That was—well, as you can imagine, it was very upsetting. We ran into the dining room and it took a minute for me to realize what to do next."

"Which was to call 911."

"Yes."

"Because that's what you do when you find someone's been hurt or killed."

"It's not always easy to know," I started. My throat was dry.

Makina cut me off. "But Ms. Bingham called you, then she called Doug Zieman at least fifteen times in the forty-five minutes between her call to you and your call to us."

"She was supposed to meet him. She was concerned for his safety."

"But she never called the police," he said. "And when I asked her about that, she told me her phone had died. That couldn't have been true."

I was blank. I'd gone about as far in this as I could go. "Vera is worried that Doug did it," I said. "You have to understand. She's a romantic. She's lonely. She met Doug and he's obviously taken advantage of her."

"You think he's a con man?"

"I think he's . . ." I needed to be careful. Was he baiting me? I couldn't tell. "I don't know." I said. "What I do know is that Vera didn't kill anyone. She got to the restaurant, she found Erik already dead. She's trying to protect Doug. Find Doug and you've found the killer."

"Just that simple?"

I wasn't getting anywhere with him, and my frustration was showing. "I don't know everything that happened that night, Detective Makina. And neither do you. But I do know that Vera found that man already dead. She's incapable of killing someone," I said. "And she didn't have time, anyway. I was with her for at least fifteen minutes before we called you. We were scared and upset. We didn't think straight. You need to look for the real killer."

He finished his water and put the empty glass in my sink. "You seem like a smart lady, Mrs. Conway, and I'm sure that you think you're helping your friend. But the truth is you were at Dugan prison all day, drove home, got a phone call, and went to meet Ms. Bingham. You couldn't have been at that place for more than five minutes before you called 911."

"I was there longer than five minutes," I said. "I rushed there because I was concerned about Vera. She said there was something off about the tone in Doug's voice. Maybe if Doug didn't do it, he knows who killed Erik."

"You were so concerned that you stopped for a burger on the way?" He smiled. "Do your friends a favor, Mrs. Conway. Tell them to come clean now. Maybe this Victor Pilot guy can avoid jail time if he tells us that he didn't know what Ms. Bingham was planning. And, if she's smart, she'll claim emotional distress and take a manslaughter plea."

"If you're so sure that Vera is guilty, why haven't you arrested her?"

"I'm waiting on the autopsy results," he said, "and I want to tie up some loose ends."

"Like?"

"Like the argument Ms. Bingham had with the victim. I want to find out what it was really about."

"It was about Erik's interview with me. She was concerned he came off looking like a jerk, and that by extension the restaurant would look bad."

"Is that what she told you?"

"No, that's what Erik told me." The words came out without my thinking. I would like to say I did it to protect Vera. That, at least, would be noble. Misguided, but noble. But I did it because Makina was a jerk who thought he'd outsmarted me. How lying to the police was going to prove him wrong, I hadn't figured out yet. "He asked me if I would leave that portion of his interview out of the show," I said. "He told me Vera made him realize how he might be misunderstood. I told him I'd think about it."

Makina stepped a few inches closer to me, and looked carefully. I stared back. It was high noon without the gunfights and mood music. Finally, he blinked. "Well, I guess that backs up Ms. Bingham's story."

I didn't say anything else. I just stayed in the kitchen as Detective Makina walked down my hall, into my living room, and out my front door. I was afraid if I moved, I would drop.

Thirty

In television, even in reality TV—no, make that especially in reality TV—the truth is massaged, it's pushed, it's kneaded and manipulated, and in some cases, it's invented. Producers tell the guests on all of those shock-TV talk shows that when the secret is revealed, they should get up and yell, throw a chair, look ready to punch someone. We tell cops on true crime shows to pretend they didn't know who the killer was right away, even though they did, just to stretch out the story. We rehearse surprises, we start arguments, and we create dramatic situations—all so people will stick around through the commercial break.

I've never been proud of my role in that, but I've never been ashamed either. The truth, I've often said, is subjective. But today, away from cameras and the comforting thought that it was just a television show, the truth wasn't subjective. Erik had never said anything about his argument with Vera. In fact, after he drove away that day I never saw him alive again. But it wasn't really a lie, I told myself. Vera had told me that was what the argument was about. And I believed Vera.

Didn't I?

I wanted to call and scream at her for not dialing 911 the minute she'd found Erik, but after my encounter with Makina, I was half certain that our phones were bugged. I'd never worked on a single true crime show in which the cops had bugged a suspect's phone, but it happened in the fictional TV versions of crime shows all the time, and I didn't want to take the chance.

Not knowing what else to do, I called Andres.

"I need to meet you for a drink somewhere," I said. "Now."

"There's a quiet place about halfway between my house and yours," he said, without asking for another bit of information. "I think it's called Cavan's."

Thirty minutes later, I was taking a sip out of a pint of Guinness in the back corner booth of a small Irish pub. Andres's face was white, his drink untouched; he was still in shock from everything I'd told him.

"Shit, Kate. It's bad enough that Vera's mixed up in it, but she kind brought it on herself. Victor . . . well, we have to get Victor out of this mess."

"I agree."

"You don't think for one second there's any truth to it, do you?" he asked.

"I don't think Vera killed Erik, and I certainly don't think she and Victor cooked up some plan for her to receive fake threats."

"It would have gotten the boyfriend's attention."

"Andres, this is Vera we're talking about. I'm as aware as anyone the lengths she'll go to when she thinks she's in love, but this isn't her style," I said. "She's a little ditzy, a little too trusting, maybe too much of a romantic, but she's not a sociopath."

Andres drank half his beer in one gulp, set it down, and picked it up again as if he might need the other half. "You're right," he said. "No, of course you're right. So what do we do?"

"I don't know. That's why I called you."

He stared into his glass a long time, and I sat watching him. I was afraid he was just as out of ideas as I was, until he looked up at me. "Remember that show we did with the family who had that big house with seven kids? Then the dad got transferred and they were moving, and the mom was completely overwhelmed by where to start?"

"Yeah, we brought in a professional organizer," I said. "Mandy something. What does that have to do with this?"

"That Mandy lady said sometimes it's a bad thing to look at the big picture. It's too much to take in; you get all psycho and give up. She said you have to break it down. Look at things one at a time."

"I don't think a murder investigation is quite the same thing as organizing your shoes."

"You're wrong," he said. "It's exactly the same thing. We have to take this one thing at a time. Each step, each suspect. Otherwise we're not going to get anywhere." He finished his beer and sat back, looking a lot more relaxed than he had a few minutes before. "The first thing we have to do is decide where to start."

"By your logic, it's simple," I said. "That Mandy woman said when you organize a house you start with the easy stuff first, like getting rid of the visual clutter. That way you feel a sense of accomplishment when you tackle the hidden clutter—the attic, the old tax files, the garage."

"I remember her saying that."

"So let's start with what's right in front of us."

\\\

Vera, Victor, Andres, and I sat in my living room and stared at the floor. Victor had taken the news that he was a suspect in a homicide investigation surprisingly well.

"I can handle prison," he said. "I've got tattoos, and guys in prison respect a good tat. We've done enough shows in prison that I know how things work, so nobody has to worry that I'll wig out or anything."

"It's not going to come to that, Victor," I said. "It's just that we have to go over everything that's happened step-by-step and maybe we'll figure something out."

Victor and Vera exchanged a guilty glance. "There's a little more to the story," Victor said.

I could feel a headache coming on. "Of course there is," I said.

Victor looked down at his shoes, at Vera, then at the wall. Everywhere but at Andres and me. "I know that I haven't been as, you know, as on top of my game as I usually am, but it's because of, well, because I was a little short on money—"

"How could you be short of money?" Andres jumped in. "We've been working practically every day and you don't have any expenses. You live on other people's couches; you drive a twenty-year-old car." Andres was getting quite worked up.

Victor looked over at him. "The new band. We're trying to do a tour, trying to get money together for a van and some new equipment. I've been moonlighting at a bar on Rush Street."

"So that's why you've been so off," I said. "You've been tired."

He nodded. "So, when we started doing this show at Vera's restaurant . . ."

I looked over at Vera. "You gave Victor some money?"

"I'm an investor in the band," she said. "I gave Victor ten thousand for new equipment, and I bought a van."

"I didn't want to take it," Victor said. "Vera offered that first day we worked together, and I said I had to think about it."

"He did," Vera agreed. "I told him if he let me help, he could quit working at the bar and Andres wouldn't be angry with him anymore. So finally, he let me help."

"When?" I asked.

"The day I got the call about being slashed," she said.

Andres shook his head. "It's going to look bad if Makina finds out. He'll think she was paying Victor off."

"He already knows," I said.

"Are you sure?" Victor asked.

"He seemed very stuck on the idea that you were working with Vera. When I mentioned your name, he had this cat-that-ate-the-canary grin on his face," I said. "That has to be why."

"But all this questioning is normal, isn't it?" Vera looked frightened and tired. "They have to look at everyone involved with Erik before they pick a suspect."

"The police already have a suspect," I reminded her. "They have you. And once they have a suspect—"

Victor jumped in. "Like the guy in that DNA show we did, who did, like, twenty-five years for murder and then it turned out that he wasn't guilty."

Vera's face went pale.

"That's not going to happen here. We're going to figure this out," I said, though, to be honest, I didn't feel all that confident.

"What if the police are watching the house?" Vera asked. "Should we all be meeting like this? It will just drag Andres into it."

"Let them watch," Andres said. "We haven't killed anybody."

"This has gotten out of hand," I said. "We're just getting paranoid, and Victor is already planning his prison break. Vera, maybe you should just get a lawyer."

"I have one," she said. "Ascoli and Lowe. It's a firm my family has on retainer. I talked to one of the senior partners this afternoon. Basically, he told me to shut up and direct all police questions to him. I told him about calling you after I found the body, and I said I should go to the police and explain everything, but he said at this point altering my story would just make me look like I'd killed Erik."

"What about Victor?" Andres asked.

Vera looked toward Victor. "I'll pay for your lawyer. I got you into this mess."

Victor shook his head. "That's not our way out. Our way out is to figure out who killed the guy. Once the police have their killer it's not going to matter that you waited to call, or that you told a little lie."

Vera was on the verge of tears. "But who would kill Erik? Everyone liked him."

"I didn't," Victor said.

"Me neither," Andres added.

"Yeah, I'm with the boys on this one," I told Vera. "And clearly there's at least one more person who didn't like him. We don't really need to know who the killer is; we just have to find a plausible suspect. Someone with a better reason to kill him than Makina thinks you have."

"Erik was pretty cozy with Ilena that first day, remember?" Victor said.

I nodded. "So that puts Roman on the list if he's the jealous type, and Ilena if Erik wanted to end things."

"And he had that disagreement with Walt about the food," Andres added. "Erik was getting a little too involved in the menu."

"Would you kill someone over that?" I asked, then conceded his point. Dugan was populated with men who'd killed for far less.

"We should split them up," Andres suggested. "Each take a suspect. That way we can each question one of them. It'll save time."

"But what excuse would we have to see them again?" I asked. "The show is canceled."

"Did the Business Channel call you?" Andres asked.

"No," I admitted. It had just occurred to me that maybe I should call them. "But they're not going to let us tape with one investor dead, another missing and a third that's a suspect."

"It would be good television, wouldn't it?" Victor said.

It would be. But I didn't think the police would consider that reason enough to let us continue with the show.

"Roman is the only one with any possible criminal activity in his background," Andres said. "I think he's our guy."

"Those are only rumors," Vera said. "I just don't see any of them killing Erik. It's a business. If you don't want to be in business anymore, you leave, you quit, you sue . . . but you don't kill someone. None of the investors would kill Erik. They're not like those people in Dugan."

"I remember talking to a cop when we were working for Crime TV," I said. "I asked him how someone goes from never having a traffic ticket to killing a person. The cop said that there are lots of people in the world with a sense of entitlement. They cut you off in traffic, push ahead in line, that sort of thing. They want what they want, and to hell with who it hurts. So, when they want custody of the kids, or the insurance money, or out of a bad business deal, it's not that they want the other person dead; it's just that the victim is in their way. Lawsuits take years; divorces are messy. For a certain kind of person, murder is fast and easy. The cop said it's more about being selfish than being evil."

"That description pretty much fits that entire crowd," Victor said.

Vera wasn't buying it. "They're all smart people. Any one of them would know if you kill someone, you get caught."

"I don't think anyone who commits murder thinks they're going to get caught," I said to her. "Especially this killer. Whoever did it has done a damn good job of making you look guilty. The trick is to think like the killer thinks."

"But you're not that kind of person, Kate. You don't push ahead in line or cut people off in traffic. You don't know how a killer would think," she said.

I sat back and sighed. Vera was right. I didn't know how a killer would think. But, I realized, I did know a killer. In fact, I knew two.

Thirty-one

I'm afraid you've wasted a trip," Russell told me after I'd been in Dugan's waiting room for almost a half hour. "Brick took sick this morning. Stomach pains. He's in the infirmary."

After our little meeting broke up, I'd stayed awake thinking of what to do. Then I tried sleeping for a few hours. At six in the morning I got out of bed and called the prison to make sure that it would be okay to meet with Brick in the visitors room. I told Joanie Rheinbeck I had some general questions about prison life I needed for the show. I wouldn't be bringing my crew, I said, so it wouldn't be the usual intrusion. Brick was having breakfast when I called; based on what I'd seen of the food that was probably where he got sick. A guard got word to him and asked if my visit would be okay. Inmates don't get to say yes or no to many things, but they do get to decide if they want to see a visitor. Brick said yes to me.

I had no idea what I was going to ask him, but it made sense to me that he could provide a better insight into the criminal mind than a producer, an heiress, and a television crew. I just hoped the idea wouldn't insult him so much that he'd throw me out of there; I still had two more days of shooting on the documentary.

Now, though, the trip had been for nothing. I thanked Russell and tried not to seem too disappointed.

"If it's just some general questions you need answers to, I could ask Tim," Russell said. "He's got a visitor right now, but I'm sure they'd let him have another one. Especially since you've already been to the prison so much and know everyone."

"That would be okay," I said. I felt more comfortable talking to Brick about Erik's murder, partly because he already knew some of it, but also because he was more straightforward. With Tim I always felt slightly off balance as he switched between happy camper and penitent sinner. But I needed to talk to a killer, and Tim was the only one on offer.

Russell led me to the visitors room and sat with me at one of the empty tables. It was more crowded than it had been on the day I'd visited with Brick. Russell told me that a lot of people from out of town visit on Fridays. They take the day off work and spend the weekend going back and forth from a motel to the prison, because it could be months before they can afford to come back.

The visitors were almost all women. Some were clearly mothers, the others were wives or girlfriends with children underfoot, and then there was a sprinkling of what could almost be called sexual encounters: women pulling their tops low to expose as much breast as possible without getting kicked out; the inmate on the receiving end of the show leering and laughing, making the sort of small talk that made me want to cover the children's ears.

As a producer, I get to sit with the inmate in a quiet room for an hour or more, talking about whatever I like, shaking hands, even going into their cells. But for their family members, no such privileges are allowed.

"It must be hard," I said to Russell, "to not be able to touch each other."

"They find ways. There are even a couple of closets that rent out for twenty bucks for ten minutes of privacy." He could see I looked surprised, and then he added, "I don't condone it, and I don't participate, but then I don't condemn it either. It calms the men and I guess it helps the ladies too."

"I can't imagine coming to visit someone who's going to be here twenty years, or forty, or an entire lifetime."

"I know what you mean. I think it's easier to forget. And most do. The friends don't stick around past the trial, the siblings come once or twice, the wives and girlfriends eventually fade away. Even the fathers, they give up," Russell said. "But not the mothers. They come until they can't anymore. Until they're dead. Then nobody comes." He pointed toward a table at the other end of the room. "I think Tim's visit is ending. Wait here."

I saw Russell walk over to Tim and chat for a moment. Tim got up from the table. A young woman, much younger than Tim, got up too. All three walked toward me.

"Hey there, Kate." Tim was all smiles. "Heard about Brick. Can't handle his oatmeal." He turned to the woman with him. "This is Angela. She's from Peoria. She's my cousin on my dad's side. Come up to visit me. Ain't that nice of her?"

"It is." I reached out my hand and the woman shook it limply.

"Angela is here for the weekend. We visited yesterday and today and we're gonna visit more tomorrow," he said. "And Russell says you have a problem with the show you needed to talk about. I'm all ears."

As Russell led Angela out of the room, Tim sat opposite me.

"Your cousin?" She would have been three or four when Tim went to prison, so it seemed odd, family or not, that she would drive more than two hours to see him.

Tim laughed. "Hand to God, Kate. She's my cousin. Well, my cousin's daughter. But she's family. She's a shy little thing but likes to do good deeds. A churchgoer. She heard from my mom that I don't get too much mail, so she started writing me. And after about a year of that, she decided to come up and say hello."

"I thought you didn't want to have women believing you could take long walks on the beach."

"Good Lord, you are a skeptic. She's my cousin. And almost a child. Can't be more than twenty-three or -four. You can ask her if you like."

"No." I was getting off track. "I'm here about something else."

"The show," he said.

"Not the show."

"Oh." He lowered his voice a little. "Did somethin' happen?"

"There was another show I was working on. A restaurant show. And someone connected with it was murdered."

"The Club Car guy?"

"You watch the Channel Nine news too?"

"Channel Seven, but I guess the story's the same. Some guy opening a big restaurant was killed there the night of the snowstorm."

"Yes, that's it." I looked around but no one was paying attention. They were all too wrapped up in their own visits to listen in. "One of the other investors is a suspect. She's a nice woman and there's simply no way she did it, but she found the body and she didn't call the police for forty-five minutes."

"That was stupid."

"Yes, I think she realizes that now."

"It ain't you, is it, Kate? Whenever anybody says, 'it was a friend' . . ."

"No." I laughed, releasing a little of the tension in my throat. This whole thing had become absurd. "This must sound crazy," I said, "and forgive me, but I don't really know what else to do."

"You want to help this woman?"

"I guess I do. I think she's being taken for a ride, and that bugs me."

He leaned in. "Okay, Kate. What do you need?"

I took a deep breath and tried to figure out why I was really there, other than I'd run out of places to go. I told him what I knew about Erik, Roman, and the others. Tim was listening intently, as if he were memorizing every word. "Roman Papadakis was involved in an arson murder some years ago, when someone set fire to the home of his business partner and cousin," I said. "A lot of people think he did it, but another man was sent to prison. His name was John Fletcher. I can't find any record of him in the prisoner database."

"That could mean he's done his time."

I shook my head. "Life sentence, plus a hundred."

"Or he's dead."

"Someone told me that he'd been in Pontiac. I know you were in Pontiac. . . ."

Tim's smile widened to a toothy grin. "It ain't a fraternity, Kate. We don't have a secret handshake or an alumni directory." He laughed. "Well, I guess the parole board kinda does, but just because we were in the same place don't mean we knew each other. In case you hadn't noticed, these places are huge and packed to the rafters."

I sighed. "I understand."

"When was he there?" Tim leaned forward, his hand nearly touching mine.

"The murder was in eighty-nine, and he was arrested quickly, convicted quickly."

"I've heard that tune. Somebody with connections commits a murder and somebody with no connections and no money goes to prison."

"I know that's a bit of an urban myth, but it might have actually happened in this case," I said.

"It's no myth. It happens. Happens more than ya think."

I looked at Tim. The grin was gone. He was staring at me with soft, sad eyes. I was almost afraid to ask. "Who are you talking about, Tim?"

"You hear stories, is all," he said. He was resting his arms on the table, one hand on top of the other. He looked relaxed, except his hands were tightly clenched.

I didn't want to ask. I didn't want to get more involved in other people's problems than I already was, but I asked anyway. "Did you kill your wife?"

"We talked about that in the interview," he said. "I told you what I done."

"You told me you were responsible. You told me you didn't remember. You skirted the answer."

Tim looked frightened for a moment, then tears formed in the corners of his eyes. He blinked them away. "No. I didn't kill Jenny."

"What happened?"

"Kate, I spent years tryin' to get someone to believe me. It nearly killed me. It don't matter now. Too much time has passed to really change anything," he said. When he saw I was about to protest, he waved me off. "Please, just leave it alone."

"But if—"

He shook his head. "No." He was adamant. "The justice system is an imperfect mistress. We all want to believe that if we tell the truth we will be believed."

"What if we lie?"

He looked back at me. "Well, then we get what we deserve."

Thirty-two

By the time I left the prison I was exhausted, and it was only two o'clock. Tim hadn't wanted my help, so I had no choice but to shake off the depressing possibility that he was wasting away in prison, wrongfully convicted of his wife's murder, and get on with the mess of my own life.

It was noon on the West Coast, I reminded myself, and I had a call to make. I was hoping Ralph would be at an early lunch and I could just leave a message, but on the second ring, he picked up.

"Ralph Johnson," he said. He sounded chipper.

"It's Kate Conway."

"Kate." He elongated my name, seeming sad and worried. Kind of like Ellen does. "Is everything okay?"

"You heard."

"I got a call from some police detective in Chicago, looking to confirm that we'd been taping a show there," he said. "It's awful. I talked to Erik Price a couple of times when we were setting this up. He had such high hopes for the place. They all did. And now . . ." he left the sentence unfinished. "It's just terrible."

"It is," I agreed. More terrible than Ralph could imagine.

"Would have made a great show, though, if we could have finished it with this," he said. "When do you ever get an angle like this on a business show?"

"So it's definitely canceled?"

Ralph didn't answer. I could hear him breathing, so I knew he hadn't hung up. My guess was that the silence was due to a tug-of-war between his personal ethics and his professional instincts. He wanted to be disgusted by the idea of using someone's death as a ratings ploy, but instead he was intrigued by it. I understood his dilemma. I was feeling much the same way myself.

"Do you think any of them would give us an interview?" Ralph said finally. "Maybe explain what happened, where the investors go from here. Does the restaurant still open or does Erik's death kill the dream? That kind of thing."

"I don't know. I could ask."

He paused again. "I'll have to check with my boss, see what he thinks, but if you set things up on your end, I'll set things up here," he said. "It would be a shame to scrap the footage after all that shooting."

"It would." For the first time since Erik's murder I felt relief. If the show went forward, and if people agreed to be interviewed, then maybe it would be the simplest way to get answers without raising any suspicion.

"Maybe even Detective Makina would do an interview," Ralph said, his voice back to being chipper. "Give him a call and see."

The relief was gone.

\\\

I sat in my car and made four phone calls. Walt said he'd do the interview, but only if I had dinner with him. Ilena said yes before I'd finished asking. Roman laughed, muttered something about vultures picking the bones clean, but he also said yes, and Doug didn't answer either his cell or home phone.

I had a fifth phone call to make, but I wasn't in a hurry to speak with Detective Makina. So instead I considered my options. The smart move was to just produce the last day of the restaurant show as if it were any other: ask the questions that would get me the predictable Business Channel responses Ralph was looking for, and not ask anything designed to smoke out a killer. When did I become Nancy Drew, anyway? The smarter move would be to call Ralph back and tell him the participants weren't available, and wash my hands of the whole thing.

Then there was the dumb move, the one I was destined to make. And that was to get even more deeply involved in this mess than I already was. It would either get Vera, Victor, and I out of trouble, or drag Andres down with us. I didn't need to present Makina with the killer; I just needed to throw him off our scent. And whether Vera liked it or not, I knew exactly who that person was.

I called Doug again. When he didn't answer, I dialed another number. Vera answered on the third ring.

"You know where Doug lives, don't you?" I asked.

"He has a house in Oak Park."

"Ever been to it?"

"A couple of times. Why?"

I dug through the paperwork I had for the show and found a copy of the release form that all of the show's participants had signed. The address Doug had given was in Oak Park. "Meet me at his house in an hour," I said.

I had no idea what we would find there, but I needed Vera on board for Doug as the killer if my plan was going to work. If he was home dodging phone calls, it was probably best that Vera was there to see it for herself.

Thirty-three

Except he wasn't there. The house, a Craftsman-style bungalow, was locked up tight. The snow from earlier in the week had piled up on the steps, mail sat in the mailbox, and several days' worth of papers were frozen to the porch.

"I guess he's fled the jurisdiction," I said to Vera.

"I think he's dead."

I looked over at her. She was staring at the living room window, covered with thick blue drapes that didn't let in even a sliver of light.

"That would suck," I said. "He's our best suspect."

I pulled on the door handle again. No give. It wasn't as if I was considering breaking in, but if the door just gave way and I could walk in, that would be another story. But no luck, even on the third try.

"Everything okay there?" I turned and saw a woman around seventy, a small, yappity dog at her feet who began barking and growling. I guess even dog's can have a Napoleon complex. The woman was standing on the sidewalk, blocking a quick getaway to my car.

"We're looking for Doug Zieman," I said.

"He's not home."

"I guess not." I pushed Vera slightly in front of me, and I stood with my back to the mailbox. "Do you know where he is?"

"No," she said. "Are you friends or something?"

"I'm Vera Bingham. Doug's girlfriend," Vera said. "And I've been calling him for days and he's not calling back. I'm really worried about him. It's just not like Doug."

"Oh." The woman seemed a little unsure how to take that information. "I didn't know Douglas had a lady friend."

The woman looked up the street, almost as if she were hoping for another neighbor to consult. As she looked away, I reached back, grabbed the mail from the mailbox, and stuck it under my coat.

"Are you his neighbor?" Vera asked.

The woman pointed to a house several doors down. "Going on five years. He's a quiet man. I didn't know he . . . socialized much."

"We met online," Vera told her. "We've only known each other for a couple of months but we've been really close. We're investors in a restaurant together."

It was way more information than I would share with a stranger, but it seemed to be working. The woman softened her stance. Even the yappy dog stopped barking.

"I'm glad to see he met someone," she said. "I thought he might be lonely, in that house by himself. No family or anything."

"When did you last see him?" I asked the neighbor.

She stood for a moment, thinking. "The afternoon before the storm," she said finally. "I remember we were talking about the reports that we might get twenty inches. He told me he'd come over in the morning to help shovel my path, like he does after every big snow, but he never showed up. Not like Doug."

"No it isn't," Vera agreed.

I walked down the front steps, nearly slipping a few times, and didn't stop until I was a few inches past the neighbor. Then I reached in my purse and pulled out my business card.

"This has my cell phone on it," I told her. "If you hear from him, will you call me?"

She studied the card. "Kate Conway, Producer," she read. "Who are you to Doug?"

"I'm a friend of Vera's. I just want to make sure she's okay, and she wants to make sure Doug's okay."

The woman nodded. "It's very nice of you to care so much about your friend."

I smiled at the compliment, tightened my arms around my coat so that Doug's mail wouldn't fall out and headed to my car.

\\\

Vera followed me to the nearest Starbucks, and we sat at the one available table, drinking hot chocolate and going piece by piece through Doug's mail. I'd expected a lot of flak about stealing it, or cautions against breaking federal regulations, but Vera didn't say a word. She just took her half of the pile and went through it.

"There isn't anything," she said after only a few minutes. "It's all junk mail and two bills."

"For what?"

"Electricity and cable."

"Either of them late?"

"No," she said. "He's current on both. What does that tell you?"

"Nothing, I suppose."

Vera scowled. "It tells you he pays his bills. He's lived in the same house for at least five years and he's nice enough to shovel his neighbor's driveway. That's not a con man."

"Maybe."

My prospects for pointing Makina toward Doug as the killer were looking grim. Doug was every bit as dull a human being as he'd appeared the day I'd met him. In my pile of mail there was a gardening catalog and an invitation to a book signing at a comic book store. A credit card bill had a zero revolving balance. The current charges were for a half dozen meals at a diner on Addison and a gym membership.

"So what now?" Vera asked.

I looked through my pile again. "I don't know. All we've got so far is that Doug probably hasn't been home since the murder."

"I think he's dead somewhere," she said, her voice cracking. "It's the only thing that explains why he hasn't called or been to his house."

"So where's his body? The killer left Erik's body right where we could find it. Why move Doug's to a hidden location?" I asked. I glanced down at the credit card statement. "Where's his office?"

"On Jackson and Wells. Why?"

"He went to a diner called Terry's near Wrigley Field six times last month."

"Maybe he's a Cubs fan."

"In winter?"

Vera sighed. "So maybe it's got great coffee."

"Or maybe he's meeting someone there and wants to keep it private." There was a small part of me that was a little pleased that Vera was now the one unraveling the secret life of a man she trusted. But being pleased only made me feel bad. I knew how much it hurt to love someone who'd betrayed you, and I didn't want that for anyone, even Vera.

"We're not going to get anywhere staring at his mail," I said. "Besides, I have to meet Walt for dinner."

Vera's face lit up. "Really?"

"I think he wants to talk about Erik's murder," I said. "He probably wants to spin it so he looks good in the final piece. A guy like him could end up a TV host if he plays his cards right. My bet is he's looking to feel me out about how he makes that leap."

She seemed to want more details, but I was only interested in what I wanted—another plausible suspect. And that meant asking Walt about his secret meeting with Ilena and Roman.

Thirty-four

Walt had chosen a German restaurant on Lincoln Avenue, one of those places that have been around since the 1950s and haven't changed anything since opening day. The wallpaper and red leather booths looked a little worse for the wear, but the food was amazing.

"You like it?" he asked, a nervous smile on his face.

"I've always been a sucker for bratwurst and spaetzle," I said. "But this doesn't seem like the sort of place you would like. Paintings of Bavaria on the wall, lace decorations, framed family photographs—it all seems a little sweet for the chef of the century."

He blushed a little. "I like good food and this is good food," he said. "My mom is from Alabama. Her folks owned a little restaurant and she learned to cook all the traditional Southern dishes. And my dad grew up near Taylor Street. His grandparents were from a little town in Southern Italy. They both loved to cook, so I was raised on soul food and pasta. And lots of good conversation. I guess that's how I relate to people, through food."

"So you had to feed me before you could talk to me."

"I suppose so." He laughed. "I would have cooked for you at my place but I thought that might be a little much for a first date."

I coughed. "A date?" I tried to say it casually, but all the confusion and surprise I felt came out in my voice.

"Vera said you weren't seeing anyone," Walt said. "I guess . . . well, I thought that you knew I was asking you out."

"I didn't," I admitted. "I guess I just . . ." I'd embarrassed Walt and felt stupid. "I haven't been asked on a date in so long I didn't recognize the invitation."

"Why did you think I wanted to have dinner with you?"

This was not the time to mention the secret meeting with Ilena and Roman, or my assumption that Walt had ambitions for a TV career.

"I thought you were nervous about what to say about Erik during the interview," I said.

"Oh."

"Look, Walt, it's my fault. And I'm flattered—"

"But not interested."

"It's not that." I wasn't about to tell him that I'd dated only one man in my entire life. Frank and I had met at sixteen and had been together until Vera came into the picture. I'd noticed that when I'd mentioned to other people I had only been with Frank, I was greeted with the same alarmed expression usually saved for circus freaks. "I haven't seen anyone since my husband died."

"I didn't know," Walt said, stumbling. "Vera didn't tell me you were . . . well, she didn't say anything about your husband. She just told me you were unattached."

"She's trying to help, I guess."

"People in love are always trying to fix up everyone else." He shrugged and dug into his sauerkraut.

"You think Vera is in love with Doug?"

"I think she wants to be."

"Do you think Doug is in love with Vera?"

He considered the question. "Doug's kind of a geek. Not that it's a bad thing. But he's the kind of guy who eats spaghetti on Tuesday. Every Tuesday for the last thirty years."

"A creature of habit."

"Yeah. Someone who thinks ordering the chef's special is taking one of life's big risks. I just don't see him being the kind of person who suddenly changes his life to include a free spirit like Vera."

"But they were dating."

He didn't seem convinced. "They're what my mother likes to call 'keeping company.' I don't see it leading to marriage," he said. "Is that what Vera wants?"

"I have no idea," I said. "But why does a guy who plays it safe invest a lot of money in a restaurant? Erik said it would take a long time, if ever, before anyone saw any profit from it."

"I wondered that myself. I even asked Roman about it." Walt put his fork down and signaled the waitress. "You want dessert, Kate? They make a great *bienenstich*. It's a cake with honeyed almonds baked onto the top and then filled with vanilla custard."

"Sounds delicious. What did Roman say?" I asked.

The waitress came over, and Walt chatted with her about the cake, ordered us two slices and coffee, then asked how business was. It felt like the seasons were changing while I waited to get Walt's attention again.

When he finally turned back to me, he said, "You're going to love this cake."

"What about Roman?"

"What?"

"Before you ordered dessert, you said you asked Roman about why Doug invested."

"Yeah."

"What did he say?" If I had been interested in dating, this would have been the moment when I pulled the plug. On the slim chance I ever let a man into my life again, he would have to be capable of getting to the point.

"He said Doug had made a low-risk investment."

"What does that mean?"

"Who knows? Roman likes to be opaque."

The waitress, a tall, slim blonde of about thirty, arrived with our cake and coffee, and while I had to admit the cake was delicious, I didn't want to waste time eating it. I wanted to ask questions.

"Did you ask Ilena about what Roman said? You two are close."

Walt's eyes widened slightly, then relaxed. "Not really. Personally, I like to stay away from both of them."

"So you don't socialize with them at all?"

"Why would I? Erik was my contact at the restaurant. We were the ones who were actually going to be working there. The rest of them were just investors." He bit into his cake. "It's good, isn't it? I've tried a couple of recipes but I can't seem to make my Bienenstich as good as this place."

He smiled, and I smiled back. I wanted to push further, but I'd decided that I'd like to have his reaction on tape. "You must be sad about Erik," I said instead.

"I am. He was a good guy," he said, hesitating before finishing his thought. "Not to be disrespectful to his memory, but restaurant managers are a dime a dozen. It's the chef people talk about."

"But Erik had a vision for the place."

He scowled. "He was all caught up in bringing glamour back, but I think he lost sight of the fact that this is a new era. When people think of movie stars they don't think of Clark Gable. They don't even know who he was. Erik's plan had us running uphill with bricks on our back."

"Excuse me?"

"He was making everything harder than it had to be."

"So the place is better off without him?"

Walt shook his head. "That's not what I meant. But Erik thought the restaurant experience wasn't about the food. What kind of thinking is that? If you don't want great food, then go to a bar, go to the movies." He waved his arms around. "He wanted to be the star of the show."

"And that's your job."

I'd ruffled him. "I just think we can simplify matters and make the place profitable," he said.

"So the restaurant is still opening?"

"You really are bad at dates, Kate. This feels more like another TV interview than a conversation."

"Sorry about that," I said. "But it is an interesting question."

Walt signaled the waitress for more coffee. When she brought the pot over to us, it created another opportunity for the two of them to chat about the restaurant business, and an invitation for Walt to meet the chef.

Walt excused himself quickly with a tepid invitation to join him in the kitchen, which I declined. I waited until my cake was finished and my coffee had gone cold, but there was no sign of either Walt or the waitress. When he didn't return after about fifteen minutes, I left the restaurant alone.

I wasn't sure if he was dumping me for the waitress, had a genuine desire to exchange recipes with the restaurant's chef, or was just avoiding my questions. Any way you looked at it, though, my first date with a new man in twenty-one years was a washout. It was a good thing I hadn't bothered to shave my legs.

Thirty-five

I resisted the temptation to call Vera and enlighten her on the results of matchmaking, because I knew in her own way she was just trying to help. Just as when I'd lied to Makina I'd been trying to help her. Both of us had screwed up, giving me two more examples of why it's best just to stay out of other people's affairs.

Not that I imagined for a second I had any choice anymore. I'd been home only twenty minutes when the disposable phone rang, giving me another chance to help someone. And get it wrong.

"Will you accept a collect call from Dugan Correctional Center?" It was a recording. "Tim Campbell would like to speak with you."

"Yes," I said into the phone.

It was too much to hope that he'd already figured out who had the motive for murder.

"Kate," Tim said in an exaggerated version of his usual "good ole boy" drawl. "Drive home go okay?"

"Yes, it went fine, Tim. I'll be back at Dugan on Monday if you want to talk then about what we discussed this morning."

"Actually it's related but I think it's okay to talk now. That lady, the friend, she's a wealthy woman. I read something about her in the *Sun-Times* today after you left."

"Her family has money."

"Well, that's the thing that's always been missing for me, you see. I couldn't mount the right defense because that takes experts, and DNA tests and big-time lawyers. That takes money."

"What are you saying?" I asked, even though I was pretty sure I already knew where this conversation was headed.

"Maybe you could talk to her about helping me, since I'm helping her."

"You haven't actually helped her yet."

"But I will, Kate. I have some information I got from somewhere about one of her friends at that restaurant."

"That's pretty vague."

"I can get more specific when I see you. I have a few people I can talk to, but it's not an easy conversation to have. It looks like your friend jumped into the deep end of the pool on this, and if she wants rescuing . . ."

"It's going to cost money," I finished for him.

"No, Kate. I'll help her because she's your friend and you're a nice lady. But I'm just saying that if she thinks she can help me, I sure could use the help."

I took a deep breath. "I'll talk to her, Tim. And we'll talk on Monday." I hung up.

\\\

I climbed into bed and sat with my arms wrapped around my knees. For someone who had been accused of spending too much time alone, I was sure making a lot of new friends. And all of them were the wrong friends. They had problems, complications. They wanted things from me, and I wasn't in a giving mood. Maybe Tim was innocent of murdering his wife. Maybe Doug was a decent guy lying dead in a ditch somewhere. And maybe Walt had wanted nothing more from me than a nice conversation and a good-night kiss. Maybe.

I opened the drawer to my nightstand and pulled out the one picture of Frank and me that wasn't in a box in the garage. For some reason, when I'd put away his photos after he left me, I'd held on to this one. It wasn't from any special event—not our wedding or Christmas or even a favorite vacation. It had been taken at a barbecue at my brother-in-law's house about three years before we split up. Frank was sitting on a plastic lawn chair, beer in one hand, hot dog in the other. He looked relaxed. He was smiling, almost laughing. Frank had a nice smile, wide and unassuming. He didn't pretend to be happy when he wasn't, and didn't hold back his happiness when he felt it. It was a trait I'd always envied. I'd built my career on being able to express emotions I didn't really feel—sympathy, warmth, affection. Sometimes I wasn't sure what I actually felt. Especially these days.

In the photo, I was leaning into Frank, my shoulder against his, my head touching his head. I was smiling too. Maybe not as widely, but I looked happy. I told myself I'd kept this picture in my nightstand because it was a good picture of the both of us, particularly me. My waist looked really thin in it, and for once my dark red hair didn't overwhelm my face. But I realized looking at it now that it wasn't my waistline, or Frank's smile. It was the ordinariness of the moment it captured, one of a thousand barbecues we'd attended as a couple. That's why I kept it. My life with Frank had had a rhythm to it, a routine. Sometimes I'd hated that routine while I was living it, but I craved it now.

Being a freelance television producer means never knowing what I'm going to be working on, or where, or with whom. It means never knowing how much money I'll make in a month, or when I'll get paid for the work I do. When I was married, there were certainties—family barbecues, a date for New Year's Eve, arguments over where to spend Thanksgiving, a warm body next to me at night.

Now I had no routine, no certainty. I'd just drifted the past seven months, expecting things to fall into place. But they hadn't. I missed Frank's sense of humor, his talent, and the love we'd shared for at least some of our marriage, but mostly I missed knowing he was there at the end of the day. If Frank were alive I wouldn't be caught up in all this mess. I'd never had the energy for other people's craziness. I'd had too much of my own. I'd had an unhappy marriage to obsess about, in-laws to dislike, and family parties I'd been forced to attend. But that was gone now. And staring at this photo of us, I saw that I hadn't created a life without Frank; I'd avoided one.

\\\

I stretched out in the bed and covered myself with the comforter. I could hear the wind outside, and a tree branch scratching against the window, but I didn't care. I was warm and safe and in my own bed.

I tried to think of Frank, and of some of the happy nights we'd been together in this bed, but the present kept getting in the way. If Tim hadn't killed his wife, then he'd spent twenty years away from these small comforts for a crime he hadn't committed. It wasn't something I would wish on anyone, including Vera.

Thirty-six

There was a loud banging on my door. I could see daylight through my window, and when I looked at my alarm clock it was after noon. I hadn't slept well, so noon or not, I wasn't about to get up. Instead I waited, staying in bed under the warm covers, hoping it was just some overenthusiastic Jehovah's Witness or a Girl Scout with a strong belief in sales quotas. But the banging wouldn't stop.

I put my feet on the cold floor, cursing whomever was at my door. I looked around until I found a pair of discarded socks under a chair and put them on, then grabbed a chunky cable-knit cardigan with a coffee stain on the front, threw it over my sweats and T-shirt, and headed for the front door.

"I'm not interested in whatever you're selling," I announced as I opened the door.

It was Ellen. "Good Lord, Kate, is that how you dress to answer the door?" She walked into the living room. "What happened in here?"

"Nothing." The living room looked fine to me. Messy, but fine.

"I had no idea it was this bad."

"What's this bad? I've been working a lot," I said. "I haven't had time to clean. I bet if I showed up uninvited to your house, I'd find a reason to nitpick."

Ellen picked a pizza box up off the couch and set it on the coffee table next to the empty beer bottle. "How long have these been here?"

It had been two days. Or three. I couldn't remember. "Last night," I said. "I had some friends over and we hung out and watched television." I silently prayed she wouldn't ask me which friends or what television show. It was one thing to lie to a cop. I had a chance of getting away with that. But I knew my sister wouldn't be as gullible.

Ellen grabbed my arm and led me to the couch. "I know you've been depressed—"

"I'm not depressed. I'm tired," I tried to explain. "I've been working on two shows at the same time and on one of them there was a homicide, so it's been a bit crazy. We've been trying to arrange additional interviews, which as you can imagine takes a lot of time. Plus I've been driving back and forth to Dugan Correctional, so I've been getting home late a lot."

I was rambling, but it didn't matter. She wasn't listening.

"We're going to sit here and talk," Ellen said, "and then we're going to come up with a plan that will help you. Tony is taking the kids to his mother's, so I don't have a thing to do but be with you all day."

"Wow," was all I could think of. "The thing is, Ellen, I do have things to do today. All day. I can't just sit around and talk, much as I'd like to. I don't know why you came over but—"

"You missed your hair appointment yesterday," she said. "And today you were supposed to meet me at Mom's."

"Dividing up her knickknacks." I remembered. Damn, I was never going to hear the end of this. I took a deep breath and looked Ellen square in the eye, doing my best to sound tough. "As important as it is to decide right now which one of us gets Mom and Dad's souvenir plate from their honeymoon at Niagara Falls, I really do have stuff to do."

I got up from the couch, hoping to signal to her that it was time to go, but I couldn't even take a step. Ellen had a death grip on my hand.

"Like what?"

"Like . . . stuff," I said. "What difference does it make? I don't have time to go through Mom's house picking out valuables in some macabre version of *Antiques Roadshow*. Why don't you and Mom pick out the things you think I'll like and don't tell me what you've chosen? That way when she dies, I'll be surprised. It'll be like Christmas morning, only with caskets and burial plots."

"You know Mom and I planned this to cheer you up." Concern had become pouting, Ellen's favorite tactic for getting her way.

"How is talking about Mom's death supposed to cheer me up?" I snapped. It was a tactical error. The angrier I got, the more evidence Ellen had that I was in crisis. I tried to sound calm. "Ellen, I was up late. I'm crabby and I have a lot to do. I appreciate your being concerned, but I just don't have the time for it right now."

"At least make the time for a shower." She sniffed, and finally let go of my hand. She got up from the couch and walked toward the door, tsking and shaking her head the entire way. "I know you don't think I understand your situation because my marriage is happy and I have children, but I've been lonely, Kate. And I don't want that for you." It was a petty dig and genuine concern in one sentence. I stood back in awe at her skill.

"I know you do, Ellen. But I'm fine. Really I am."

She nodded, but there was skepticism in her eyes. "By the way, your neighbor is a creep. I'd watch out for him."

"My neighbor is a seventy-nine-year-old woman," I said.

Ellen rolled her eyes. "Your neighbor on the other side."

"That house is empty. It's been on the market for months but it hasn't sold."

"No. The guy who lives right there." Ellen pointed to the empty house, refusing as always to admit she was wrong. "When I was walking to your door, he was standing on the lawn of that house looking at your house. I went right up to him, told him I was your sister, and asked him who he was. He told me he lives there."

"No one lives in that house, Ellen." I looked out the window, but whoever had been there was gone. "What did he look like?"

"Big guy. Bald. Maybe in his late fifties. He tried to pretend he was going to clear the path, but he didn't have a shovel and he was standing in the snow in really expensive shoes. I'd have to be a moron to buy that story. Is he peeping in your windows?"

"Oh, that's the guy who used to live there," I lied, hoping if I didn't make eye contact I'd get away with it. "He's probably got an open house or something."

"Well, you're lucky he's moving away. If you ask me, there's something kind of angry about him."

Ellen imagined she had a near-perfect ability to find the psychopath in a roomful of normal people. She said it came from years of teaching seventh graders. But in this case she was probably right. Roman Papadakis had found out where I lived and, for some reason, had come to see me.

Thirty-seven

I used to love winter when I was a kid. My friends and I would put on snowsuits and build igloos and spend hours running around in the cold. Years later, when I was digging out my car and praying I could get out of the parking space without getting stuck, I griped occasionally, but I still liked it. I'd thought people who took up residence in Florida from November to March were cowards.

But this year winter was getting to me. I felt a near-constant chill. Spring—which usually came to Chicago around Memorial Day, lasted an hour, and then turned into a three-month heat wave—couldn't come fast enough.

Winter did have one advantage, though: footprints in the snow. As soon as Ellen left, I took her advice and showered. Then I bundled up and went looking for evidence of Roman. In the middle of my neighbor's lawn were footsteps. They were large, very large, which immediately prompted me to wonder if that old wives' tale was true. If it was, perhaps Ilena had married Roman for more than his money.

They were also pointed directly at my house, just as Ellen had said. He'd walked toward my door, then doubled back, stepped on the lawn next door, and stood there for who knows how long, looking at my front door. And then he'd left, I guessed, after Ellen spoke with him. I could see the footprints moving toward the street.

Damn it. I was stuck in it now. Possible murderers, arsonists, my sister . . . everyone was showing up at my door, and there was no ignoring it. I did the only thing I could do in this situation: I went to the neighborhood bakery, got a hot chocolate and a cinnamon roll, and silently berated myself for caring about what happened to Vera. I blamed Frank for it. Although he'd been dead since July, it didn't stop him from screwing with me. And somebody was going to pay for that. Someone aside from me.

I'd left my tote bag in the backseat of the car. I grabbed my files on the show, found the address I was looking for, and drove to one of

Chicago's wealthiest suburbs, Lake Forest. Turnabout, someone once said, is fair play. And it was the only idea I had.

\\\

The house looked like it was on steroids. It was large, made from stone and a muddy brown brick. There were wings coming off each side, and a garage that looked bigger than my three-bedroom bungalow. I drove into the long circular driveway and parked my car close to the front door. I didn't have a plan, but I was annoyed and sleep deprived, and that would have to do.

Ilena answered the door. "Kate? What brings you here?"

"Your husband came to see me this morning so I'm here to find out why."

"He came to see you?" She was holding the front door open only enough to see me, but not enough for me to see inside.

"It's twenty degrees outside," I said.

"I'm a little busy right now. Perhaps we can meet for coffee later."

"I'm writing the script for the show later, and in it I reveal your affair with Erik. I think the audience will really enjoy seeing what a hotbed of sex and lies your restaurant really is."

Ilena glanced behind her, then bit her lip. "You can't say things you can't prove."

"You'd be amazed by what I can say. Are you going to let me in?"

She stood back and let me walk past her into a large center hallway that looked as though a gold mine had thrown up on it. Every piece of furniture had gilding, statues of Greek gods stood on either side of the front door, two ornate chandeliers hung from a high ceiling, and the floor was a dark veined marble. It was Vegas, but with less restraint.

"Nice home," I said.

"Thanks. I put a lot of myself into it." She pointed toward a room to her left. It turned out to be a living room the size of a football field, with four couches, a grand piano, and a ten-foot painting of Roman and Ilena with two dogs at their feet.

"Where's your husband?" I asked as I sat down.

"I'm not sure. He didn't come home last night."

"Is that usual?"

"We have a place in the city, on Lake Shore Drive," she said. "When he works late he stays there."

"Has he called you today?"

"No. Is something wrong? You said he came to see you. What did he want?"

"I don't know. He apparently stood outside my house this morning for a while, until my sister chased him away."

She smiled. "Is your sister so intimidating she could scare Roman?"

"She is, actually."

"Good for her. She has to tell me her secret sometime," Ilena said. "I don't see how I can help you."

"Did you kill Erik?"

"Are you serious?"

"You were having an affair with him."

Her eyes narrowed and she looked on the verge of throwing me out. "Can I offer you some coffee?" Without waiting for me to answer, she walked to a small intercom, pressed a button, and asked someone named Maria to bring two coffees to the sitting room.

"Ilena, I'm really not interested in who you sleep with," I said. "But I am interested in who killed Erik."

"You barely knew him. I doubt the Business Channel cares. They just want a wrap-up, if I understand it. A statement from each of us about Erik's passing and some kind of announcement about whether we'll continue without him."

"You spoke to someone there."

"I did. So explain to me why any of this concerns you beyond getting those statements."

"Because the police think Vera killed Erik."

Ilena laughed. I wasn't sure if she was laughing at the absurdity of Vera being a suspect or at my caring that Vera was a suspect. I was about to ask when Maria came in with a sterling silver coffee service for two.

Ilena poured my coffee. "This is a dark-roast mix of beans from the best plantations in the world. Would you like cream and sugar?"

"Black."

"Just like Roman," she said. "Personally, I can't stand the taste of coffee unless it's got lots of cream and sugar in it."

"If you don't like it, why drink it?"

She cocked her head. "It's what refined people drink in the morning."

I couldn't help myself. As I sipped my coffee I felt sorry for Ilena. The rich husband had turned out to be a domineering bully, the house clearly intended to impress was in all likelihood the eyesore of this sophisticated neighborhood, the business that was supposed to buy her freedom was crumbling around her, and the man she'd taken to her bed was now lying in the morgue.

But that didn't mean she was a victim. If she couldn't help me with why Roman had come to my house, there were other questions she could answer.

"What were you and Walt doing last week at the restaurant? It was late. There was candlelight and wine."

"Now you're asking me if I'm sleeping with Walt?"

"Well, if you are, I'm even more curious why Roman was there."

She blinked, looking a little confused. "How do you know that?"

"I was spying on you."

Ilena put her coffee on the tray, scratched her neck, and patted her hair. She was looking toward me but not at me. Buying time, searching for a response.

"Why?" she finally asked.

"I was in the neighborhood."

"Well, you misunderstood what you think you might have seen."

"That's quite a lot of qualifiers, Ilena."

"I'm not really sure I want to do the show," she said suddenly, and stood up.

"Speaking of the show, I have one person who I still need to book for an interview. Detective Makina," I said. "I need to drive over to talk to him, give him a rundown on everything I know."

She said nothing. For a moment I thought maybe she'd pull a gun, like what happened in all of Humphrey Bogart's movies. Ilena had a vintage dame quality about her, the kind of woman in all the black-and-whites from the forties. But there was no gun, no sudden moves, no rapid-fire dialogue. She just stood there.

"My husband is a very powerful man," she said finally. "He doesn't like people who get in the way of his business."

"Is that supposed to frighten me?" I asked.

"It frightens me," she said.

Thirty-eight

The Makina thing had been a bluff. I didn't want to go anywhere near the guy. But still, I knew I needed him for the interview, and given Ilena's veiled threat, it was probably a good idea to share some of what I knew with him.

When I called he suggested I meet him at his office at Area Four headquarters, but when I got there he seemed surprised to see me.

"The last person I expected to see," he said as he led me to a small room. There was a desk and two chairs, but little else.

"I called and told you I was coming."

He smiled a little. "That's what I didn't expect. You didn't seem interested in cooperating with this investigation."

"I'm interested in the right person being arrested," I said. "And I hope you are too."

"Would you like some coffee?"

"No thanks," I said. "I've had enough caffeine for today."

He motioned for me to sit down, and as I did, he sat across from me. He seemed a little shy. He'd pegged me as an uncooperative witness, and now my coming to see him, I could tell, was throwing him. "What can I do for you?" he asked.

"I'm working on a television show about the restaurant," I said.

"I know that."

"I'd like to interview you about the investigation into Erik Price's death."

"It's an open case, Mrs. Conway," he said. "There's very little I can share with you."

"I'm sure my bosses will be happy even if all I get is a quote saying that you're doing everything you can to find the person who shot him."

"What makes you think he was shot?"

"I don't know a lot about bullet wounds," I said, "but he did have holes in his body, so I figured that was what happened."

"And Ms. Bingham owns a gun," he said a little smugly, correctly guessing why I'd assumed Erik had been shot. "Mr. Price was stabbed. Eleven times."

"Any defensive wounds?"

"A few. Why?"

"Someone must have been pretty angry with him. Someone strong enough to stab him without Erik getting the knife," I explained.

"That depends on where he was stabbed first. He was on his feet for three of the wounds, then the M.E. says he was on the ground for the last eight."

"Sounds like a crime of passion."

"Does it?" Detective Makina sat back, crossing his arms and looking at me. "So you want me to do an interview?"

"Yes."

"On one condition. You have to answer a question for me."

"I'll do my best," I said.

"Why are you protecting Ms. Bingham?"

"I didn't know I was."

"But you like her."

"I really don't know whether I do or not. She's not a friend, exactly. She's just . . . I don't know, but you'd have to know her. She means well, and she's so . . . guileless, I guess, she makes you want to make sure she's okay."

"You don't think she could be taking advantage of you?"

"You think I'm that stupid?" It was, despite my indelicate wording, a sincere question. Maybe I was that stupid.

"I don't think that. But if, as you say, Ms. Bingham is so guileless, maybe you thought by backing up her story you could help her."

"Trust me, Detective, I'm not one of those people who like to help," I said. "I mute the TV when those commercials come on to sponsor hungry children. I walk right past homeless people even when I have change in my pocket. I'm not helping Vera because I need to help. I'm helping—" I stopped myself. I was on the verge of confessing to a lie. "I believe Vera is innocent because I saw her the night Erik died. She was every bit as freaked out as I was. Besides, she doesn't have a motive."

"She has two hundred and fifty thousand motives."

He had me there. "Vera is a very wealthy woman," I tried again. "She's heir to Knutson Foods. Did you know that?"

"So?"

"Two hundred and fifty thousand dollars is hardly going to be a game changer for her. She probably spends more on shoes every year," I said. "And it wouldn't be the first time Vera's given money to a friend starting a business. She's never killed anyone over it before, so why start now?"

I don't play chess, but I sensed I'd just captured his queen. He shifted in his chair and changed his line of questioning. "You mentioned that Erik spoke to you about his argument with Ms. Bingham," he said.

"He did." I placed my hands in my lap and dug my fingernails into my palms. I knew what was coming.

"When?"

I'd planned for this moment. Every lie needs a backup plan, which is why lies are so difficult to keep up when someone applies pressure. "Erik drove away right after the argument, and then Vera got one of those threatening calls."

"The call Victor Pilot recorded."

"Yes," I said. "Naturally we were all focused on Vera at that point. We checked her car, because we believed the reference to slashing had to do with her tires, but that wasn't the case. So then we went back to the restaurant. When we were leaving a few hours later, I saw Erik's car parked down the street. I walked over to it and saw Erik inside. That's when he told me."

"He didn't call you or ask you to meet him?"

"No." I knew Makina would be checking phone records, so there was no point in pretending there had been a call.

"Why did he come back to the restaurant but not go inside?"

"I would say you should ask him but obviously that's not an option," I said. "He was having an affair with Ilena. Maybe that's who he was waiting for."

"You know this?"

"Don't you?" I asked. "Maybe he broke it off. Or maybe she did, and he threatened to tell her husband. She's terrified of Roman. I'm a little afraid of him too. He's apparently stalking me. My sister saw him lurking outside my house this morning."

Makina leaned forward in his chair, an amused expression on his face. "Why not Walt Russo, the chef?"

"What about Walt?"

"So far you've handed me Doug Zieman, Roman Papadakis, and now Ilena. All possible suspects far more likely to be killers than Vera Bingham. So why not try and distract me with Mr. Russo?"

I tried to seemed scandalized by the suggestion, but I think I just looked caught. "I'm not trying to distract you. I'm trying to help you."

"I thought you don't like to help."

I hated when my own words bit me in the ass. "You will probably just think I'm making this up," I said, "but I saw Walt, Ilena, and Roman in the restaurant having a secret meeting. Walt signed some papers. Ilena was very upset when I asked her about it."

"What were the papers?"

"I don't know," I said. "But it was clearly something they were hiding from the others."

"Okay, thanks." He studied me for a moment. What he was looking for, I couldn't tell, but I tried to be blank and innocent.

"I need to do the interview next week," I said as I got up. "Friday afternoon okay? We can do it here."

"I'll confirm with my lieutenant, but I don't think it will be a problem." He shook my hand. "If there's anything else you want to share with me . . ."

"Not at the moment," I said. "Have you found Doug Zieman? He hasn't been home since the murder."

"No. But two nice women went by his house and picked up his mail."

I gave him my best Mona Lisa smile. "While you were checking the mailbox, did you search his house?"

"He's not there. And nothing is missing as far as the neighbor could tell," he said. "The dog is annoying but she's a very nice woman, isn't she?"

Nice try, but I didn't answer. "So you didn't find anything?"

"We did find something. He had a list of things he wanted to do. Number twenty-six was owning a high-end restaurant."

"Let me guess, he also had an entry on surviving a zombie attack."

"That was one of my favorites."

"What's number forty-two?"

Makina sifted through some files on his desk until he found what he wanted. "Number forty-two," he said as he scanned the paper. "'Fall in love again.' Why?"

"It was on a card Doug sent Vera with a dozen roses." I felt a pang of pity for Vera. I didn't know which was worse, loving a man who was setting her up for murder, or loving a man who loved her back but was missing and probably dead.

"There's another item that your friend might be interested in. Number thirty-four." Makina handed me the list.

After items as whimsical as "Land on the moon" and as practical as "Lose thirty pounds," I found number thirty-four. "Find a rich woman to buy me whatever I want." Pity changed into anger.

"That would give Ms. Bingham an interesting motive if something has happened to Mr. Zieman," Makina said.

"Doug may have told her about having a bucket list. He told me," I said. "But do you honestly think he shared number thirty-four with Vera?"

"No. But can you be sure she didn't stumble across the list herself? It was on a bulletin board in his home office. She could have seen it."

"She didn't."

"You sure?"

I met Makina's eyes. All the fear he'd managed to instill in me was, at least temporarily, gone. I was the person who always saw the worst in others. I prided myself on it, but I knew Vera. Despite trying for more than a year to see her as a bad person, I knew she wasn't a killer. "I'm sure," I said.

Thirty-nine

I'm sorry about the other day." Brick looked tired, and some of his usual bravado was missing. We sat on a bench in the exercise area while Andres and Victor set up the equipment.

"If you're not up to this," I said, "we can shoot you reading in your cell or something."

"No, that's okay. I can walk around a little. Show you how we keep in shape."

He laughed, and he had reason to. The "exercise" area was a small outdoor section with a broken basketball hoop, some mismatched weights, and a track running along the edges that measured less than a quarter mile. I wasn't sure what footage we could get of him here, but at least it gave us a chance to talk. The guard was busy with Andres, too fascinated by the video equipment to pay much attention to Brick.

"What happened to you on Friday?" I asked. "Did you have food poisoning?"

"My stomach can handle a lot but I just didn't feel too good after breakfast. Went to the infirmary and had a few unpleasant hours but I'm good as gold now," he said. "So what was so important you needed to see me without your boys?"

"It's this other show I'm working on. I'm trying to find out about a guy who was in Pontiac for a while. His name was John Fletcher. He was in for arson and murder."

"Short dude, white, older. He'd spent a lot of time in the joint."

"You knew him?" I couldn't believe my luck.

"Yeah. Not well, but I knew him. He was hard to miss."

"Why's that?"

"He was kind of a preacher, tryin' to save souls from eternal damnation. That kind of shit. He'd go from one guy to the next, didn't give a damn about gangs, or gettin' himself messed up; he'd just preach and preach."

"Sounds annoying."

"He didn't mean no harm. I don't think he was all there, you know what I mean? He used to talk about seein' the fires of hell."

"He was an arsonist, so he'd know," I said. "I was thinking that maybe he was set up. That he hadn't actually committed the murder he was convicted of."

Brick shrugged. "If that was the case, he didn't say nothin' to me about it. He just asked me if he could save my soul."

"What did you tell him?"

"If he could find it, he could save it." He laughed.

"Where is he now—do you know?"

"Dead. Right before I left Pontiac to come here. He had cancer all over his body," he said. "How's he connected with your dead friend at the restaurant?"

"He might not be," I admitted. "But the police are looking at a woman I know, and I don't think she's the one."

"You tryin' to help?"

"Unfortunately."

Brick nudged me in the ribs. "Kate Conway has a soft side," he said. "I'm gonna tuck that away for later."

"How does my alleged soft side help you?"

"We all con artists. Killers, thieves, drug dealers . . ."

"TV producers . . ."

"We try and get people to do what we want," he said. "And we all want somethin'."

"I want to get the police away from this woman and from me."

"You stepped in it, didn't you?" He shook his head. "What'd you do? Alibi her?"

It was probably a dumb move, which I'd been making a lot of lately, but I felt an odd kinship with this man, trapped in a life he didn't want by a past he couldn't escape. "Kind of," I admitted. "I maybe helped her a little with the time line."

"Shit, Kate. Stupid. You sure she didn't kill the guy?"

"Yes. Mostly sure," I said. "He was stabbed. She owned a gun, so if she were going to kill him why not use that?"

"Guns are traceable. Besides, she might not have been thinkin' straight."

I hesitated, wanting to ask Brick a question that had been on my mind since I saw Erik's body. "What's it like to kill someone?" I finally asked.

"Depends, I think. For some people it's like swattin' a fly."

"For you?"

Brick looked down at his hands. "A gun puts some distance between the killer and the other guy. Kind of like that camera puts distance between you and whoever you talkin' to. It makes it easier to do something disagreeable."

"But a knife?"

He sighed. "I never stabbed no one. I gotta think it's real intimate, looking that person in the eye, watching the surprise they feel when the knife first goes in. Then the pain, the fear. Watching as their eyes go blank. Somethin' fierce about it, somethin' desperate. You have to want that person real dead to do something like that." We sat quietly for a while before Brick spoke. "I answered your question. Now you answer mine. Why'd you alibi that friend of yours?"

"It just started with a small lie and kind of snowballed."

"It always does. You want my advice?" he asked.

"Why not?"

"Stop. Back off, shut up, and let your friend get herself out of it."

"Good advice."

"You ain't gonna follow it, are ya?"

"Probably not."

"Okay then, I got another piece of advice for you. You need to ask yourself why this dude got shanked. What was he up to? In my experience, if a brother gets himself killed, probably he did somethin' to cause it."

"That makes sense," I said.

"That's probably what Tim told you, right?"

"Not really," I admitted. "And he said he didn't know John Fletcher."

Brick considered it. "Maybe he didn't. Fletcher told me he only preached to the sinners. Maybe he didn't think Tim made the cut."

\\\

We spent about twenty minutes getting footage of Brick shooting hoops by himself and sitting on the bench, staring up at the sky. He called it his meditation time, when he let himself get lost in his thoughts. Afterward I asked him what thoughts he was lost in, but he declined to share. Instead, he offered one last piece of advice.

"Carin' about people is a slippery slope, Kate," he said. "You let someone into your world, there's no tellin' what you might do to protect them. You just better watch yourself."

"You do the same," I said. "And remember we have one more interview left."

"I'll pencil you into my busy social calendar." Brick nodded toward the crew. "See you guys."

Andres and Victor waved at Brick, who stood quietly while the guard handcuffed him and led him inside. Andres looked over at me.

"Everything okay?" he asked.

"Yeah," I said. Knowing that Brick had killed three people and regretted only one weirdly made him easier to trust. It made him seem honest, in a kind of twisted way. "We're getting footage of Tim at the library," I told Andres. "He works there every afternoon."

\\\

Tim rolled a cart down a short aisle in the chaotically organized library. He put books on shelves, he took them off again, he paged through them, and he chatted with two other inmates who were checking out books—all at Andres's direction. Tim barely looked at me, but I couldn't take my eyes off him. I was looking for signs of the con artist that he appeared to be now that he was crying innocence. All I saw was the same laid backed guy I'd met the first day.

When Andres had all the shots we needed, I told him to break down the equipment while I waited back with Tim.

"So what did you find out?" I asked.

"You mad at me, Kate?"

"You're attempting to extort money from someone, Tim."

"No." He shook his head slowly, confusion mixed with concern. "You asked me for help, and I asked you for help. That kind of thing is done on the outside all the time. It's just business, right?"

"I suppose. What's your help?"

"I talked to a bunch of guys I know from Chicago and one of them had heard of that Papa guy."

"Roman Papadakis."

"Yeah. This guy had done some work for him."

"In his restaurant?"

Tim looked around. "Kind of. He provided backup when things got sticky. He told me that your guy Roman was looking to unload a package." Tim said it as if the meaning were obvious.

"What's a package?" I finally asked. My years shooting documentaries in prison only took me so far.

"A . . . you know, a person."

"Kill someone?" My voice elevated and Tim's eyes widened. I lowered my voice. "Did he say who this package was?"

"No, but this guy I talked to, he's only been here six months, so the information is pretty fresh." Tim was whispering. "He told me that he might be able to get in touch with some people on the outside and find out more. But there's a catch."

"Money."

He nodded. "Not a lot. Maybe a grand. No one in here does something for nothing."

"Who does this money go to?" I asked.

"You give it to me and I give it to him. You can bring it in cash. They don't search you, do they? Not like family members." Tim took a few steps back from me, as if he were trying to uncross the line he'd just crossed. "You can check out the story or you can just ignore it. I'm just telling you what I know."

"Well, thanks, I guess," I said, reeling a little from this new information. "I don't know about getting any money, but I'll look into it. If it turns out to be something, I'll get back to you."

"I'm sorry, Kate," Tim said. "I'm not good at the right thing to say, and I think you got the worst possible idea about me."

"You put yourself in a position for me to think the worst."

"I get that. I ain't learned a lot of social skills in here. If you want to just forget what I asked you, about your friend helpin' me, that would be okay, but what I told you is true."

I wanted to walk out of there, to just shake his hand, make arrangements for our last interview, and leave. But I didn't. And it wasn't just because an innocent man locked in prison for twenty years would make a perfect ending to the documentary, though it would. It was because if he was innocent . . . I didn't want to finish the thought. It was just too sad to consider.

"If you didn't kill your wife, then what are you doing in prison?" I asked.

"I was there when it happened, in the apartment. I was half passed out, and I saw Cody trying to take advantage of Jenny."

"Cody, your drug dealer," I said.

"Yeah. I didn't do anything to stop it 'cause we didn't have enough money to pay for the drugs and I figured it was kind of a trade." He kept his eyes toward the floor. "But Jenny wasn't inclined to go along with it, and something got out of hand and Cody just stabbed her. I tried to stop it." He cleared his throat, seemed almost ready to cry but didn't. "I grabbed the knife from Cody but it was too late. Jenny reached up to me for help but I couldn't do nothin' by then. The damage was done. I just stood there and watched her die."

"Did you tell the police what had happened when they arrested you?"

He shook his head. "I told 'em it was my fault. And it was. And I was so drugged out I didn't make any right choices. By the time I sobered up, it was too late. I had an appointed attorney, and he didn't give a damn. He didn't even stay awake during half the testimony."

"And Cody?"

"His family knew people. His daddy was on the city council. I was a nobody with a knife in my hand, a drug addiction, and a dead wife."

"And all the years since?"

"I didn't care if I lived or died."

"So why care now?"

He looked at me. "My little cousin, the one who visited me, she told me that Cody is dealin' again. He was straight for a while, but he tried to put the moves on my cousin, get her to try some meth. I'm gonna do what I can to stop him."

I looked for the telltale signs of a lie—I've seen them all, the broken eye contact, the extraneous detail—but there were none. Tim looked straight at me, his eyes sad but sincere. "I'll do what I can," I said.

He smiled a little, then turned toward the guard, who handcuffed him and took him back to his cell.

Forty

It's a good story," Andres said.

Andres, Victor, Vera, and I sat in Vera's kitchen, eating deep-dish pizza, drinking beer, and trying to figure out what to do. Vera had spent the better part of ten minutes staring off into space, so I wasn't sure if she was even listening.

"I can call Makina, tell him what Tim said," I suggested.

Victor sneered. "That guy has his head up his ass."

"You've already told him about Roman," Andres pointed out. "Told him about the fire, about his cousin's murder, about Ilena being afraid of him. Haven't you?"

"Yeah."

"And what's he done with that information?"

"Nothing," Victor answered for me. "He's too busy going after two completely innocent people. I say you give him nothing."

"Victor's right." Andres patted his old friend's back, the first friendly gesture between the two of them in weeks. "It's a prison rumor given to you by a convicted killer looking for cash. Is Makina really going to take that seriously?"

"Especially since it may not be true," I agreed. "I told Tim about the fire. I practically handed him Roman as a suspect. He could have just made up the whole thing."

"I don't think we can take a chance on whether it's true or isn't," Vera said, finally turning to face the rest of us. "If Roman killed Erik, then we have to prove it. If he gets arrested, Doug can come out of hiding. If he's okay."

"That's a lot of ifs," I said. Including the one she'd left out: If Roman had planned to hire someone to get rid of one "package," couldn't he hire someone to get rid of us? I looked over at Vera, who looked as worried as I felt. "I suppose we can try," I told her. That cheered her up, but she had a lot more confidence in my detective skills than I did. "It would be something if Tim has given us the break we need to find Doug and wrap this damn thing up."

"That poor man," Vera said. "Tim, I mean. All these years to carry around that guilt about his wife, and to be in prison for something he didn't do."

"*If* he didn't do it," I reminded her, and myself. "All we have is his word. And as Brick said, all these guys are con men."

"He would know," Andres interrupted. "What is it with you and that guy, Kate? My wife does the same thing. She has faith in the most ridiculous people."

"Quite a character flaw," I said.

"You never saw the good in people before," he told me, actually sounding concerned. "It was your best quality."

"Tim gave us information that we can use to find Erik's killer," Vera answered for me. "And the deal Kate made was we would help in return, so that's what we're going to do."

"That's only one part of this," I reminded her. "Brick said that if we want to know who killed Erik we have to know more about him."

Andres rolled his eyes, and even Victor shook his head, but Vera smiled approvingly. Regardless of what any of them thought, what Brick had said made sense. Instead of focusing on the suspects, which so far was getting us nowhere, we had to focus on the victim. It's an unfortunate reality that in true crime shows, and in life, it's the victim who gets lost in the shuffle while the killer gets all the attention.

When I tell friends I've sat across from people who've committed horrible acts of violence, even the mildest of my friends are riveted by my stories. But no one asks me what it's like to sit with the families of murder victims. No one asks me about the victims at all. And I was just as bad. I'd barely spent any time thinking about Erik Price. It was as if his death was an annoyance to me, getting in the way of my sleep and keeping me involved with Vera.

"I'm going to look into Erik's background, see what I can find," I said.

"Because Brick said so?" Andres asked. "Kate—"

"Andres," I said, stopping him. "I'm not enamored by a prison inmate, if that's what you're getting at, and I'm not doing his bidding."

"But you trust him," Vera cut in. "You like him."

"As a person, yes," I admitted. "I'm not going to be his pen pal or anything, but I like how straightforward he is. I like that he understands what it's like."

"To be lonely," Vera said.

"To be a killer," I corrected her. "He's helping me understand how Erik's killer might think."

\\\

Andres and Victor left, refusing to admit that I was on the right track. We would be shooting together in a few days. I was scheduled to do the interviews with some of the Club Car investors, so whatever ill feelings there were among us would have to blow over by then, but I was annoyed. It was as if the whole world was concerned about the fragile state of my emotions and no one was able to see that my emotions were perfectly fine. Except Vera, who seemed to have gone to the other extreme.

"So, Detective Kate, what's the plan?" Vera asked as she put the pizza box and beer bottles in the recycling bin.

"I'll start by searching for info on Erik online, and see what I have in my file on past employment. Maybe someone at one of the restaurants he's worked at will know if he had any enemies."

"And Doug?"

"There were those charges on the credit card for the diner near Wrigley Field. I guess we can look there," I said. "And I can go by his office and see if he's been in."

"I did that," she said, as her face turned red.

"When?"

"A couple of days ago. I didn't want to tell you because I thought you would be mad, that if the police found out it would look like I was planting evidence or something."

"Let's hope the police don't find out," I said. "So what happened?"

"It's a small office. Just Doug and a computer, basically. I thought he might have gone back. But it was empty."

"No Doug?"

"No anything. There was a desk, but his files, his computer, anything that could hint at where he is was cleared out."

"How did you get in?"

"I told the manager that Doug had asked me to pay the rent for him."

"It's February twelfth," I said. "How did you know Doug hadn't already paid the rent?"

"I took a chance."

"And he hadn't?" I asked.

She shook her head. "After I paid it, I asked the manager to let me into the office to pick up some stuff for Doug."

"And naturally, the guy wasn't going to give you a hard time, especially since you just gave him money."

She smiled. "He let me right into the place. I was worried he would stick around and I wouldn't be able to snoop, but he just left me all alone. It was kind of fun."

"It would have been more fun if Doug hadn't cleared everything out."

"Or someone else."

She had a point. "I'll need a photo of Doug I can show around," I told her.

"I have a bunch of them."

"That will help."

"And we have to find out about Tim's wife," Vera said.

"That's third on the list, after Doug and Erik."

"Why? Tim is sitting in prison while the real killer is walking around free."

"That could be us, unless we find out who killed Erik," I reminded her. "And if I have to choose between saving Tim's neck and saving my own—"

"You'll save mine," Vera interrupted. "You had a choice and you chose to help me, even though it put you in a tough spot with the police." She moved toward me, her arms dangerously close to hugging position.

"I wasn't thinking that night," I told her. "If I had—"

"You would have done the same thing."

"You don't know me as well as you think," I said. "I'm not that giving a person."

"Maybe you didn't used to be. Maybe you're changing."

"That's a terrible thing to say," I blurted out.

Forty-one

That night I thought about Vera's words, about my changing into someone kinder. And Andres's accusation that I was seeing the best in people, even people who were in prison for murder. I love my family, more or less. I loved Frank, most of the time. I'm pretty fond of Andres and Victor, and I love, without hesitation, the chef at my neighborhood British pub, who makes a chicken and mushroom pie that is comfort food and elegant dining in one.

But strangers? Did I care about strangers, or near-strangers like Tim and Brick? Or Vera? Like Brick said, it's a slippery slope. You start caring about people, start worrying about them, wanting things to work out for them, and the next thing you know, you're unable to produce a television show.

I've dipped a toe in the waters of empathy, and it's never worked out well for me. I ended up in ugly bridesmaid dresses for girlfriends I didn't really like. I got roped into a friendship with Vera. And worst, I've screwed up on stories because I wanted the subjects to look good, to seem sane and reasonable, at the expense of entertaining television. It's harder to lie to interview subjects when you like them, or talk them into crying or, better yet, screaming, on camera. If you can't get what you need, then you don't get hired for the next job. And that means no money for mortgage payments, or health insurance, or chicken and mushroom pie.

Everyone was wrong about everything, I decided. And mostly they were wrong about me. I didn't care about Tim or Brick. I didn't. But I did wonder what it would be like to be in prison for a lifetime, paying for choices that were more than twenty years old.

\\\

In the morning I made coffee, fixed some toast with a little peanut butter, and cut a banana into thin slices and layered it on the toast. It was something my mom used to do when I stayed home from school with a cold. Then I shoveled the path from yet another snowfall, checked my e-mail for sales coupons, and even scrubbed away the hard water stains on my shower stall, which had been there for years.

Procrastination is highly underrated. If more politicians thinking of starting a war said, "I'll decide tomorrow," we'd be in better shape. But unfortunately even the most noble of procrastination efforts have to be called off eventually. So when I couldn't stand it any longer, I started a computer search.

I could find little on Doug's background, except an office address, which I already had. It's amazing that even in these days of Facebook, Google, and a thousand other sites that invade our privacy and record every fleeting thought for eternity, there are still some people who manage to keep a low cyber profile. Doug was one of them.

Next I tried Walt, and this time I got tons of hits, but all of them were about what a great chef he was. The fire at his former restaurant was listed as electrical, with the owners hoping to rebuild. Once again, nothing that I didn't already know.

I changed tactics and looked up Tim and came up just as empty as I had with Doug. The story of Tim's 1991 arrest and trial wasn't widely covered on the Internet. As Tim said, he was just another guy with a drug problem and a dead wife. But I was hoping for a little background information before I went to the trouble and considerable expense of ordering trial transcripts, so I called the *Peoria Sun* newspaper and asked for archives.

Newspapers keep archives of all their stories, even the old ones, like Tim's, that aren't posted on the websites. Problem is, newspaper people have a tendency to look down on the true crime television producers. With good reason, I'll grant you, but also because they're jealous. I make more money, have more free time, and my industry may be choking on its own vomit, but, unlike newspapers, TV's not becoming as irrelevant as a globe with the USSR printed on it.

The woman who answered my call didn't seem aware that her profession was on its way out. She seemed hurried and nearly out of breath. "We're really busy here," she said once I'd explained what I needed. "You'll have to put a request in writing on the letterhead of the company you work for, with a detailed account of the dates and headlines you're interested in, and we'll get back to you in six to eight weeks."

"I don't work for a company," I explained. "I'm freelance. And I'm kind of screwed. My boss moved up the deadline by three weeks, so I'm scrambling to get everything together, or else I'll probably be replaced on the project."

"Can't you just ask for more time?" She sounded a little less annoyed and just a tiny bit more helpful. It was my opening.

"Has your boss ever given you more time?"

She laughed. "Good point."

"I'm living day to day, just waiting to get replaced with a computer," I said. "I've got a mortgage and an ex who doesn't pay child support—" She grunted. I'd hit the right nerve. "And if I get fired, I'm going to have to move my kids in with my parents."

"Listen," she whispered into the phone, "what you can do is get a code for the archive files on the Internet. Then you can have everything immediately."

"How do I get that?"

"You have to have business with the paper. I can't just give it to you."

She wanted to help—I could hear it in her voice—but she also couldn't break the rules. At least without a really good reason. So I pushed a little harder.

"I totally get it." I used my most empathetic voice. "They have all these inflexible rules you have to follow. It puts you in a bind when it shouldn't. I guess I can see if my ex can watch the kids for a day or two, and drive down to Peoria. Then I can go through your archives in person, right?"

"Yeah. If that's what you want to do."

"It's not, but I'm stuck between an asshole boss and a creep of an ex-husband. What can I do? The most important thing to me is my kids. I'd do anything for them. I just hope they know that."

"They do," she said, the urgency from earlier becoming the fatigue of working moms everywhere. "I know my kids get frustrated with my schedule, but they know everything I'm doing is for them."

"Absolutely." I had her. "It just sucks when I have to keep letting them down." I sniffed a little. Maybe that was overdoing it, but it worked. She gave me the code to the Internet search after getting me to swear I'd never reveal to anyone where I'd gotten it. I swore, and at least that part was the truth. I didn't feel good about it, but I didn't feel good about most things, so it was just another item to add to the list.

"Care about people, my ass," I said after I hung up. I poured myself another cup of coffee before punching in the code and digging into the arrest and trial of Tim Campbell.

\\\

It was pretty much as he'd described it. Hours after his wife's death, Tim was arrested for her murder. Twenty-year-old Jenny Campbell had died of multiple stab wounds from a kitchen knife, in the kitchen of the apartment she'd shared with Tim. Their neighbor, Cody Daniels, son of a prominent local politician, was the only witness to the crime. A photo of a much younger Tim staring at the ground as he was led away in handcuffs was just below the headline DRUG-RELATED MURDERS ON THE RISE IN PEORIA. Even as he was led to jail he was already being turned from person to statistic.

Subsequent stories covering the trial were brief and perfunctory. The prosecution put Cody on the stand, along with a forensic expert and Jenny's mother. Tim's lawyer didn't call any witnesses for the defense. Tim was convicted in two hours, just long enough for the jury to have lunch and take a single vote. Six months later, Tim's lawyer appeared in another newspaper story. He'd been convicted of drunk driving, his third, and was subsequently disbarred.

Maybe Tim hadn't done it. Maybe he had spent twenty years in jail for a murder committed by a well-connected neighbor. Of course, Tim wasn't entirely innocent. Even in his own version of events, he was willing to let his wife be taken advantage of as payment for drugs. Hardly a good guy, but that's not what Tim was claiming to be.

I once interviewed a reverend for one of those TV churches who said that everyone's a sinner, but no one's beyond redemption. Later he was convicted of tax fraud. But even with his own sinning, it was possible the TV reverend had been right. Maybe Tim could be redeemed, and maybe I could redeem him.

But if I did, then Vera was right. I was changing into someone nicer. And that wasn't the image I'd spent a lifetime creating.

Forty-two

One of the sad, sick truths of our judicial system is that if you go on trial for something, you are very likely to be convicted. Prosecutors don't go to trial unless they feel confident, because state's attorneys don't like to screw up their conviction rates. Juries have an unconscious bias that if you're a defendant, you must have done something wrong. Most defense attorneys don't have the zeal of Perry Mason, and most defendants don't have the money to pay for the ones who do.

Once convicted, the chances of getting out on appeal are almost zero. New evidence, even evidence that proves innocence, is often ignored by the courts. Once Tim had been led away in handcuffs, he was on a short path to Dugan, guilty or not.

Still, I reminded myself, I had more important people to protect. Myself, for one. After I was done with the few articles available on Tim, I satisfied myself that I was at least trying to do the right thing and returned to the more relevant job of finding someone to blame for Erik's murder. I looked through the tape of Erik's interview and wrote down the names of the restaurants he'd mentioned to impress me. Two were in New York, and calls to both got me nowhere. One had closed and at the other, the management had changed several times. No one knew Erik Price or cared much that he was dead. A third restaurant was in France, but my French was rusty. I could say, "Je m'appelle Kate," but after I said my name, I'd be stuck, so I didn't bother trying.

The fourth and final restaurant was a trendy bistro type in Old Town, a section of the city where at least two-thirds of the businesses are trendy bistros. I called, but after the seventh ring I gave up, wrapped myself up for the subzero weather, and headed out.

"I'm looking for someone who knew Erik Price," I said to the leggy blond hostess with an eating disorder and four-hundred-dollar shoes. The phone next to her was ringing but she seemed oblivious to it, and barely aware of me. "Excuse me," I said a little more loudly. "I'm looking for someone who can talk to me about a former employee, Erik Price."

She looked at me, blinking slowly, as if my words had no meaning. Then she bent her head slightly, glanced at a large book in front of her, and looked up at me again. "I'm sorry," she said, "but we don't have a reservation for an Erik Price, and you really have to have a reservation."

"He's not eating here. He used to work here."

"Well, if he *used* to work here, then he's probably not here now."

I smiled. I wanted to slap her, but even a light tap probably would have broken a few bones.

"He's dead," I explained. "Murdered. I need to talk to someone here who knew him."

She blinked even more slowly. "I can call someone."

"What a delightful skill."

"Excuse me?" She glanced toward the artsy types, the young professionals, the moneyed moms with strollers filling up the tables. She was probably debating if I would cause a scene and ruin the ambience. I was trying to convey with my crossed arms and loud sighs that I would. "I'll call Thomas." She said this as if everyone knew Thomas and was appropriately awed by him. I showed no awe, which clearly irked her. She pressed one number on the phone, chatted for a moment. It seemed to exhaust her, so she sat on a stool next to the hostess station and stared off into space, ignoring the couple who had walked in looking for a seat. Nearly every chic eatery in the city had a woman like her as gatekeeper, which is why I preferred takeout food and diners to chic eateries.

A few minutes later, an older man with gelled hair and a perfectly tailored gray suit came from the back of the restaurant.

"I'm Thomas Knight. I'm the owner." He held out his hand and shook mine. "You were asking about Erik?"

"Yes. He recently passed away."

"I heard about it. It's tragic. Why don't you come to my office?"

He showed me to a small room at the back of the restaurant that had little more than a desk and two chairs. Restaurants, even fancy ones, save all their decor for the front of the house. Kitchens and offices are all business.

"I'm sorry things are a bit disorganized," he said. "I need to concentrate my efforts on sorting through all of this . . . stuff, but you know how it is. So many other things to be done. You're a friend of Erik's?"

"We didn't know each other well, but I liked him," I said. "I'm putting together a video." It was vague but honest, and seemed like a better reason than "I'm trying to get my friend off the hook for his murder." I sat down on the wooden café chair that was wedged between the door and the desk. "You knew Erik?"

"For fifteen years," he said. "He came here after a few years working in kitchens around the Midwest."

"Not Paris and New York?"

He laughed. "Indianapolis, if I remember correctly."

"And he worked as a sous chef here?"

"No. I don't think he ever worked as a sous chef. Maybe worked the line at some point, but it wasn't in him."

"What wasn't?"

"The art. He wanted desperately to be a chef, and he had the technical skills, but he didn't have the touch. He couldn't make a sauce sing."

"I didn't know they sang," I said.

"The good ones do." He smiled at me. "You aren't a foodie."

Unlike most people who consider food the ultimate life experience, he didn't say it as an insult, which made me immediately like him.

"No, I'm not a foodie," I admitted. "I have to dress, but I don't care about designer labels. I have to eat, but I don't really care about chefs, or great restaurants, or ambience. Not that I don't enjoy a good meal," I added as a sort of apology.

"Pity. Are you putting together the video for a memorial service?"

"No," I admitted. "I'm working on a television show about the Club Car, the restaurant—"

Thomas nodded. "With Walt Russo and Roman Papadakis."

"Yes. Do you know them?"

"Walt, yes. A wonderful chef. Wasting his talents at that place. But Roman I've never met. He has a reputation, of course, but we haven't crossed paths."

"What's his reputation?"

"Hard businessman. Someone who knows how to get things done. Absolutely necessary if you're going to succeed in restaurants."

"You know anything about his cousin dying in a fire some years back?"

He hesitated. "I heard about it, of course. You should ask his wife. She was his bookkeeper at the time. Mousy little thing then, from what I've heard."

"Why would she know?"

"Rumor was she told the police Roman was with her the night of the fire," he said. "Which was interesting since everyone knew was he was dating one of his waitresses, and hadn't even noticed Ilena. But they got married three weeks later."

"Do you think she lied about where he was that night?"

He shrugged. "The police didn't think so—why should I?"

"If you don't know Roman, how do you know he was with Ilena the night his cousin died?" I asked.

"It's a small industry. We work odd hours, spend a lot of time together talking food and drinking good liquor. You would think people in the restaurant business live for food, but it's gossip that keeps our world humming."

It was fascinating stuff, but it still told me nothing about Erik. I was losing track of the victim again. "If Erik didn't work in the kitchen, what did he do here?"

"Assistant manager. He did that for two years, then became the manager. Then he left for Shoulders. Do you know it?"

I shook my head.

"It was a wonderful restaurant in Lincoln Park. The chef deconstructed food. Brought it down to its bare elements. Very daring."

"Sounds like it." I didn't bother asking how you deconstruct food. Or why.

Thomas laughed. "The public felt the way you do. It closed after two years. Erik and I kept in touch. His passion was infectious. It reminded me why I started in this business."

"Do you remember when he started here?"

"Not off the top of my head, but I keep pretty good records." He jumped up from his chair and spent several minutes going through papers in a dusty metal file cabinet. Finally he had what he was looking for. He handed me a slim manila file folder with Erik's name written at the top.

I leafed through it. There was little there, aside from a résumé with an address in Muncie, Indiana, and a few notations on raises. There were two requests for days off, and at least a dozen memos with Erik's suggestions on changes to improve the look and image of the restaurant.

"Was he good at his job?" I asked.

"He was wonderful at it," he said. "He loved talking to people, earning their trust, knowing their tastes. He was here even on days when he didn't have a shift." Thomas shook his head. "Of course, it was easy for him to do that. His job was all he had."

"I know he wasn't married, but didn't he have someone in his life?"

"Not that I knew. Erik was a bit of a loner. Lived alone, spent his time away from work alone."

"He had friends, didn't he?"

"His friends were all work friends. And the people who came to eat here. Of course, the patrons served a purpose for Erik. He was in control around them. He didn't really care about the patrons, of course, but he was good at pretending he did."

Erik, for all his fancy watches and expensive suits, was beginning to sound a lot like me. "So you didn't know anyone who might have wanted to do him harm?" I asked.

"No." Thomas seemed to wince at the idea. "He was a lonely man. And now that he's gone, he'll be forgotten," he said. "It's a shame, isn't it?"

"We're all forgotten eventually," I said.

"Yes, but some sooner than others."

Forty-three

Thomas made a copy of Erik's file for me, and I tucked the papers into my tote bag. As I did, I saw the photo of Doug I'd borrowed from Vera. It was a long shot, but I showed it to him. It didn't pay off. Thomas had never seen Doug, nor did he know of his involvement in Club Car.

"I don't really pay attention when civilians invest," he told me. "It's usually some fantasy they have of walking around to the tables, offering free glasses of wine to pretty girls. People with no experience in the business have no idea how hard it is. When you open a new restaurant, investors are lining up to give you their money. But they don't stay long. Within two years, they've usually lost their investment or sold out."

"Why not just get a bank loan?"

Thomas seemed amused at the suggestion. "Banks don't often loan money to restaurants just starting out. Too risky. Too many closings. And too many uncontrollable factors, like an unreliable chef or a bad review," he said. "We get our capital from investors. Hopefully investors who know what they're getting into. But a desperate restaurateur will take money from amateurs too. Parents, friends, lovers . . . anyone with a checkbook."

"What if the amateur gets cold feet, wants to back out before the place has even opened?" I asked.

"It could kill the deal," he said.

"Someone could get very upset about that."

He smiled. "Those of us who have been around a long time understand that it's a gamble, and sometimes you lose," he said. "And if it's just business, you can live with that."

"But if it's your dream?"

He threw up his hands. "Then people have a hard time letting go, don't they?"

\\\

When I got home I saw that someone from Dugan had called my temporary cell, but there was no message. It had to be Tim. Joanie and the
warden had my real phone number. Only Tim and Brick had the throwaway. I was tempted to call, but he was probably just trying to play some
new angle, get money for something. And while I felt sorrier for him
after reading the newspaper stories, I wasn't going to be led around by
the nose because of it.

Instead, I sat in the kitchen, studying the folder from Erik's time at the
Old Town restaurant. According to his résumé he was from Muncie,
Indiana. Nothing wrong with Muncie, but it's a long way from the
designer suits image he'd been presenting. I called information but
couldn't find anyone named Price in the area. It was frustrating until it
occurred to me that Price was probably not his real last name—just something that sounded good to him. Then I started calling high schools.

There were six. With each new school, I tried to explain who I was
and that I was looking for information on someone who may or may
not have been named Erik Price and who may have been around thirty-
five, putting him half a lifetime away from a high school senior. One
person chuckled, two thought I was nuts, and one guy told me he was
busy and hung up. Each time I just went to the next school on my list
and hoped for the best. At number five, I got lucky.

"Erik? Lived in Chicago, worked at a restaurant?" An older-
sounding woman repeated what I said. "He went to school here."

"He was about thirty-five," I explained, trying to be helpful.

"Thirty-seven," she said. "He's Don Pritzker's kid. Passed away
recently."

"Yes," I said. "He was murdered."

"No. Heart disease. He had heart trouble for years and Erik never
came to see him. Didn't even come for the funeral."

"Erik's dead," I said. "He was murdered."

"Oh." There was quiet as it sank in. "That's too bad."

"I was wondering if you have any information on him."

"I can send you a yearbook. We have copies of all the years. You can
use it in your TV show."

"That would be great."

"There's a nice picture of Erik his senior year." She put me on hold for several minutes before she came back and read to me. "Under his picture it says his ambition was to be famous. I guess you're going to do that for him."

"Kind of a hollow victory," I said.

I gave her my address, then went back to the folder I had on Erik Pritzker/Price. His suggestions for improvements fascinated me. He had grand ideas for the place, but none of them seemed practical. In one memo he suggested a baby grand for the corner that even I could see would require getting rid of at least a third of the tables. Another called for a complete and expensive remodel. A third suggested cutting the menu in half, which must have gone over well with the chef. And a fourth was a list of ways to provide the kind of ambience that encouraged guests to linger. Most restaurants don't want guests to linger. They want turnover, particularly in a busy neighborhood like Old Town.

Erik was trying to provide an experience at the expense of profits. And it looked like his philosophy hadn't changed by the time he took on the role of manager at Club Car. But guys like Roman Papadakis wouldn't be interested in experiences, *especially* at the expense of profit. It might have been a big issue between them, but was it reason to kill someone? I decided that would be the first question I'd ask at the interview in the morning.

Forty-four

But it wasn't. When Roman showed up at the restaurant the next day as my first interview subject, he had a sling on his arm.

"What happened?" I asked.

"Slipped on the ice." He was curt, grumpy. He sat in the chair opposite me and glanced toward Andres, who was still working on the lights. "How long is this going to take? I have a couple of appointments this morning and I need to get this over with."

"Twenty minutes," I said, just to give him a number. "It depends on you, really. I'm looking for insights into Erik as a person."

"I'm the wrong one to ask."

I waited. Andres finished with the lights, Victor put a mic on Roman, and I sat back until the camera was rolling. "If you're the wrong one to ask," I said, "who would be the right person? Your wife?"

Roman cocked his head to the side. "You mean that business at the restaurant? The giggling? Ilena is like that."

"Like what?"

"Insecure about her looks. She was a little plain when I first met her, felt that men didn't notice her. But she's put more effort into it as the years have gone on and she enjoys the attention it gets her."

"So what got you interested in her?"

"She's ballsy. You know Ilena. She doesn't scare easily. A lot of women find me intimidating." He chuckled a little.

"Some people are easily intimidated," I said. "I heard that you were dating a waitress at the time, and only started spending time with Ilena after your cousin's death in a fire."

He grunted a little. Roman only liked to play if it was on his terms. "People break up and date other people." He punched every syllable.

"Yes they do," I said. "And you ended up happy."

"Yes."

"Except . . ." I hesitated. Not because I was nervous about asking, but because I wanted to dangle the question, let him know I was in control of the interview. "Was Ilena having an affair with Erik?"

"The Business Channel wants to know that?" He seemed mad, but he was trying to hide it under the guise of being amused. "Or is that just your curiosity?"

"A little of both. We're always looking for an interesting angle on television. And Erik was murdered," I pointed out. "I think the audience will want to know who might have killed him."

"Well, I didn't."

"But you had a motive."

"What motive?"

"Why aren't you listed as an owner of Club Car?"

"I am."

"Not according to the application for a liquor license."

"This is bullshit," he said. The look of amusement was gone. "I came here to say that we're all sorry about the passing of our colleague. We're hoping to continue the restaurant without him, but that's something that has yet to be determined. Erik was an important member of the team. Irreplaceable."

"Walt said he was very replaceable."

"Walt has different priorities than I do."

"Erik's ideas for the restaurant were expensive. In fact, you had a fight with him about it."

"The uniforms? So what? He special-ordered a bunch of uniforms. Expensive stuff that would have taken eight weeks to come in. We didn't even have a waitstaff hired. We would have had to hire people who fit the clothes. How crazy is that? I canceled the order, and told him that he had to run all the decisions by me."

"It sounds like he was costing you money."

"All my managers cost me money," he said. "They're like kids. They think there's an unlimited amount of cash just sitting there waiting to be spent."

"Must be aggravating."

"Listen, lady, I've been in this business for thirty years. I know how to deal with aggravation. I make it go away."

I curled the corners of my mouth into a smile. This was fun. No one ever threatens me on home-decorating shows. "You said Vera and Erik were having a lovers' quarrel. Why?"

He looked confused. I like changing up the subject matter during a testy interview. It keeps me focused and my subject off his game. Roman, though, recovered more quickly than most. "That's what someone told me," he said. He stood up. "Are we done?"

I stood up too. This interview would be over when I said it was over. "Why were you at my house the other day? You were standing in the snow staring at my front door."

"Your sister is crazy. I wasn't at your house."

"I didn't say it was my sister who saw you."

"I have a call to make."

"You have to finish the interview."

Roman came toward me. His body was easily twice mine, and he was used to bullying people. I saw Victor stand up, ready to jump in, but I stood my ground. "Or what?" he spit out.

"Or I'll make you look bad on television."

He stopped.

"I hear the restaurant business thrives on juicy gossip," I continued, "so I imagine they'll get a kick out of carefully edited clips showing up on YouTube. All the stuff that makes you and your restaurant look ridiculous."

Roman clenched his jaw and leaned toward me. "You're a bitch."

"Like that, for example."

He grabbed his cell phone from his pocket and shook it at me. "When I finish with this call, you have five minutes."

"As long as you stay in the room, you have a deal."

Victor stepped toward him, but I waved him away. Roman walked toward the other side of the room, near the bar. He turned his back to us.

"Keep the camera rolling, Andres."

Andres moved the camera so it was pointed at Roman, then backed away. He threw his arm around me. "This is the Kate Conway I love and fear," he said.

We waited until Roman finished his call. Victor kept his headphones on, nodding excitedly, but Andres and I couldn't hear what was so exciting. Didn't matter. With the camera rolling and his mic still on, everything Roman said in that phone call was being recorded.

The rest of Roman's interview netted me three grunts, a pat rewording of the sentence about Erik's passing, and a noncommittal answer about whether the restaurant would stay open. As he got up to leave, throwing his microphone on the chair, he looked victorious.

"You should be careful, lady," he said. "The world is full of animals. You try to corner one and you may just find your smart mouth doesn't get you out of a jam."

"Someone gave me similar advice. He's in Dugan for three murders."

"You have interesting friends."

"So does he. The guy in Dugan was a good friend of John Fletcher. Said that John used to talk his ear off about fires."

Roman's face went white. "I have appointments," he mumbled and walked out.

As soon as he was gone, I turned to Victor. "So what have we got?"

"Listen for yourself."

Andres rewound the tape to the moment when Roman went to the bar to make his call.

"We need to stop," Roman was saying into the phone. "I don't think we can hide this anymore. . . . Listen, this was your idea to begin with and I went along with it because . . . I'm not saying that. I'm saying that we have to stop. Now. . . . Because this TV bitch is worse than her. She might actually find something. . . . I'm going to do what has to be done. Don't I always?" Then he ended the call.

The three of us looked at each other.

"He's guilty," Victor declared.

"Of what? It doesn't sound like he's talking about Erik's murder," I said. "It's something ongoing."

"You're obviously the TV bitch," Andres said. "Is 'her' Vera?"

"It has to be," I said. I was getting under his skin, a compliment any TV producer would love. "This has to be about the offshore accounts. Vera talked about it when she was first getting threats."

"Where is she?" Andres asked.

"Home, I guess."

"Call her." Andres looked worried. "Roman said he was going to do what had to be done. If he's figured out the threats didn't work, then what if killing Vera was that appointment he was talking about?"

I called Vera, but just got voice mail on both her home and cell phones. I left messages trying to sound urgent without sounding worried. If Roman came to her door, I knew Vera would let him in. And injured arm or not, Roman looked capable of just about anything.

"Who was he talking to?" I asked.

"Ilena," Victor said. "Has to be."

"You think? She seems like she's trying to get away from him." Andres was adjusting the lights for the next interview, but his mind seemed to be more on the investigation than on the show.

"We're about to find out," I said. "She's next."

"I love watching you skewer a hapless victim," Victor said. "It's sweet, man, like watching Michael Jordan at the top of his game. Poetry in action."

Andres nodded approvingly. No one was making comments about shapeless turtlenecks or a stray gray hair now, I noticed. And it felt so good, I was ready for more.

Forty-five

Mrs. Conway?" Detective Makina walked into the restaurant and looked around. It was still theoretically under construction, although nothing had been done to it since the first day I'd been there. Of course, for the past week they had a good excuse. Until yesterday, the police had considered it an active crime scene and kept everyone out. The kitchen was still off-limits, which wasn't a problem. Wild horses couldn't have dragged me to the spot where Erik had died. Makina stood near the door and looked toward me. "Can I talk with you a minute?"

"Your interview isn't until the day after tomorrow," I said.

"This isn't about my interview." His face was, if possible, more serious than I'd ever seen it.

"Vera." The word popped out of my mouth, and suddenly I could see her lying in a pool of blood as clearly as I'd seen Erik. She hadn't been home when I called. She believed Doug was innocent. She'd uncovered something. One worst-case scenario after another went through my head. "Where is Vera?"

Makina didn't answer. He took a few steps toward Andres, Victor, and me.

"Where's Vera?" Victor said from just steps behind me. He and Andres were literally at my back.

"I don't know where she is. I'm not here about Ms. Bingham. You're Mr. Pilot, aren't you?" Makina asked. "I've been trying to get ahold of you."

"I'm not hard to find," Victor said.

"We need to talk," Makina told him. "As soon as possible."

"Roman Papadakis was just here. He made a threat against Kate," Andres said, changing the subject. "And he mentioned another woman. We assume he meant Vera."

Makina looked at me. "What kind of threat, Mrs. Conway?"

I didn't want to play the recording for him. It wasn't technically illegal—Roman, it could be argued, knew he was being recorded; he had a mic on. But if I played it, Makina would most likely want to take the tape, and before I gave it to the police I wanted the chance to use it on TV. What I'd said about making Roman look bad wasn't a threat. It was a prediction.

"Nothing," I said. "He called me a bitch."

"Was that the first time someone called you that?" Makina smiled a little.

"First time today," I said. "My guys are just protective of me."

"And of Vera," Victor said. I wanted to tell Victor to shut up, but you can never tell Victor something like that. I just took a deep breath and hoped it wasn't one more reason Makina would connect him to the harassing phone calls.

Makina didn't say anything. But he stared at Victor a long time before returning his eyes to me. "There's a problem with your statement, Mrs. Conway. I'm wondering if you have a minute to discuss it."

If Roman's display of machismo had slightly unnerved me, Makina's quiet authority scared me to my toes. "I'm working right now," I said. "Ilena is about to come in."

"This will only take a minute."

"Okay." I didn't know what else to say.

Makina motioned for me to come toward him. I took a few steps, swallowed hard, and tried to remember how I'd felt just a few moments before when I'd, as Victor put it, "skewered" Roman. Makina and I walked to the door of the restaurant. I stood there, waiting.

"You said you chatted with Erik Price after the confrontation he had with Ms. Bingham," Makina said.

"Yes. I told you. In his car."

"What time was that?"

"I don't recall." Never be specific. It's the wet dream of prosecutors and cops. Keep your answers vague and changeable. Wait for the facts, then tell a story to fit them. That's what a defense lawyer told me once in an interview.

"Ballpark it for me."

"I'm not much of a baseball player."

Makina clenched his jaw. "See, the problem is, Mrs. Conway, we have footage of Erik Price driving through an ATM about twenty minutes after he left here. Then he makes several calls from his cell phone, all of which can be traced to a location near Addison and Irving Park. Then, according to several witnesses, he had coffee at a small place called Terry's. Then more calls. Then he went home. Nothing puts him outside the restaurant the rest of the day, so I'm wondering how it's possible you saw him here and had that conversation about his argument with Ms. Bingham."

The verbal sparring with Roman had been fun. This was not fun. "Can you account for every minute of his day?" I tried to sound calm.

"No. Not every minute, but nearly."

"Then you have your answer."

"It would be helpful, though, especially as it corroborates Ms. Bingham's account of the events, if you could be more specific about the time line."

"I'm sure it would be," I said. "But as I've told you, I don't know exactly when I spoke with Erik."

"But you are still claiming that you did."

I wriggled my toes a little in my shoes. I had a moment wondering if I should run like one of those idiots in high speed car chases. Except instead of a car, I'd be running in kitten heels. I decided it was too late for that. "I'm only trying to be helpful," I said.

"Yes, you are. And I'm sure she appreciates it."

"If you think I'm lying then prove me wrong; otherwise I have to work." It was a dare. A stupid dare. In an effort to sound tough I'd challenged Makina, and he seemed pleased by it.

"Three o'clock, Friday," he said.

Was that the time of my arrest? "What's at three o'clock Friday?" I asked. My voice was hollow. I'm sure I didn't sound so tough now.

"My interview."

"Absolutely," I replied, trying to smile. "Looking forward to it."

Forty-six

By the time Ilena arrived I was pretty much done for the day, but there was no delaying this interview. I slapped on some lipstick, tried to shake the fear from my eyes, and greeted her when she came through the door.

Ilena's face was dewy fresh, her eyebrows perfectly plucked, and her nails polished a brick red. She was in black, head to toe, with a long, colorful paisley scarf wrapped several times around her neck. "Awful to be back here," she said, staring toward the door to the kitchen. "I haven't been back since, you know. I don't know if I ever want to be here again."

"Does that mean you'll scrap your plans for this place?"

"It's not really my decision."

"Then whose decision is it?" I asked.

"If we lose Walt, then—"

"Why would you lose Walt?"

"I heard he's let it be known he's available. He and Erik were so close," she said. "I don't think he can continue without him."

The word "bullshit" nearly spilled out of my mouth, but I held my tongue. "I had no idea," I said. "They didn't seem close."

"They were practically brothers," she continued. "Such a shame."

Andres signaled that he was ready for us to begin. Ilena looked at the chairs set out for the interview, one next to the camera and the other directly facing it, just a few inches apart.

She pointed toward the one facing the camera. "Is this where you want me to sit?" She sounded as if this was the first time she'd been interviewed.

"Just like last time," I said, to make clear I wasn't falling for the nervous act. Her lies had calmed me, reminded me that I wasn't the only one with something to hide. "Your husband didn't like my questions."

"Was he here?"

"Yes," I said. "Just before you. He called you before he left."

"Before he left here?" She seemed genuinely nervous now. "He didn't leave a message."

"He talked to you."

She shook her head slowly. "He didn't talk to me. I was getting my hair done." She reached into her purse and pulled out a cell phone, as if this offered some proof. "I had the sound off. My hairdresser doesn't like it if I take calls in the middle of a cut."

I wasn't sure I believed her, but it didn't matter. "I want to ask you about Erik," I said.

With the camera rolling, Ilena's voice deepened, took on a melancholy tone. She really was a master at playing to the room. "Erik was a showman," she said. "The best. He had plans to turn Club Car into a world-class restaurant, making each dinner a night our guests would remember for the rest of their lives. His talent was staggering."

"His ideas were expensive."

"They were worth it."

"Roman didn't think so," I said. "He and Erik argued about it."

"Roman argues with the mailbox. He argues with the television. He'll argue with anything. It's his way."

"What if he doesn't win?"

"Roman always wins."

"Sounds frightening."

I watched as Ilena considered her next move. If she wanted to get rid of Roman, implying he might be guilty of Erik's murder was one way to do it. But if it didn't work, she'd pay for it, one way or another. I could see her weighing her options. "Roman is all talk," she said, trying to sound light. "He's a teddy bear, really, and he thought Erik was a genius."

"Where were you the night he was killed?"

She laughed. "You sound like one of those cheap TV detectives," she said. "I was far away from here, thank goodness, having dinner with a friend."

"And you can back up your story."

"I don't need to," she said. "The police are the only ones who have the right to expect a full and honest accounting of my time."

"So I've been told," I said. "Can you give it to them?"

"I can do whatever I have to," she said.

\\\

That was all I could get from her. After the interview, Victor tried Vera again, but no luck. I promised to stop by her house to check on her, though I was sure I'd find her rewriting her will to give millions to a poodle, or whatever it was rich people did with their time. That wasn't fair, I scolded myself. Vera wasn't *that* kind of rich person. But given that I'd lied myself into a problem with Detective Makina in order to protect her, I wasn't in a mood for kind thoughts.

There was one stop I had to make before I could go to Vera's. The heat in my car decided not to work, so I shivered my way north, until I got to Terry's, the Wrigleyville diner that had shown up on Doug's credit card statement.

According to Makina, Terry's was also the restaurant Erik had gone to a few days before his murder. I was dying to see what made it so popular, but I was a little disappointed. It was one of those new diners made to look old, with silver flashing everywhere and bright red leather booths. The menus had pictures on them, and the waitresses were in crisp-looking tan uniforms, with red aprons and white handkerchiefs in their pockets.

"Coffee?" my waitress asked me. Without waiting, she poured me a cup.

"Yes, thanks," I said. "It's freezing."

"Then you need pie. Heated up. We got a nice apple that goes good with a side of whipped cream."

"Perfect."

She brought me the pie, which I ate quickly. I drank the coffee and a second cup. Then I brought out Doug's photo. I gave it to my waitress and she stared at it for a long time.

"He doesn't have a memorable face," she said. She handed it back to me. "Even if I waited on him, I'd forget him the minute he walked out the door." Then she smiled. "You I'd remember."

"Yeah? Why?"

"Red hair with a few streaks of gray, a ratty sweater. Take some advice. You'd look pretty if you fixed yourself up."

"You're not the first person to say that," I told her. "This guy, the one in the picture, he charged several meals here." I grabbed the credit card bill and showed her the charges. "He's gone missing and my aunt is really worried. He's my cousin. Maybe I'm grasping at straws here, but I have to try everything."

The waitress patted my shoulder, took the credit card bill, and walked to the counter. I watched her chatting with another woman, then she headed to the kitchen. I was beginning to wonder if she'd left with my evidence, but after a few minutes she returned with a third woman, a tall, heavyset waitress. "This is Anne," my waitress told me. "I figured out why I don't know your guy. These dates are all Sundays and I don't work Sundays. But Anne works Sundays."

Anne handed me back the credit card statement. I showed her the photo of Doug. "Do you know him?" I asked. The bigger question was, even if she did, so what? I'd proven that Doug liked this place. And why shouldn't he? The pie was delicious.

"Yeah," Anne said after examining the photo. "He comes in here for dinner. Doesn't talk much, but he tips pretty good."

"Does he come in alone?"

"Usually. But the last couple of times he's had dinner with a friend."

"A tall woman in her forties?"

"No. Not a woman. A man. Young, good-looking black guy. He asked for the recipe for our banana cream pie."

Walt. But why would Walt and Doug meet at a diner? Why would they meet at all?

"Do you know what they were talking about?" I asked.

"I don't listen to conversations," she said.

"I understand." I looked down at the ground, dejected. It was half put on, but it worked.

"Well, I did hear something," she said. "Something about the investors. Your cousin, he said there were ten and the other man seemed surprised. But that was all I heard."

"Do you know where they went from here?"

She shook her head. "I did hear the other man, Banana Cream Pie, say that he lived nearby."

Walt's address, at least according to the release form he'd signed, was miles from here. "He didn't say where?" I asked.

"No. But I think they were going there together."

I paid my bill and tucked the photo back into my tote bag. "When's the last time you saw my cousin?"

"Sunday," she said.

"Are you sure?"

"Sure I'm sure. It was just a few days ago. I'm not that old."

"Was he alone?"

"Nope. The same man was with him."

"Sorry to be asking all these questions," I said, leaving a large tip on the table. "But there was another man. His name was Erik Price; he was recently murdered at a restaurant—"

"The one in the fancy suit?" My waitress turned to the other. "I told you. When I saw his picture in the paper, I said I'd waited on him just the day before."

"She did," Anne confirmed.

"Did he meet anyone here? Doug or the other man?"

"No," my waitress said. "He ate alone. But he was like you, asking a lot of questions."

Forty-seven

As soon as I left the restaurant I dialed Walt's number. He didn't pick up. I was dying to know about Doug, but it didn't seem the kind of thing to leave on a voice mail, so I consoled myself with the idea that in a couple of days I'd have a camera rolling. I would ask him when I could get a reaction for all the world to see. At least all the world that watches the Business Channel, one of the least watched cable channels out there.

Then I called Vera. Also no answer. I got back into my freezing car and headed to her Gold Coast brownstone. I tried calling her a couple of times on the way, but whenever I put the phone to my ear a cop would suddenly pull up next to me.

When I got to her house, no one answered the bell. And when I knocked, the door pushed open. I hadn't been too concerned on the drive over, but now I was starting to worry.

"Vera?" I called out from the front steps. The house was suspiciously silent. Her dogs hadn't run to greet me, or barked, or done any of the house-protecting things that dogs are supposed to be good for. "Vera," I said again, louder.

Nothing. I walked in a few steps. On one hand, if Vera were dead in a pool of blood, I wouldn't have to protect her anymore and could just tell Makina the truth. On the other hand, if I was the one to find her body, I'd probably end up convicted of her murder. Given the many times I'd thought of killing her after Frank left, maybe it would be a kind of justice.

"Vera! Dammit!" This time I yelled.

"What?"

I jumped.

Vera was coming through the back door with the dogs, and all three were covered in snow.

"Your front door is open."

"I know. Victor called a few minutes ago. He said you were trying to find me, that you were on your way over. I thought I'd leave the front door open just in case we were still playing in the yard," she said. "I can't hear the bell ring from the back."

"Vera, on a good day leaving your door open is really stupid. But someone has been making threats against you, remember?"

"I remember. But Victor said you were on your way over. Would it have been better to just leave you standing in the cold?"

"Yes."

"I'll know for next time," she said, without a hint of sarcasm in her voice. How does a person survive forty years in the big city without sarcasm, mockery, or disdain?

She grabbed an old towel and wiped the dogs' fur, then let them loose in the rest of the house. She motioned for me to sit in the living room. It was the first time I'd sat in the room. It was filled with a mish-mash of antiques from various periods, as well as several modern paintings I guessed were originals. The room should have looked like a decorating disaster, but instead the mix of styles and periods worked. It was comfortable and unique.

"What's Doug's relationship with Walt?" I asked once she came into the room with coffee.

"I don't know," she said. "They were nice to each other. Is that what you mean?"

"They've been seen together several times, including since Doug disappeared," I said.

"Doug's alive?"

"Oh, yeah, sorry. I should have said that first."

Vera took a deep breath. When she spoke again, her voice cracked. "Do you know where he is? Is he okay?"

"I don't know where he is now, but a waitress overheard him talking to Walt about investors. How many investors are there?"

"You've met them all. Doug, Ilena, Roman, and me. Walt isn't an investor but also has a percentage of the restaurant, as did Erik."

"Your two hundred and fifty thousand, what did that get you?"

"Ten percent of the restaurant."

"And you said Doug invested the same as you, so that's another ten. Roman has fifty percent. That's seventy, right there. What does Ilena have?"

"She started with thirty."

"So that's a hundred. So how do Walt and Erik get a piece of the action if the entire restaurant is already spoken for?"

"Out of Roman's, I guess," Vera suggested. "Or Ilena's. She gave up points for Walt."

"And if there are more investors?"

"Silent partners?" Vera asked. "That would mean someone was selling off bits of their share."

"And that would be bad?"

"Depending on who was selling their shares, yes. Roman's reputation, and Walt as the chef, those are the big draws. If they lost interest in the project, it could kill the whole thing. Restaurant people are waiting to see what they create together. That's the excitement. And of course what Erik would have done."

"But no one in the restaurant world was dying to see Erik's vision come to life?"

She shook her head, just slightly. "I don't think he was quite at that level yet. Maybe he could have gotten there. I'm sure he would have, poor guy."

"So what happens to Erik's percentage now?"

"It reverts to Roman, I think. Erik hadn't put up any money. He was just getting a token percentage as part of his compensation."

"What about insurance?"

"Life insurance?" she asked. "Erik was pretty much an employee. As far as I know there wouldn't have been any life insurance on him that would go to the restaurant."

"He was replaceable."

"That sounds bad," she said. "But yes, in terms of the business, he was." She started tapping the coffee table in that annoying way she has when she's hesitant to ask me something.

"I don't know anything more about Doug," I said. "Just that he was there, meeting with Walt."

"Okay," she said. "Why hasn't he called me?"

"Because . . ." I wanted to say, *Because he's using you*, but I couldn't. If I'd learned anything from my marriage it's that women don't see what's wrong with the man they love, no matter how many times their friends point it out. "Because he's hiding for some reason. Maybe he's protecting you."

"You think?"

"Why not?" I said.

"Do you really believe that, Kate?"

A quick reassurance was one thing, but I wasn't about to sign up for group therapy. "Vera, I'm trying to be nice here. Doug's alive. That's something. We can find out the rest in due time."

"You're right," she said. "It's enough to know that he's alive. The rest can wait." She didn't sound sure, but at least we could move the conversation forward. "And I found out something too," she added. "Since you said you didn't want to look into Tim's situation, I decided to. This morning I made some calls and I got the name of the detective that investigated the murder. He's still on the force. I also found out that Tim's neighbor, Cody, had a police record for assault."

"Who did you call?"

"The family attorney. The one representing me. He called the police down there and got the information."

"That was helpful."

Vera smiled. "I really feel we're getting somewhere."

"It isn't all good news," I told her. "Makina doesn't believe a word we've told him."

"So let's not talk to him anymore."

"I'm doing an interview with him on Friday."

"But that doesn't count," she said. "You'll be the one asking questions."

Somehow that didn't make me feel better about it.

Forty-eight

I'll go to Peoria after I interview Walt and Makina," I said. "If this detective will talk to me, then we'll have an answer on Tim."

"And we'll get him out of prison."

"Vera, that's a long shot. Even if he didn't do it."

"But what about all the new technology? All the ways they're proving people are innocent?"

"Tim admits to being there. His wife's blood was on him, so DNA isn't going to help us. We need someone to say that evidence was planted, or that statements were made about Cody that were ignored because of his family."

"Or a confession."

"That would be nice."

"I'll go with you," Vera said, suddenly brightening. "It would be fun to take a road trip."

"It's really not a good idea to double-team a police detective," I said. "It's better if I go alone. It makes sense for me to ask; I'm doing a documentary on the guy. But I couldn't really explain your presence." Mostly, though, I just didn't want to spend a full day with her.

Vera nodded. "I'm hungry," she said and jumped off the couch. When she came back she had a bottle of wine, some cheese, crackers, and a handful of Oreos. "If we're going to help spring a man from prison, we need sustenance."

"Cheese and crackers. I think that's what Darrow ate during the Leopold and Loeb trial."

"Really?"

"Sarcasm, Vera."

"Oh."

She poured me a glass of wine and then got one for herself. I let mine sit on the coffee table, but she drank hers quickly.

"Strange about Doug."

I knew eventually she'd get back to Doug, but that didn't mean I had to indulge her. "I'll be at Dugan tomorrow. Is there's something you want me to ask Tim?"

Vera wasn't listening. "I think if he cared about me, even if he were in trouble, he'd have found a way to let me know he was okay. Don't you think so?"

It would have been easier to lie, to be comforting. But I didn't think it was fair. "You'd been getting those calls," I said. "If Doug is in danger, he would have to assume you are too. And probably by the same person. So, yeah, I think he left you out to dry. You're better off without him."

She considered it a long time. "Don't you want to be with someone?"

"I was with someone for more than twenty years. From just a few weeks after my sixteenth birthday until, well, until it was over. I don't mind the idea of being alone for a while."

"You seem to be doing fine," she said. "Better than I do."

"Do I? I suppose that's good."

"But?"

"But what?" I asked.

"But something. You seem like you want to add something."

Maybe I did. Maybe I wanted to say that I was floundering, that I wanted some certainty in my life, some people I could count on, aside from Victor and Andres, who, let's face it, were paid to be around me most of the time.

"I didn't want to add anything," I said.

Vera took a long sip from a second glass. "We were sold a bill of goods, weren't we?"

"Which time? The American dream, the idea that justice prevails . . . ?"

"No, that someday your prince will come."

"Oh, that one. Yeah," I agreed. "We were pretty much lied to about that. And by our own mothers."

"Exactly. What was that about?"

"They wanted it to be true."

"So did I. And look where that got me. Divorced, lonely, dating men who don't care about me." Vera emptied her glass. "Look where it got you."

"Don't drag me into this," I said. "We had some good years, Frank and I. We probably had ten solid good years, maybe fifteen if you include the years we dated. Not all together, but in there somewhere."

She smiled. "Well, that's something." She grabbed the wine to pour herself another glass.

"You'll find someone," I said, digging out the same line that has been used over and over, always believed and often untrue. "You just have to know your own worth. Even if it's hard, it's better to be alone than to be with someone who doesn't deserve you."

Vera smiled at me. "You sound like this shrink I went to after my divorce. My father is this very dominant presence in my life. He uses his money to control me, the way he did with my mother. The shrink said I look for men's approval as a substitute for the approval I can never get from my father."

"What do you think?"

She grabbed a slice of cheese and picked through the crackers, finding one of the less soggy ones. "I think . . . we find Doug, and if he's guilty of Erik's murder, we nail the bastard to the wall."

I laughed. "You're a bit of a hard-ass when you want to be."

"I'm learning from the best."

About two hours later, I left Vera asleep on the couch, curled up with her dogs at her feet. If someone was odd in a good way, my grandmother would say, "That person is a kick and a half." She would have said that about Vera.

\\\

I had an early start the next day, but I wasn't ready to go home. Something was nagging at me. Everyone involved in the restaurant seemed to be lying about something: Roman about coming to my house, Ilena about Erik and Walt's friendship, Walt about his address, and Doug, well, he was probably lying about everything. I know people who live in glass houses aren't supposed to throw stones, but I hate it when people lie to me.

If I was going to catch one of them in a lie, I would have to start with the weak link. I'd already tried Ilena and Roman. Doug was out there somewhere but I didn't know where. That left one person. I grabbed my folder and found the address, at least the one he'd given me on the first day, and headed to Walt's apartment.

I wasn't sure what I'd find there, but I couldn't just show up demanding the truth. If my going there would make any sense, I would need to rely on Walt's interest in me.

My plan was to lull him into a false sense of security with my feminine charms—unless I could think of something more believable.

Forty-nine

Apartment 3G," I confirmed before I parked the car on the tidy block of Walt's Evanston neighborhood. It was one of those large doorman buildings, blocks from the beach and fairly imposing. Something that had been there eighty years or more but had lost none of its elegance.

"I'm looking for Walt Russo," I told the doorman.

He looked a little puzzled. I've asked a lot of questions over the years, and studied the facial expressions of the people on the receiving end. I'd gotten good at it, and right then my producer's instinct told me that he was about to tell me there was no one by that name living there. Even though the round trip was more than an hour, I was kind of relieved the whole thing was a bust.

"I think he just got home," he said instead. "Let me buzz him."

So much for my producer's instinct.

\\\

Walt's apartment was a mess of boxes and misplaced furniture.

"Moving in or out?"

He laughed. "It's been like this for over a year. I can't seem to find the time to settle into the place."

"Where did you live before this?"

"Down the street at a smaller building."

I looked around. "I hope I'm not interrupting anything."

"Nothing. The news." He grabbed the remote and switched off the TV, one of those monster flat screens that take up a whole wall. "What brought you up here?"

This was it. The story I'd been concocting the whole way. "I was thinking about the night we had dinner. I made such an idiot of myself."

"No, you were fine. I just . . . I came out of the kitchen and you were gone. It was really rude of me to leave you sitting at the table."

"An invitation to view another chef's kitchen must be irresistible."

"It is." He moved some newspapers from the couch and offered me a seat. "Wine? Coffee?"

"Nothing, thanks." I sat down. Walt sat next to me. Close. I was showing up at his apartment without a reason at nearly ten o'clock at night. Obviously he'd come up with a reason, so at least that part of my plan was working.

"I'm still on for Friday?" he asked, putting his arm behind me on the couch. It was a high school move, but since my last first date had been in high school, it seemed about right. "For the interview."

"Yes," I said. "You in the morning and Detective Makina in the afternoon. Have you spoken with him?"

"Makina, yeah. Just the day after, you know. I made a statement about Erik."

"What did you say?"

"Nothing. I didn't know Erik very well. Aside from work."

"Ilena said you were like brothers."

Walt leaned a little closer. "Remember when I said the other night that you were bad at the dating stuff? You're still bad at it."

"I'm not used to dating."

"I get that. I think that's cool. Vera said you were married for a long time."

"Dated for six, married for fifteen."

"Wow."

"Vera's really nice, isn't she?" I said. "But I think you were right about her being in over her head. I think the other investors have to be more savvy."

"You mean Roman and Ilena?"

"No, I mean all ten investors."

Walt sat back on the couch. "I think I'll make coffee," he said. He got up and left the room, just like he had on our first date.

This time I followed him.

\\\

Like the rest of the apartment, the kitchen was a mess of boxes and newspapers.

"You should tell me what you know," I said.

"I don't know anything, Kate."

"You know where Doug is."

"I don't get it," he said. "I thought you just wanted some stuff about opening a restaurant. I didn't think you were Woodward and Bernstein."

"I'm not."

"So why do you care?"

"Where's Doug?"

"He didn't kill Erik."

"How do you know?"

For a second I thought he was going to tell me, but he just looked at me.

"Who are the ten investors?" I asked.

"I don't know. Doug was looking through the financial papers, and he found some stuff about the money that didn't add up."

"What stuff?"

"The investors." He seemed confused. "I thought you knew about all of it."

If I admitted I didn't, Walt would likely clam up, but I didn't have anything else to bluff with, so I changed tactics. "What I don't know," I said, "is where Doug is."

"He's at an apartment on Irving Park," Walt said. "A buddy of mine is out of town, so Doug's been staying there."

"Why?"

"So Roman doesn't kill him."

"Do you think Roman killed Erik?"

"Don't you?"

"I don't know," I said. "But if you think so, why not tell the police? At the moment, Makina is chasing a theory that Vera killed Erik."

Walt laughed. "Why would she kill Erik?"

"She found the body."

"No, she didn't," Walt said. "I found the body. I heard Vera come into the restaurant and I ran out the back."

I hadn't expected that. I wasn't sure where to go next. "Does Makina know?" I asked.

Walt shook his head.

"You have to tell him. You might have heard something or seen something."

"I didn't."

"You still have to tell the police." If Walt could place himself at the scene before Vera, that let her, and me, off the hook. Walt would look guilty and I could forget about who killed Erik and just get the sound bites I needed. This was working out better than I'd expected.

"I'm not saying anything," Walt said. "Maybe that makes me look bad, but I'm not saying anything to the police."

"Okay." There was no point in pushing him. I would tell Makina in the morning. "Why did you run?"

"I didn't know it was Vera," Walt said. "Not then. I thought it might be the killer."

"What were you doing there?"

"I'd left some stuff. My knife roll and some notes. I wanted to get them but when I saw Erik's body, I just freaked out and left."

"Why? You could have left them at the restaurant." I looked at Walt, who wasn't meeting my eyes. "Unless you weren't going back to the restaurant. Unless you were quitting. Ilena said you were putting the word out you were available. She said it was because of Erik's murder. But maybe you had made up your mind about leaving before Erik was killed."

"It doesn't really matter."

"It does if Erik realized he was losing the city's hottest young chef. It might mean losing his dream. If you fought, and in the heat of the argument you grabbed one of your knives . . ."

"That didn't happen."

"But you were quitting."

"I was . . . keeping my options open."

"What about the three extra points you got? Wasn't that an incentive to stay?"

"How do you know—"

"The late-night meeting with Ilena and Roman."

"You sure are a fly on the wall, Kate." He seemed defeated. "Those points were a reward for information."

"What information?"

"There's something you don't already know?" He tried to laugh but it came out as a nervous cough. "Roman approached me about this deal about eight months ago, but I couldn't get out of my contract. And then—" he stopped.

"And then the fire."

"Right. That happened and I was free, so I jumped on board. But right away there were problems. I don't think Ilena wanted my kind of cooking. She kept changing her mind about things. And then she got Erik involved, who wanted to make the restaurant about the front of the house instead of what Roman and I wanted, which was a place all about the food." He took a breath, seemed to rethink what he wanted to say. "It's part of the process, though, right? The creative differences. Erik had a point about the atmosphere. And Ilena's done a hell of a job with promotion." He gestured toward me. "Getting a TV show . . . I mean, that shows you her push."

"How does Doug fit into all of this?"

"I don't know."

"Come on, Walt," I said. "You were having secret meetings with him at Terry's restaurant. What were they about?"

"He was concerned about the money. He said there wasn't enough money in the accounts to complete the restaurant, and there should have been because there were ten silent partners."

"People other than Doug and Vera and the others I've met."

"Yeah. He wanted to know if I knew anything about them. I told him I didn't."

"Why did he come to you?"

"Doug's a careful guy. He only had access to the investor side of things, but he got ahold of the books and it didn't look good. He thought Erik was probably blowing the money. Only Erik, Roman, and Ilena had access to the accounts. I didn't have access, so Doug said I was above suspicion."

"But instead of helping Doug, you told Ilena and Roman about his investigation. And got three additional points of the restaurant because of it."

"I just want to cook. I don't want to get in the middle of the business stuff. So I told them. But I saw the way Roman was cornering Doug about money. He's got a reputation. You know, for . . . getting his way. It really freaked me out. So I told Doug to lay low. Gave him the keys to my friend's place."

"That was nice."

I was being sarcastic, but Walt didn't pick up on it. He moved toward me a little, reached his hand out and stroked my arm. "I'm just trying to be loyal to people who've been loyal to me. I'm a loyal guy."

I felt his fingers tickling my shoulder and moving slowly toward my neck. I was talking about murder, and he was hitting on me.

Fifty

I managed to get the address of the apartment where Doug was staying from Walt, and then I left. Walt, like all masters of delusion, had convinced himself he was a good guy caught in an impossible situation. His desires somehow allowed for any lapse in ethics, since he was only doing his job. Just because I'd said the same thing to myself dozens of times didn't let Walt off the hook.

The address he'd given me was only blocks away from Terry's Diner and, lucky for me, on my way home. It was above a sports bar, and as I walked up the steps to the third floor, the ground was vibrating with the screams of Blackhawks fans below.

There were two apartments on the third floor. Walt hadn't given me an apartment number, just the third floor, so I knocked on the door closest to the stairs. The man who answered wasn't Doug; he was the reincarnation of Kurt Cobain. A stoned-looking twentysomething in a ripped flannel shirt peeked out from a barely open door, not even bothering to hide the bong in his hand.

"Hey. What's up?" He looked me up and down, and clearly decided I was a little old for him. He coughed and widened his eyes. "What can I help you with, ma'am?"

"I'm looking for a man named Doug Zieman. Balding, a little overweight, maybe fifty."

"You lookin' for the dude across the hall?"

"I guess so."

"Well, you missed the action. There was all kinds of shit goin' on in that apartment."

"What do you mean by 'shit'?"

"Shit."

Helpful. I walked across the hall to the other apartment and knocked.

"I don't think there's anyone there," the Kurt look-alike said.

I tried the doorknob. "It's locked," I said. "I guess I'll come back tomorrow."

"The locks here are really bad. You just have to push against it."

"I'm not going to break into this guy's apartment."

The guy walked out of his apartment toward me. The bong wasn't the only thing he wasn't hiding.

"You're not wearing any pants," I said.

"Yeah, sorry. Didn't think you'd notice."

"Very little escapes my notice."

"It's not little."

"You want to have a discussion with a total stranger about the size—"

My half-naked friend had put his shoulder against the doorjamb, and with one good push he opened the door. Then he turned toward me, smiling, giving me a full display of his talents. But I wasn't looking at him. I was looking at the mess inside the apartment. The guy turned to see what had caught my attention.

"Damn," he said.

"What time was the shit that happened?"

"A few minutes ago. Like right before you got here," he said. "Sorry, lady, but you're on your own." In seconds he was back in his apartment. I could hear the dead bolt lock.

I took a step inside Doug's place, but I didn't bother calling out his name. It was pretty clear that if he was inside, he wasn't in a position to talk. The apartment, sparsely furnished and badly decorated to begin with, was in disarray. Clothes, dishes, papers, and everything else that wasn't nailed down was on the floor. I've never seen anything ransacked, but my guess was this was the dictionary definition of it.

I stepped back into the hallway. The sensible thing was to run, take a long hot shower to get the smell of pot out of my hair, and pray that the worst thing I would see tonight was a stranger's junk.

But.

I stood in the hall, trying to change my own mind. Trying to will myself to leave. But I couldn't. Either Doug was in the apartment hurt or possibly dead, or someone had grabbed him. Either way I couldn't just pretend I didn't know, much as I wanted to. Especially if there was a chance to help him. The jerk.

"Damn it."

I called Detective Makina.

\\\

"So tell me again how you came by this place?" Makina asked me after a search of the apartment had turned up nothing.

"I've told you three times." My eyes hurt from the fluorescent lights in the hallway and the drifts of smoke wafting under the door of the naked guy's place. "You know the guy across the hall is smoking weed? You should arrest him and I'll go home and get some sleep."

"I'm homicide. I don't care what drugs that guy is doing as long as he's breathing in the morning."

"Good to know."

"Mrs. Conway, you seem to be in the middle of this case, and I want to understand why."

"Am I a suspect?"

He sighed. "You're a busybody."

At least being a suspect has some glamour to it. He'd made me out to be Gladys Kravitz. "I'm not just snooping, Detective. I'm doing my job. I'm a journalist working on a show about the opening of a restaurant. The homicide and Doug's disappearance are part of that show."

I'm not a journalist. I have no First Amendment protection, nor do I really care about the truth, so it wasn't a statement that would hold up in court. But to call me a busybody? That was just rude.

"Who else knew that Doug was here?" Makina asked.

"Walt. I told you."

"Aside from Walt."

"No one."

"Not even Ms. Bingham."

"No."

"Did she have any idea that Walt knew where Doug Zieman was?"

It would be my third lie regarding Vera's involvement in this mess. But at that point I didn't care. "What's your hang-up about her, anyway?" I asked.

"She's the only one of the suspects who's lied to me."

"Really? Everybody's lied to me. Roman, Ilena, Walt, even you."

"What have I lied about?"

"Knowing Erik's whereabouts the day he fought with Vera."

It had nagged at me. Erik's former boss had called Erik a loner, someone whose only friends were work friends. No wife, no girlfriend. He probably didn't even have a cat. Yet Makina had said Erik went home after the diner. Who would have known that?

It was just a guess, but Makina blinked. For a full ten seconds he stared at his notebook.

"Withholding information material to a homicide is illegal, Mrs. Conway," he said, his voice just a little less cocky. "I'm sure as a journalist, you understand that."

"I called you, didn't I?"

"Only after you went looking for Mr. Zieman alone. Why did you do that? Were you hoping to get some information from him? Does he know something about Ms. Bingham's involvement in the murder of Erik Price?"

"Aren't you the least bit suspicious of Doug?" I asked.

"This isn't a two-way street, Mrs. Conway. What I think about Mr. Zieman is my business. So let me ask you again, what information were you hoping to get from him?"

The adrenaline from finding Doug's hideout was ebbing. I was suddenly very tired, and Makina's voice was giving me a headache. "No more questions tonight." I said it forcefully, and was surprised at how little Makina's latest theories scared me.

"When?"

"I'll see you Friday," I said. "I'll conduct my interview and you can conduct yours. Seem fair?"

Before he had a chance to answer I started down the stairs and out the door, into a fresh onslaught of snow.

Fifty-one

The next morning, earlier than I needed to, I got into my car. Not only didn't the heat work; the car wouldn't start. I called Andres and asked him to swing by and pick me up.

While I waited, I called a tow truck and played my messages from the night before. I was hoping one of them was Makina letting me know that someone—someone other than Vera—was under arrest for Erik's murder. But no luck. All the messages were from Ellen, and each one was more alarmed than the last. I'd missed my nephew's game and he was, apparently, devastated. My nephew said hello to me only when instructed to do so, but by not being in the crowd to cheer him on, I'd ruined his childhood. At least according to my sister. I'd add it to the list of things I was screwing up, including Erik's murder investigation, the documentary on life in prison, and my life.

As my car was being towed to the repair shop, Andres and Victor pulled up outside. When I got to the van, they both looked worried.

"What happened?" I asked.

"Nothing," Victor said. "It's cool. It's all going to be fine."

"Going to be fine?"

"Get in," Andres instructed. "We'll tell you on the way."

Victor got in the back and I jumped into the passenger seat. Both of them seemed uncertain where to start.

"We have a problem," Andres finally said.

"Vera?"

Andres shook his head and sighed.

"What?" I yelled. "Did something happen to Brick or Tim?"

"You're worried about them?" Andres asked.

"I'm worried about the shoot."

He didn't seem convinced. "No. It's about genius here, sticking his nose into another mess."

Victor rolled his eyes. "I didn't have a choice."

"What did you do?" I asked Victor.

"Vera called me last night," he said. "She told me that you said Doug was alive. So she started calling his number, over and over. Like an obsession."

"Did she reach him?"

"Yeah. Eventually he picked up. Said he was staying at a friend's place. Told her to get out of town," Victor said. "I mean, if a guy just wants to break up with a girl, he says, 'It's not you, it's me,' right? This asshole has a whole covert operation going on."

"What time did she reach him?" I asked.

"About ten, I think. Why?"

"Never mind," I said. "How do you fit into this?"

"I'm getting to that. Vera calls me. She said you had gone home and looked like you needed a good night's sleep so she didn't want to keep bothering you. She asked me what to do. And I know a lot of computer stuff—"

"So you found Doug."

"No," Andres interrupted. "Only it looks like he did. Victor started doing some kind of search on his computer trying to locate the guy by what he told Vera."

Victor nodded. "Doug made some comment about walking three blocks in the snow to get a hot dog at Byron's, so that had to be the Wrigleyville area," Victor said. "And he told Vera to talk louder because the Blackhawks game was on in the bar below his apartment. There are six sports bars within three blocks of Byron's that have apartments above them."

"And?"

"That's as far as I got. I was going to figure out the rest today, after the shoot. Then Makina called Vera, and he took it wrong."

Andres shook his head. "Kate, this is out of control. Something must have happened to Doug last night."

"And Makina thinks Vera and Victor did it," I finished for him.

"The police took my laptop this morning," Victor said. "I have some of my own tunes on that, so I better get it back."

"I don't think that's your biggest problem," Andres told him. Then he looked at me. "So what now?"

I thought it over. "We finish the shoot with Tim and Brick, I guess. There isn't anything else we can do. We talk to Vera after we're done, and when I interview Makina I'll see if we can straighten it out."

\\\

It sounded like I had a plan, but I was as much at a loss as Andres. When we got to Dugan the guys set up for the final interviews and I stayed outside and tried to reach Vera. She answered on the third try, whispered something about calling me back, and hung up. She didn't need to say it. Makina was with her.

Fifty-two

I sat in the small drab prison room, waiting for Andres and Victor to set up the lights. It might seem like I'm pulling rank by not helping, but I've learned it's faster if I just stay out of the way. And I get coffee for my guys, who begged for caffeine but would probably have been better off with water, because they were both already pretty jumpy. The guard brought us three Styrofoam cups of the thickest coffee I'd ever seen, a handful of nondairy creamers, and a dozen packets of sugar.

I grabbed my cup and walked over to the lone window in the room, dirty and covered by metal bars. Outside the sky was gray. More snow. I felt claustrophobic just being in this place, but the choking feeling in my throat wasn't, I knew, coming from the prison.

\\\

When Brick arrived, he seemed angry. I looked to Russell, who circled his fingers around his own wrist, which I took as a question: Did I want Brick to stay cuffed for the interview? I shook my head, so Russell uncuffed him. But he stayed close.

"What's wrong?" I asked.

Brick just stared at me.

"Brick, if you don't want to do this—"

"Don't you need the interview for your show?"

"Yes, but—"

"What we gonna talk about today?"

"Growing old here."

He laughed, but there was no joy in it. "Don't think I need to worry 'bout that."

"Not yet, but someday. I mean, you will grow old here."

"Not necessarily." He shifted in his chair, seemed to relax a little. "How's that other matter comin' along?"

"Badly," I admitted. "But I have cameras rolling, so we're not here to talk about me."

"I'll give you what you want; we can skip to the end of this shit."

"Okay."

"I don't care about growing old, or dyin'. It's all the same to me." He looked at the camera, then at me. "That it? We done with this?"

I leaned toward him a little, trying to get him to focus only on me. It would be easier to get a better answer if he thought he was talking to a friend and not a TV audience. "That's a bullshit answer. I want how you really feel about dying here."

"Oh, how I really feel?" he said, imitating my inflection. Only he combined it with a mocking tone and undisguised hostility. "Shit, Kate. You really care that I'm going to die here?"

"I do," I said. In the same moment that I realized that I was being sincere, I saw that Brick realized it too. I signaled for Andres to turn off the camera so I could talk freely. "You've been straight with me, Brick, so I'm being straight back. You've killed at least three people, and I don't think there's any excuse you could give me that would make me forget that, could make me forget there was a little girl named Tara Quinn who didn't get to grow up because of you. You made a choice, and it's ruined lives, yours included. But I also think you're not the same man you were twenty years ago. And the man you are now has become a friend. I don't give a damn what you say on tape; just give me something I can use. But between you and me, I do care that you're going to die here. I'm sorry about that." I signaled Andres, and he turned the camera back on.

Brick looked at me, shifted again, stared off into the distance, as if he was searching for the words outside himself. Then he looked back at me. His eyes changed half a dozen times in just seconds: angry, sad, tired, hopeful. I wasn't sure if he was going to continue with the interview or just go back to his cell. I waited. We all waited for what seemed like quite a long time.

When he finally spoke, he seemed on the verge of tears. "I see the old guys, the ones in wheelchairs, or with, what you call 'em, walkers. They can't even remember what it is they done that brought 'em here. They're frightened of the outside. You tell one of those guys, 'You goin' home today,' and they start shakin'. This is their home. They don't want freedom. They don't want choices. They want to be told when to eat, when to piss. The whole idea of a world out there, that's like Mars to them, it's been so long. They don't want nothin' to do with it." He hesitated. "One day, I'm gonna be one of those old guys. That's my fate."

We sat in silence for a moment. "Thanks," I said. My voice cracked. I didn't know what else to say.

"What about you, Kate? What's gonna happen with you?"

"I don't know."

"You gonna be old someday too."

"Yes."

"You gonna be alone?"

"I don't know."

He looked at me a long time. "We done now?"

"I guess so," I said. "I have my sound bite."

Behind me, Andres shut off the camera.

"So what's goin' on with your dead man and your friend?" Brick asked.

"It's just getting worse and worse."

"What can I do?"

I almost said, "Nothing." It's a reflexive response to an offer of help, but I knew Brick wouldn't take it that way. He would take it as an indication that I saw him as powerless. But there really was nothing he could do. At least not about Erik's murder and Vera's and my imminent arrests.

"I want to ask you about Tim."

I heard Andres grunt. Brick noticed it too, and smiled. "Tim botherin' you?"

"No. He's . . ." I didn't know how much was appropriate to say, but I wanted an answer. "He's reached out for help, legal help."

"You're no lawyer."

"No, but I have access to them. He seems to feel there's been an error in his case that the right lawyer can help him with. He didn't have good legal counsel in his trial."

"Who did? You walk through this place and I promise you, you ain't gonna meet a lot of rich folks. We all had shit lawyers, all had bad breaks. I'm not cryin'—why should he?"

"I think he's just interested in the possibility. A lot of guys in here spend time going over their cases, don't they?"

"Yeah, it's a hobby for some, an obsession for others. What does he want?"

"What *I* want is to know his reputation in here."

"He don't have one."

"You told me once that all you wanted from me was books, and you implied Tim wanted more."

"He likes the ladies."

"No, Brick. You like the ladies. Tim hasn't shown the least bit of interest in me that way. What did you mean?"

"I like to look. I like to imagine." He stretched out the last word. "Tim likes to play games."

"What kind of games?"

"You sure he's not playin' one with you right now?"

Fifty-three

Victor left Dugan and bought sandwiches at a nearby deli, and we ate sitting huddled around the camera. While he was out, he had called Vera. She was home, said everything was fine. Sounded normal, Victor reported. Though she had mentioned that Makina wanted to talk to Victor before the end of the day.

"Brick got one thing right," Andres said. "There aren't rich people in places like this. Vera's rich; Victor's not. We keep Victor the hell away from Makina."

"Until tomorrow," I reminded him. "What do we do then?"

"We'll figure that out tomorrow," Andres said.

I patted Victor's arm, and he smiled. There we were, Mom and Dad making decisions to protect our only child, our tattooed, pierced, nearly homeless twentysomething musician-child.

"What are you going to say to Tim?" Victor asked. "Are you going to help him?"

"I don't know," I admitted. "He's either a sociopathic con artist or an innocent guy who's gotten a little warped by twenty years in the system."

"Can you walk away without knowing which one?" Andres asked.

I didn't have an answer. At least not one that I liked.

\\\

They say the eyes are the windows to the soul. Assuming you have one. When Tim came in and sat down, I looked into his eyes, and they didn't reveal a thing. Even the sadness from the other day was gone. He was the same friendly good ole boy he'd always been.

"Growin' old in here?" Tim repeated my question. "A lot of the anger has left me from when I first got here. I'm used to this place. It was like movin' to a foreign country when I first went to prison. I didn't speak the language, didn't know the customs. But now this is all

I know." He took a long, deep breath. "I'd like to visit Jenny's grave. I'd like to say I'm sorry. But if that don't happen, if I'm here, I guess I'll just grow old like I been doin'. Wait out my time on this earth, do what I have to do every day and then die. The outside has changed a lot. I can see that on TV, but I don't suppose dyin' is much different in here than it is on the outside. It's still lookin' into God's eyes, isn't it?"

"I suppose."

He nodded. "Don't think I believe in God, though."

"I thought you were born again. It's in your file."

"It was a phase. A reaction to the death penalty bein' lifted. I thought it meant I wasn't supposed to die here. Some guys got depressed after the ban, you know. Felt like they'd been holdin' their breath for years waitin', and then when the death penalty was gone, they didn't know what to do with themselves. Knowin' you gonna die, well, everybody's got to deal with that. But havin' the date circled on the calendar? That's a weird feelin', is all. You get used to it. You get scared, you get ready, you get scared again. Then, all of a sudden, you might be here fifty years."

"So you found Jesus."

"Yeah. Then I let him go again. I didn't feel anything, prayin'. I didn't feel better," he said. "My life has been wasted and no amount of Bible verses gonna change that."

I sat quietly for a moment. I didn't have another question. I didn't want to ask anything else. I just wanted out of there. I wanted to lie on my couch and order takeout Chinese food for two, watch reruns, and forget that places like Dugan existed. And people like Brick and Tim. And Erik. All lives wasted. And no amount of anything was going to change that.

Instead, once the cameras were off, I promised Tim I would look into the matter. I told him Vera was willing to help as long as we could confirm the details of his story.

"How you gonna do that?"

"I'm going to talk to the police detective in charge of your case."

"He's gonna lie to you."

"Probably, but I still need to talk to him," I said. "I did find that your lawyer was a drunk who was disbarred. Maybe there's something in that. Vera has access to much better lawyers." I didn't mention she was currently using them herself. "They'll look at your case, and see what motions can still be filed."

He reached out and touched my shoulder. Russell stepped forward and Tim pulled his hand away. "Thanks, Kate. Thanks. Whatever happens, thanks."

Fifty-four

While the guys loaded up the van, I said good-bye to Joanie Rheinbeck.

"You get what you need?" she asked.

"Yes, I think so. Maybe more than I need."

"As long as it's honest," she said. "This is a sad place full of sad people."

"I think that will be clear."

She shook my hand. "Well, if that's all . . ."

"Actually," I said, "I do want one more thing. I'd like to look at your visitors log."

"Kate Conway, you're becoming like one of my inmates—I give you an inch and you take a mile." She sighed. "But if this is it, then okay."

\\\

On the drive to Vera's house, I sat in the passenger seat staring out the window. Somewhere deep inside me were tears. Maybe they were for what Brick and Tim had said, maybe they were for me, or maybe they were just the result of tiredness and stress. Whatever the cause, I didn't want the guys to catch me.

Andres took my silence as annoyance and started making jokes. When they didn't work, he tapped my shoulder. "You know I feel bad for these guys too," he said. "But you can't save them."

"I'm not trying to save them," I said. "But it's nice to see that you've softened your stance."

He shrugged. "We all make bad decisions. Maybe not as bad as theirs, but we all make them."

"What bad decisions have you made, Andres? A good wife who loves you, nice kids, a house you can more or less afford. It seems to me you've made all the right choices."

"I started working with you." He smiled. "And that's been no end of trouble."

I laughed, and for the time at least, the tears receded.

\\\

"Hi guys." Vera greeted us at the door, her two dogs at her side, flanking her like bodyguards.

"Are you alone?" I asked as Andres, Victor, and I moved past the dogs into the house.

"Yes. He's gone," Vera said. "He had to leave. I told him he had to direct any questions to my lawyer."

Finally, a little common sense.

"I also hired a lawyer for Victor," she continued. Victor began to protest, but Vera wouldn't hear of it. "I know you don't think you need one, but you do."

"It's just so . . ." Victor was at a rare loss for words.

"Adult," I said.

"Necessary," added Andres.

"Freakin' chicken," Victor jumped in. "Like I gotta hide behind someone."

"He's at a different firm than my lawyer, and he has a very good reputation. He comes highly recommended," Vera told him. "I've given him a retainer and he's said that you have to tell Makina that he can't speak to you without your lawyer present."

"What about tomorrow?" Victor asked. "How am I going to do my job?"

"You just have to mic the guy; you don't have to chat him up," Andres said.

Once we were all settled in the kitchen, with the dogs lounging beneath the table and all of us with coffee and those crumbly bakery cookies on our plates, Vera sat down.

"Done playing hostess?" I asked.

"Unless you need something?"

"No."

"Then I'm done."

"So . . ."

Vera smiled. "It's fine. Doug's alive. It was all a big misunderstanding. I called him after you left." She paused. "I called him quite a few times. I think the wine had something to do with it."

"It usually does," I said.

"Finally he picked up. He said that I was in no danger as long as he stayed away. He said that the restaurant was in trouble. I was right about the offshore accounts. There's some mess with the money. It's gone missing or something."

"'Or something'?"

"I didn't get the whole story. Doug had to hang up. He had to meet someone."

"Did he say who?"

"No." She looked at me. She must have seen the worry in my face, because her expression changed from optimism to panic. "What don't I know? Detective Makina came over and he wanted to talk to me but I told him he had to talk to my lawyer and I sent him away. What did he want to talk to me about?"

"After your call with Doug, something happened," I said. "Victor said you spoke to Doug around ten."

"Ten twelve." She showed me the call on her cell phone. "We talked for four minutes."

"I got to his apartment around ten forty-five, maybe a few minutes later," I said. "His place had been messed up, like someone was looking for something. And Doug was missing."

"So, he's not okay?" she asked. "What's happened to him?"

"Vera, it's more than that. You spoke to Doug at ten. Forty-five minutes later his hiding place is turned inside out and Doug is missing. Guess who the police suspect?"

"Me?"

"You and Victor."

Vera tapped the table. "So do I tell the police what I found out or do I just tell you?"

"That depends," I said. "On what you found out."

Fifty-five

Doug told me that Erik was embezzling," Vera said. "He didn't want to say anything bad about him, of course, but I made him tell me."

"How did he know that?" I asked.

"Doug was hired to help on the investment end, but he didn't have access to the checkbook. When I got those threatening calls, Doug got worried that I was right, that it did have something to do with the investors." She said. "He started looking into things."

"He told you it was an ex-girlfriend," Victor pointed out.

"He didn't want me to worry." She blushed a little, which made me want to sock her.

"You buy that?" I was too annoyed to worry about Vera's feelings. "Then why did Doug run after Erik got killed?"

"I'm getting to that," Vera said. "Erik, as the restaurant manager, did have access to the checkbook. And when Doug went to Ilena, they looked into it, and it turns out that money is missing. Lots of it. The investment account and the day-to-day checking account are almost dry."

"But Roman and Ilena can write checks too," I said. "So how do you know it's not one of them who embezzled?"

"Almost all of it is their money," Vera said. "What would be the point of embezzling from yourself?"

Andres leaned back, seeming satisfied by Vera's story. "So someone killed Erik because he took the money. That could be Roman, or Ilena. Or even Walt, if he felt it meant the restaurant wouldn't open."

"Or Doug," I said. "His money was in that bank account."

"Or Vera." Victor looked at us. "I mean, she's got the same motive as Doug, so this isn't going to get us off the hook with Makina."

Vera didn't skip a beat. She'd obviously thought of that herself. "I asked Doug about the other investors you mentioned, Kate. He said

Ilena gave him a thumb drive. It was supposed to have the numbers of an account where Roman sometimes hid money. She handed it to him at the restaurant."

"When?" Andres asked, but he looked at me. "That must have been what Ilena handed Doug during the taping."

"Why didn't she e-mail him the numbers?" Victor asked.

"A thumb drive is easier to hide from a prying husband than an e-mail account," I said.

"So why did she trust Doug?" Andres asked.

Andres, Victor, and I looked toward Vera, hoping she was reaching the same conclusion we had, that he and Ilena were more than business partners.

"Obviously Doug is trustworthy," Vera said. She caught me frowning and shrugged. "Or he's been sleeping with her. But we don't know that for certain, and if Tim's story teaches us anything it's that you shouldn't convict people without solid evidence."

"What happened to the thumb drive?" I asked. I decided to ignore the ethics lecture, as I've ignored all past ethics lectures.

"I don't know," she said. "I guess Doug still has it. The scary thing is when Doug looked at the drive, it contained a lot more than one bank account number. It had dozens of account numbers, and the names of some of Roman's associates. Doug thinks she gave it to him so he would take it to the police and get Roman arrested."

"So why didn't he?" I asked.

Vera didn't have an answer, but I did. Doug wasn't an innocent. Going to the police would get him in trouble for some reason. Or he was working with Roman, and Ilena didn't know it. Either way, he was more than a nerd with a bucket list.

"You're both assuming Doug's still alive," Victor said. Vera looked frightened at the suggestion, so I gave Victor my best "shut up" look. He shook it off. "Look, Kate, I'm just saying. Someone was at his place looking for something. It has to be the thumb drive. And if the person looking for it found it, why keep a witness around? Especially if that witness knows the identity of Erik's killer."

Vera turned to me. "That makes sense, doesn't it?"

"Shockingly, yes," I had to admit. "Victor's probably a hundred percent right."

Victor smiled. "See? I don't need a lawyer. I can just talk to Makina. I'll set him straight." Victor was getting excited. "I have a few theories about how this all went down, and I think once he hears me out, everything will be fine."

"Tomorrow is going to be fun," Andres said. "Once Victor is led away in cuffs, you want to do audio, Kate, or should I?"

"I'll do audio," I said. "You're going to have to shoot the arrest so we have an ending to the show."

\\\

That night, like so many other nights, I went home with the intention of lying on the couch, watching bad television, eating takeout, and going to bed. There was another missed called from Dugan on my throwaway cell phone, but no message. Tim probably couldn't leave a message, I decided, since it was a collect call.

There were too many things on my mind, too many people's lives I was forced to understand. I wanted a break from human interaction, and the conflict that went with it. I ordered General Tso's chicken for two, and when it arrived, I poured myself a sparkling water and settled on the couch to watch a movie. Just as I was finally relaxing, the phone rang. I went to the kitchen. It was Dugan.

"Will you accept a collect call from Joseph Tyler?" The computer voice asked.

It took me a second to remember who that was. "Yes," I said. I heard a clicking sound. "Brick?"

"Yeah. Kate," he said, "you're all done with the documentary?"

"Yes. It was our last day today," I said.

"And this number. This ain't your real number?"

"Why?"

"This is just a number you give out to guys you don't trust?"

"Why?"

"Get rid of it."

"The phone?"

"Get rid of it," he repeated. "Toss it."

"Brick, what's this about?"

Another click. Brick had hung up.

I turned the phone off and put it in a drawer, then I took it out of the drawer and turned it on again. I left it on the kitchen counter near the trash, but I couldn't decide whether to throw it away or not. After about twenty minutes of standing in my kitchen debating, I called Dugan. I didn't know what information I was looking for, so I told the guard who I was and asked if anything unusual was going on.

The guy thought I was crazy. "We don't really discuss that," he said. "Especially with TV people."

"Can I talk to Brick, Joseph Tyler? I have his inmate number somewhere," I said. "I can find it if you need it."

"It's after hours," the guard told me.

"But he just called me."

"They can call until nine p.m. It's six minutes after."

"Right. It's just six minutes after nine," I said. "I just want to . . ." I didn't really know what I wanted, so I stopped there.

"You can call in the morning if you want, but not tonight." I could hear the guard hesitate. "One of these guys harassing you or something?"

"No, it's fine. I just had a question."

"Tomorrow, after nine." He hung up.

After the call, I tried to go back to the movie, but I couldn't follow the plot. Something about a woman who becomes friends with a shy dog-walker in New York. Secretly, the guy is a prince from some made-up European country and is slumming to see how the other half lives. Naturally the two fall in love. And naturally love conquers all.

Vera was right. They had sold us a bill of goods.

Fifty-six

Walt was early for his interview, and he'd brought muffins, a recipe he'd gotten from some restaurant he'd visited in Vermont. We stood in the dusty dining area of Club Car drinking coffee and waiting for Andres and Victor to be ready with the lights.

"Do you go from kitchen to kitchen trying to get their recipes?" I asked Walt.

"Yeah." As if it was the most natural thing in the world. "It's good. Try it."

I bit into the muffin, cherry streusel, and it was good, but that wasn't the point. "Would you share your recipes with anyone who walked in off the street asking for them?"

"Any chef, yeah. Why not?" Walt glanced toward Andres. "In fact, I'll show you something. In the kitchen."

"The kitchen's off-limits," I said.

"No, they cleared it."

"When?"

"Yesterday." Walt walked toward the kitchen and I followed, nearly stopping every third step to reconsider. I couldn't imagine going in there, but as Walt disappeared behind the swinging doors, I also couldn't imagine letting my fear get the better of me.

I walked in. The kitchen was cleaned up, scrubbed. There wasn't even a stain on the floor where Erik's body had been. It was cleaner than it had been the day Walt did the tasting.

"What happened?" I asked.

"There's a service. They come into crime scenes and, you know, take care of it."

"Doesn't it creep you out?"

"A little," he said. "But what am I supposed to do? I have a kitchen to put together."

I stood in the center of the room and looked around. The place seemed bigger, or maybe just emptier. "Didn't there used to be more equipment? More boxes of things?"

Walt looked around as I had. "No. I think it's the same."

"So you're going to cook here? Inches from where Erik was killed?"

"Jeez, Kate. I'm not really thinking of it that way. I mean, if you want to, you can find a history with every inch of land. Someone died there . . . something terrible happened. If you go back far enough, you won't find any space that's free of some blood."

"I'm not talking about ancient Indian burial grounds, Walt. Erik died nine days ago," I said. "Right where you're standing."

He shrugged.

And to think he had once been my favorite of this group. "Ilena said you've put the word out that you're available for work," I said.

He bit the inside of his cheek. "Posturing. It's just a good idea to let people know you're available. It gives Roman more incentive to get this place together quickly."

"Are you getting paid while you wait?"

"No."

"So what are you living on?"

"Insurance settlement from my last restaurant. I lost personal items in there. My knives, equipment, things like that. It's pretty expensive to replace."

I pointed to the knives on the counter. "But you've obviously replaced them. So what are you living on?"

"Ilena bought those," he said. "They were a gift when I signed on to the restaurant."

I heard Andres in the next room call out that he was ready. "What did you want to show me?" I asked Walt.

"This." He handed me a box of more than a hundred tattered recipe cards with notations from restaurants around the world. "It's my collection," he said. "And if someone wanted one of my recipes, I'd give it to him in a heartbeat."

"It's nice that you're willing to share."

"There's more than enough for all of us."

\\\

He gave me a dull interview, but it had all the right sound bites about Erik, about the legacy of his vision, and about Walt's hope that the restaurant would carry on because it was Erik's dream. It was hokey, but that's what I was after.

He didn't once ask me what had happened at Doug's, and when I brought the subject up, he brushed it off.

"Makina asked me about that," he said. "I told him what I knew, of course, about you coming over and everything. Whatever went on with Doug happened while you were at my place, so you're in the clear."

"Thanks for being my alibi."

"And mine," he said. He gave me a light, awkward hug. "If you ever want a good meal, I'd be happy to cook it for you."

As Walt left, I thought about something. He wasn't my alibi. Whatever had happened to Doug had happened around ten forty-five, a few minutes before I'd arrived. I'd left Walt's place at just a few minutes past ten, got gas, and drove the streets. Could Walt have beaten me there? It would be tight, but it was possible.

I wanted to share my theory with Makina as soon as we arrived at his office for the interview, but he was pacing. He'd worn a new suit, dark blue, with a light blue tie and crisp white shirt. I sat him in the chair opposite me and chatted with him. Normally this is when I try to make my interview subject comfortable, but I didn't want to make Makina comfortable.

"I'm sure your colleagues will get a kick out of this show," I said. "I'm sure they'll all watch it. Maybe tape it."

"Uh-huh."

"You've never done TV before?"

"I usually let someone else handle it," he admitted. "But I know I'm just supposed to look at you and answer your questions."

"That's right. And I'll be paying close attention to everything you say."

Makina shifted. He tried to seem casual, but a band of red was creeping up his neck, the telltale sign of nervousness. Andres pointed the camera toward Makina, but I waited a moment before starting the interview. I wanted a minute to enjoy watching him be the one to squirm under the hot lights.

But I didn't let him sit long. I had business to discuss. I told him about Walt not having me as his alibi.

"Listen, Mrs. Conway," he said, "I appreciate the help, but—"

"There are plausible suspects that you are not considering."

"You really don't know what I'm considering." He nodded toward the camera. "These are not the kinds of things I'm prepared to discuss on videotape."

"Okay. Then tell me where you are in this investigation."

"There is nothing I can tell you beyond the fact that we're doing everything we can to apprehend Mr. Price's killer. We are following every lead, no matter how ridiculous, and we're confident that we'll have a resolution to this matter."

"Where's Doug Zieman?"

"That's a separate investigation that may or may not have anything to do with the homicide."

"How can it possibly be separate? Doug disappeared the night Erik was killed. He said to both Vera and Walt that something fishy was going on at the restaurant."

Up until then Makina had been sweating. On hearing Vera's name, he perked up. "What did he say to Ms. Bingham?"

Victor was right. Telling Makina about Doug's phone call, about Erik's embezzlement, wouldn't get Vera off the hook. It would just make her motive stronger. "My interview. My questions," I said.

"Then your interview is over," he said. "There isn't anything I can really tell you, anyway." He grabbed at the mic hidden just below the third button of his shirt. As he removed it, Victor jumped up to take it from him. "Are you ready to talk now, Mr. Pilot?" Makina asked.

Andres and I looked at Victor, who looked like a cat raising its fur to look bigger, with about as much effect. Victor looked Makina in the eye, and Makina looked back. We waited. Victor looked like he was just about to tell Makina one of this theories. Andres took a step toward him. But before he could get there, Victor spoke.

"I have a lawyer," he said. "You can only talk to me when my attorney is present."

I could hear Andres exhale.

Makina nodded. "Then I guess we're done here."

Fifty-seven

After Makina left, I tried Dugan again. I had to tell Andres and Victor that I was checking with the Business Channel about the interviews. I knew Andres wouldn't like it that I was worried about Brick, and he especially wouldn't like my justification. On the first day I interviewed him, Brick had said that at some point we have to throw away the rules and live by our instincts. According to the rules, a multiple murderer is a bad guy, but my instincts said he wasn't—at least, he wasn't trying to hurt me. And more than that, something in my gut told me he was in trouble.

But for some reason, I couldn't get anyone at Dugan to confirm it.

"We've had some issues in that block, and we've suspended phone privileges," a guard told me.

"Can I talk with Joanie Rheinbeck?"

"She's in a meeting with the warden."

"Can you at least tell me if Joseph Tyler is okay?"

"We don't give out prisoner information. Unless you're family."

I would have lied and said I was his sister, but they probably had records of his relatives, and Brick had only mentioned a brother to me. "No," I said. "But I'm the television producer—"

The guard hung up.

"Everything okay at the network?" Andres had somehow snuck up behind me. I wasn't sure how much he'd heard.

"Yes. Of course, they'd love it if we could end the show with an arrest."

"We came pretty close there with Victor," he said. "I say we end with a celebration that we didn't have an arrest today."

Just as I was about to agree, my phone rang, a number I didn't recognize. "Hello?"

"Miss Conway?" An elderly woman's voice. Not weak, but definitely older. "I'm Douglas Zieman's neighbor."

"Have you seen him?" It was abrupt, but I couldn't be bothered with pleasantries at the moment.

"Yes. We spoke. I told him his girlfriend and a Miss Conway were looking for him. He seemed very concerned. I didn't know whether I should call you, but you were so nice that day and so worried about your friend, I thought you would be able to help Douglas if he were in trouble."

"When did you talk to him?" My heart was beating just a little fast. It was almost too much to hope for.

"Fifteen minutes ago. He was on his way into his house."

I almost laughed out loud. "Thanks," I said. "Just don't tell him you called me."

I hung up and slapped Andres on the back. "Keep your camera out," I said. "We may get that arrest on tape yet."

\\\

On the way to Oak Park, I called Makina, but only once Andres and I were blocks away from Doug's. I am a law-abiding citizen . . . ish, and it was my civic duty to inform the police that a possible suspect in a homicide had been spotted. And I wanted footage of Makina taking the elusive Doug Zieman into custody.

When we got to the house, Andres parked his van across the street. He pointed the camera out the window, discreet but still a good shot, and we waited. I was tempted to go to the front door and see if Doug was there, but I didn't want to spook him. Or get killed. I'll go toe-to-toe with anyone in a verbal altercation, but my chances of winning an actual fight are somewhere around zero. Especially since it was likely that Doug still had Vera's gun.

Local police pulled up just a few minutes after we'd arrived, surrounded the house, and waited. A few minutes later, Makina and several other detectives arrived. Makina glanced toward the van and frowned.

They knocked on the door. Nothing. More knocking. More nothing. Then a nod from Makina and several Oak Park police officers broke down Doug's door. There was a rush inside. This was it—a great ending to the show and Vera off the hook for Erik's murder, all in one easy step.

A few minutes later Makina walked outside. No Doug. He chatted with a uniformed cop, pointed toward the door. The cop made a call. There was no urgency. If Doug had been inside fifteen minutes before the neighbor called me, then he'd left in the twenty minutes it had taken us to drive over.

Makina walked over to the van. "I'm afraid I'm going to have to ask you to clear the area."

I jumped out of the van and walked into the street, approaching Makina before he could reach us. Andres was still shooting every moment, and Victor's boom mic had made an appearance out the van door. How can you not believe in psychic connections when we all knew what to do without speaking?

"Why?" I asked Makina when I'd reached him. I positioned myself so he had to look toward the camera to speak to me.

"This is a crime scene." The nervousness from the interview was gone. He was back in charge and he wanted me to know it.

"You have evidence that Doug killed Erik?"

"Mrs. Conway . . ."

It took a minute. "Doug is in there. Someone is in there. Someone is dead in there."

"Mrs. Conway, you have to move the van."

"You're a Chicago detective. This is Oak Park. You have no authority here."

"I can get someone with authority."

"We're a news organization. We have the right—"

"I'm happy for you. Move the van."

Makina turned and walked back to the scene, just as an ambulance pulled up.

"Did you get everything?" I asked Andres.

"It was nice," he said. "We have the cops milling about in the background and Makina up front giving us the tough cop act. And now we have the ambulance." He tossed Victor the keys to the van and got out. "If Victor moves this down the block, I can stay here and shoot until they kick me out."

I turned to where Andres was shooting. I watched the street for a few minutes, looking at the cops milling about. The neighbor woman with her yappy dog was on the other side, looking just as confused as I was.

"We have an ambulance," I said.

"I know. I just said that."

"No, Andres. We have an ambulance. Not a coroner's van. Whoever is in there isn't dead. And they can't be that hurt, because Makina was too casual."

"Should we call Vera?"

Victor came toward us, smiling. "Already did. She's on her way."

"I don't know if that was the best idea in the world," I said.

"Why not?"

I watched as Makina approached us again. But this time he had an Oak Park police officer with him.

"I think he's about to tell us," I said. Makina came so close to me that I almost stepped back a few inches, but I didn't. I wasn't about to lose ground, symbolically or literally. "Someone inside Doug's house is hurt," I said to him.

"We're establishing a perimeter around the house," the uniformed officer was saying, but I didn't move.

"Someone is hurt, and not seriously, or you wouldn't be standing around. That's not cause to set up any perimeters."

The Oak Park cop spun around and looked about to shoot me, but Makina smiled. "One of the guys coming in from the back cut himself on some broken glass," he said. "That's why we have an ambulance."

"So why move us back?"

As I spoke, another van pulled up, forcing us all off the street and onto the sidewalk. I looked at the side. It was a coroner's van.

"Any more questions, Mrs. Conway?"

"Who is it?"

Makina wasn't listening. "Now that's an interesting development," he said. I turned to see what he was looking at, and saw Vera walking toward us, looking worried.

"We called her," I said.

"When?"

"Just now."

"Which one of you is 'we'?" Makina looked at the three of us with equal suspicion.

"I am," Victor said.

"So you called her a few minutes ago, and here she is. Unless Ms. Bingham took a helicopter from her home, she had to have been in the area when you called. By the way, the gun used inside, we recovered it next to the body. It's the same gun Ms. Bingham registered with the police."

"Of course it is." The words came out of my mouth before I had a chance to censor them.

"You guys make my job so easy," Makina almost laughed, but it came out as more of a sneer. "Move back behind the crime scene tape or I'll have someone arrest you."

This time I moved.

Fifty-eight

The local news channels were on the scene about twenty minutes later, and luckily for me, Andres and Victor freelanced for one of the stations. After a few minutes of chatting with the reporter, Andres came back with what he'd learned.

"Single victim, male. Gunshot wound to the head," he said.

"Oh, God." Vera turned pale. "Are you sure?"

"Vera, where were you when Victor called?" I asked.

"On the Eisenhower, on my way here," she said. "Doug called me. He said he was all right, but he asked for a favor. He needed me to bring him some money. He can't access his accounts right now because he's being watched."

"How much money?"

"Just a few thousand dollars," she said. "Three."

"In cash?" Victor seemed astounded.

"No," she said. "I got a bank draft and then I came out here to meet him. He said he needed to get some things."

"Did he say what happened at the apartment in Wrigleyville?" I asked her.

"He said someone is after him."

"Who?"

"Kate," Vera said, seemingly exasperated, "I didn't interrogate him. He said he needed help, so I came to help him."

"Why did he come back here if someone is after him?" Victor asked.

"His passport." I said it at the same time Vera said it.

"He told me that I was safe as long as I stayed away from him," Vera added.

"Except when he wants you to bring him money." Andres was angry. He gets all big-brother protective sometimes, and I was alternately touched and amused by it. But this time I was in agreement. Doug was either trying to set Vera up as the killer or get her killed.

The thought must have occurred to Vera, because suddenly she started to cry. Victor put his arm around her and led her farther down the street. I was glad she was out of earshot, because what I wanted to talk about wasn't pretty.

"That doesn't make sense," I said. "A gunshot to the head sounds like a suicide."

"Or a professional," Andres countered.

"Either way, at least we can make Makina see that it's not Vera. If she got a bank draft this afternoon, she has an alibi. And since it's likely that whoever killed Doug killed Erik, she's off the hook."

"And if he killed himself," Andres said, finishing the thought, "it's evidence of guilt."

"That would be tidy."

"Assuming the victim is Doug."

"Well, if it isn't, then Doug has to be the killer." I let out a breath, tried to calm myself. The adrenaline that had started with the call from the neighbor was still in control of my system. "Either way, it's really a win-win for us."

There was movement from Doug's front porch. Cops were gathering. I saw the news cameras moving closer to the scene. I looked at Andres. "I'll get what I can," he said, "but at this angle, it's going to be crap."

"Doesn't matter. Ralph Johnson is getting the Business Channel doc of the century."

"He'll probably want a murder in every one we do." Andres laughed and moved in for his shot. Knowing the way cable TV is going, Andres wasn't far off.

The small tidbit from the local news was the last piece of information we got. The police weren't talking and Makina glared at me anytime I even came close to the police tape. Andres had a parent-teacher conference at his son's school, so after another hour, we called it a day. Victor offered to spend the evening with Vera in case she needed to cry, or talk—things Victor was much better at handling than I was. Andres dropped me at the auto shop, where I paid more than five hundred dollars to get the car running. The heat would have to wait.

I tried Dugan again, but nothing had changed since the afternoon. No incoming calls were allowed on the cellblock where Tim and Brick lived. I left a message for Joanie, but she'd gone home for the day.

\\\

When I got back to the house, my phone was ringing. I picked up to Ellen saying, "Oh good, you're home." Then she clicked off.

Ten minutes later she was at my door. "Don't say this isn't a good time," she told me as she walked in. "I've brought groceries and a few other things."

"Why did you bring groceries? I can shop for myself."

"Last time I was here, there were takeout cartons everywhere." She opened my refrigerator and pointed out the contents to me as if she were entering evidence at my trial. Old milk, leftover General Tso's chicken, and a quarter pound of Fannie May fudge.

"Listen, Ellen, I'm in the middle of this story, and it looks like another person has been killed. I'm not sure if it's suicide—"

"For heaven's sake, Kate, what is your obsession with death? You do realize that it's just your way of dealing with Frank's death, don't you? You need to exercise some control over other people's lives, because recent events have made your own life feel so out of your control."

I was about to disagree, but there was a certain amount of truth to it. Besides, I've never once won an argument with Ellen. I changed the subject. "What did you bring me?"

"Food. Actual food." She filled my freezer with portioned meals she'd made, and added fresh fruit and vegetables to my fridge. She replaced the milk with a quart that was still drinkable, and handed me a brownie from a dozen or more that were in a Tupperware container. "The kids made these for you."

"Tell them thanks," I said.

"Tell them yourself. Come over for dinner anytime," she said. She put a dish of chicken and mashed potatoes into the microwave and sat down with me at the kitchen table. "So what's this about someone committing suicide?"

"It's this crazy show," I said, then I told her about Vera and the restaurant and the real identity of the man who'd been standing on my lawn. My mother always used to say sisters have a unique bond, which was just her way of trying to get Ellen and me to stop fighting. But she was also right. No one in the world drove me crazier than Ellen, but I could trust her to be honest with me in a way no one else would be. And honesty was what I needed even more than carefully portioned meals.

"Man, you get in the middle of things," she said with what I hoped was a little bit of envy. "I'd say get the hell out of it, but it's too late for that now." She opened up the Tupperware and bit into a brownie as I ate the chicken and mashed potatoes. "I think it's interesting that both of the women involved in the restaurant are getting undermined by the men," she said. "That Vera woman is obviously too insecure to go five seconds without a man—"

"That's a little harsh," I said and was rewarded with an eye roll.

"And the other one, Ilena, she's a minority investor in her own restaurant. Her husband actually controls the purse strings."

"I suppose that's true," I said. It must have irritated Ilena, I realized. The restaurant was Ilena's dream of independence, and Roman had squashed it with his constant presence.

Ellen checked her watch. "Speaking of men, if I don't get home Tony will never put the kids to bed. They pretend to obey, but then they just play in their rooms."

I walked Ellen to the front door. "Thanks," I said. "I can't remember the last time I ate a vegetable that wasn't deep-fried."

She sighed. "I knew Frank as long as you did, Kate. I know he would want you to get on with your life."

"I am," I said. But even I didn't believe it.

"If you could get in a time machine and go back to when you were sixteen, and erase Frank Conway from your life, would you?"

"Of course not. But it would be nice to erase some of my regrets."

"Don't you think you would just have different regrets?" she asked.

"I suppose."

She smiled. "Promise me your next show will be more life affirming than men in prison and murders in restaurants. Maybe a home-decorating show. Those are fun."

Fifty-nine

After Ellen left, I realized I'd forgotten my promise to drive down to check out Tim's story, and considering the situation at Doug's house, I was reluctant to go. But I told myself that it was the most constructive thing I could do until I knew the identity of the dead man.

I called Phil Garrett, the police detective in Peoria. I told him that I was working on a show about Tim Campbell. He'd been on the force for more than twenty years, mainly in homicide, but he didn't even have to think to remember who I was talking about.

"I'll meet you at the station," he said on the phone. "Show you the files. Answer your questions. If you draw a different conclusion than the one I reached, well, then I suppose I'll hear you out."

"Do you think you could have been wrong about him?" I asked.

"No, ma'am. I think I have the right boy for the murder. But if you know different . . ."

"I don't," I said. "I'm just making sure."

"Uh-huh. Well, tomorrow at nine, then."

He hung up before I had a chance to suggest a later time. Peoria is three hours from Chicago. Getting up at five a.m. might be a small price to pay for proving a man innocent of murder, but it's still a price.

Even though it was only seven thirty, I got ready for bed. Just a few weeks ago I was routinely going to bed early. Now it felt that there was too much going on, too many people to think about. Brick's warning, Tim's innocence, Doug's possible murder, Vera's emotional state. I sat on the edge of the bed and opened the drawer. I took out Frank's picture from its hiding spot under a mass market paperback.

"I'm chasing bad guys and possibly springing an innocent man from prison," I told the image of Frank.

I don't know what he would have thought. More likely than not, he would have told me to mind my own business. "Let the cops worry about bad guys," he would have said. "And by the way, we're supposed to go to my folks' for dinner this Saturday. I told my mom you'd make dessert." And that would have been the end of the discussion.

Or maybe he would have been proud. Maybe he would have talked over the details with me, gone over theories the way that I'd just done with Ellen. I'd uncovered so much about Frank after he died, I didn't know how he would feel about my life now.

I looked over at the other person in the picture, me just a few years ago. Would the woman in that photo have been proud of how I was handling my life? Or would she have seen me as stuck, afraid that moving ahead meant leaving Frank behind? I don't know. I glanced up and saw my reflection in the mirror across from the bed. One thing was sure.

"She would have said you look like shit."

I got up, headed into the bathroom, and opened up the box of Nice 'n Easy.

\\\

The next morning I woke up at five a.m., took a quick shower, and put on some makeup. I looked for a sweater that wasn't completely shapeless, and found a black cashmere V-neck that Ellen had given me for Christmas. She could be annoying as hell, especially when she was right, but she had good taste. I pulled on a pair of jeans and my favorite black half boots, and even added earrings. My hair was still in need of a cut, but the gray was gone.

"Getting there," I said to the mirror. "A facial, some eyebrow reshaping, and an exercise program and I might be okay."

I popped in a Dan Fogelberg CD as soon as I got on I-55, trying to get myself in a Peoria state of mind. It didn't work. As I passed the exit for Dugan, I made one more attempt to reach Tim and Brick. Instead I got Joanie Rheinbeck.

"I thought you were done shooting," she said.

"I am. I'm just concerned about the inmates I interviewed."

"I told the warden it was a bad idea, your coming here," she said. "It riles them up, gives them ideas. It's hard enough when family visits and reminds them of the outside. You were getting them to talk about the past."

"Are they okay?"

"Look, Kate, I'm sure you'll do a good job with this piece, but I just want to get things back to normal."

Then she hung up.

\\\

I got to the Peoria police station at just a few minutes after nine. Phil Garrett was waiting for me. He was a large man, near retirement age but still powerful-looking.

"Mrs. Conway," he said as he stretched out his hand. "I've been regretting agreeing to this ever since we spoke."

"Why?"

"Sad case," he said. He showed me to an empty interrogation room, where several file boxes were sitting on the table. "J. Campbell" was written in black marker across each box.

"She was very young," I said.

"And pregnant."

"And a drug addict. It can't be unusual for someone in her circumstances to meet an untimely death."

I sat across from Garrett at the table and waited as he pulled out the crime scene photos, pushing them over to me one by one. Jenny was lying in a pool of blood, her eyes open, her arms outstretched and marked by stab wounds. Near her was a kitchen sink with dishes and food in it, and the floor next to her body was black with dirt. It's always sad to look at crime scene photos, but this beautiful girl dead next to garbage made the photos almost painful to view.

"She was from a nice family," Garrett said. "Her parents were good people. Not rich, not poor, just good people."

"Like Tim Campbell's family," I said.

He seemed confused. "Campbell's family?"

"His father was an accountant for Caterpillar. Wasn't he?"

"Campbell tell you that?"

"Yeah."

"Ma'am, I don't know how you feel about Tim Campbell, but if I may say so, I think he's full of shit. Pardon my language."

I looked at Garrett, and knew what was coming. This was why I was here, I reminded myself. "Why?"

"His father is doing time in a federal prison. His mother is dead, at least I think she is. She was a drug addict, same as her son. Left the family when the husband went to prison. Hasn't been seen since."

I let it settle in my mind. Tim had lied. Not just about Jenny, but about his whole life. It didn't shock me. Somewhere inside me I'd known the whole time that Tim was, as Brick had warned me, just another con artist. Still, it left me feeling empty.

"What really happened?" I asked.

"The night of the murder? Oldest reason in the book."

"She was leaving him?"

"The other old reason."

"Money?"

He nodded. "Jenny turned tricks to make drug money. Once she found out she was pregnant she decided to stop, clean herself up. That's what she told their neighbor."

"Cody Daniels."

"That's the one."

"Tim said Cody was their drug dealer. He said Cody tried to rape Jenny and that's how she was killed."

Garrett frowned. "Cody Daniels was dealing. Though he probably used more than he sold. He used to get into trouble, bar fights and the like, right up until one night about three years before Jenny's murder when he pissed off the wrong guy and got shot for his trouble. He ended up in a wheelchair and he's been there ever since."

"So you're saying he couldn't have forced himself on Jenny?"

"He's got the use of his arms, so he could have grabbed at her, but nothing below the waist works on Cody, and frankly, ma'am, Jenny could have gotten away from him quick if she wanted."

"But your version is that Tim stabbed her in front of a witness?"

"That's what Cody said. Tim got mad that Jenny wouldn't go out that night, earning. They got into a fight. He picked up a knife and he went after her with it. She locked herself in the bedroom until Tim calmed down, then she came out again thinking it had blown over. That's when he stabbed her multiple times, even while she was on the floor, helpless. Cody said Jenny raised her hand to Tim as she was dying." He raised his arm in just the same way Tim had during our first interview. Then, like Tim, he let it drop. "She tried to hold his hand but Tim pushed it away and just watched her die."

"What was Cody doing there?"

"Waiting for his money. He told Tim that there wouldn't be any more drugs until he was paid what he was owed. Tim told him that Jenny would get the money that night, but of course, she wouldn't do it and things just got out of control real quick." He shook off the memory of it. "Tragic. All round. That Tim Campbell was a smart fellow. A psychopath, but as bad guys go, he was okay, if that makes any sense. Respectful, smart. Maybe could have been someone under other circumstances." He smiled sadly. "Tim was always looking for someone to latch onto, like a drowning man. Trouble is Campbell doesn't get saved. He takes the other person down with him."

I don't think he meant it as a warning, but I took it as one. I never had to go back to Dugan. I could throw the temporary cell phone in the trash and move on without ever confronting Tim about his lies. What good would it do, anyway? But I knew I wouldn't leave it alone. I wanted the confrontation I deserved, and I wanted it on tape.

Garrett reached into the box one more time and pulled out another photo. "Her high school graduation photo," he said. Jenny had straight brown hair, caramel brown eyes, and a friendly smile. A cheerleader type, except for a slightly sallow complexion that suggested to me she'd already found drugs.

"She was very pretty."

He nodded. "Too easy to forget the victim."

"Maybe I could get a copy of this," I said. "For the show. It's about Tim's time in prison, but it would be nice to have a reminder of why he's there."

Sixty

After I left the station, I looked for an address near the university. Angela Thompson, Tim's young cousin, or whoever she was, had given that address when she signed in to the visitors log. I wasn't sure what she could tell me, but I was here, so I thought I might as well ask her a few questions.

The neighborhood looked a little run down, but Angela's house was tidy. Maybe in need of some paint, but clean and well cared for. She was out front, building a snowman with a child no more than three. When I pulled up she waved, then realized I wasn't someone she knew and seemed to shrink a little.

"Do you remember me?" I asked as I approached her.

She looked at me a long time. "The TV lady?"

"Yes. Tim Campbell introduced us."

"I remember. I don't want to do any interviews. Tim said you were trying to get him to give you all the gory details on his wife's death," she said. "Said it made for good television."

"It would," I told her. "He said you were his cousin, but that isn't true, is it?"

"He didn't want you bothering me."

"You're the mother of his child." I pointed down to the little boy.

"Tim doesn't get conjugal."

"But it can be arranged, if you give money to the right person. A few minutes in a closet," I said.

"Is that what you're here about? Because it's none of your business." She wrapped her arm around her son.

"No. I'm here about Tim." I looked at the woman, so young and small-looking. She didn't look like a drug addict or a woman in crisis. Just lonely and stupid. Easy prey for the likes of Tim Campbell. He must have thought the same about me.

"What do you want to know about Tim?" she asked.

"How did you meet him?"

She smiled. "Online. There's places that inmates can post and if you want you can write 'em; you can. My girlfriend met her husband that way. He just got out after five years in Pontiac, and I figured it was worth a try. I saw Tim's post and I thought he sounded nice, you know, sweet. So I wrote."

"But he's in prison for the rest of his life."

She shrugged. "Maybe. Tim's got someone helpin' him. Some rich lady that helps wrongfully convicted people. But even if she doesn't get him out, we love each other and we'll manage."

"How does your family feel about your being with someone in prison?"

"I'm an orphan. Like Tim," she said. "We have that in common. That's how I knew I could trust him."

I debated whether to set her straight, but I knew it was pointless. She wouldn't believe me, and even if she did, Tim could find a way to justify his lies and she'd find a way to believe him. But if I couldn't tell her anything useful, maybe she could help me.

"Angela," I said, "Tim told me that you bring him things. Things he can't get in prison."

She turned red. "I don't know what you're talking about."

"It's okay. I'm not going to put it on TV. It's just that he asked me since I was coming to Peoria anyway, if you had anything that I could bring into the prison. You won't be there for a while. . . ."

She took a breath. "I usually just bring him some money, and a little weed," she said. "I don't know if he wants any more of that other stuff."

"What other stuff?"

"Magnesium citrate. It's to help Tim, you know, with constipation. They don't give him anything at the prison, so he suffers, poor thing."

"He really depends on you," I said. She lit up at that. "I think you're all that's keeping him sane. Maybe you and that little guy." I pointed to her son. "What's his name?"

"Tim junior," she said. "I think he looks just like him, but Tim says he favors me. But he's only seen him in pictures."

I patted the boy's head. "When did you bring the magnesium citrate to Tim? I can get him more if he's run out."

"The last visit."

"The day we met?"

"No, the day before. He had me go to a store near my hotel and get it. It was a bitch sneaking it into the prison. I had to pour it into sandwich bags and hide 'em in my bra," she said. "I've done it for him before. He really goes through the stuff. The constipation, it keeps him from going to work at the library sometimes, and he hates that." She shifted her weight and looked me over. "You can probably just walk it in, bein' in TV."

"Probably," I said. "I'll ask him if he needs it."

Magnesium citrate is used for constipation, so maybe Tim was telling the truth. Or maybe he'd added a couple of doses to Brick's morning juice the day I called the prison about seeing Brick for visitation. I'd said I was coming alone, without Victor or Andres or a camera. I was a lonely widow kind enough to bring Brick a dozen books just to get a good interview, and Tim knew that. I could only imagine what he'd hoped to get out of me with claims of innocence.

I didn't really have any other questions, so I said good-bye and headed to my car, but something hit me as I opened the driver's-side door. "Did Tim ever tell you he played the violin?" I asked.

She looked puzzled. "No. Why?"

"No reason. Did he tell you he played any instrument?"

"No. Tim was in the choir in high school, just like I was."

"It's like you were meant to be."

She giggled. "Isn't it?"

I watched her turn back to her son and add a scarf to the snowman, then I drove a couple of blocks in search of the expressway. I saw Avanti's, the restaurant Tim had mentioned as the place he wanted to get his last meal. I stopped in and got some pizza bread to go. The bread had a sweetness to it that went great with the salty cheese, and I finished it quickly. It was good, really good. And it was one of the only things Tim had said that turned out to be true.

Sixty-one

I stopped a few times on the way back to Chicago, getting coffee or gas, going to the bathroom, checking e-mails . . . anything to delay returning home. I was fighting with myself. The small part of me that believed in human decency was getting pummeled by the large part that knew better. Hadn't I worked enough true crime to have seen right through Tim? The fact that there had always been doubt was no comfort, because it wasn't so much that I'd believed him; it was that I'd wanted to believe him. That made me a sucker for a happy ending, an intolerable fault in my line of work.

I tried Vera on the way, but she hadn't learned anything more about what had happened to Doug and started crying whenever I tried to ask her questions, so I suggested she call her attorney and see if he could get information for her, and I got off the phone as quickly as possible.

I kept mulling over whether to call Dugan again, whether to try to see Tim. Despite my first reaction after I'd learned the truth, I knew that confronting a liar isn't as satisfying as it should be. People sometimes sputter, occasionally break down in tears, but more often than not, they just attack, weaving a new set of lies and leaving the confronter feeling confused. Even if I could get into Dugan, I told myself it wasn't worth the effort.

The thing about Tim, and me, and all other practiced liars is there's always a nugget of fact in there somewhere, a hint of truth that's just enough to make the rest plausible. Even the stories about a girl finding her prince make the point that true love matters more than beauty or castles or family connections. It covers the lie that love conquers all, that it never dies, and that once you find the man of your dreams you'll never be lonely again.

For Tim, even in a story that was an elaborate fiction of loving son and grieving husband, that nugget of fact was Jenny's outstretched arm. And maybe the sad, harsh reality that drugs had put him on the path to prison.

For Erik, the truth was that vision for Club Car. The friends, the glamour, the restaurants in New York and Paris, they were his invention. Walt's truth was his desire to run his own kitchen from the ground up, Ilena's that she wanted money of her own, Roman's that he was a legitimate businessman, and Doug's that he wanted adventures that had so far eluded him. But each one covered lies, and hiding behind one of those lies was a murderer.

I used to think that people lied for a lot of reasons, but on the drive home I saw that Brick was right. They lied for only a few. And they killed for the same ones. Love, hunger, sex, fear. Love turned into obsession, hunger into greed, sex into jealousy, and fear into hatred. Whoever had killed Erik had done it for one of those reasons.

\\\

As I pulled onto my street, tired and ready to collapse, I had a change of heart. I drove past my house and toward Area Four headquarters. I waited for Detective Makina at reception.

"Another interview?" he asked when he saw me. "Because I really don't have time for that. I've got a second homicide in the Club Car case."

"It isn't Doug. The man who was shot at the house," I said. I was guessing, but in my gut I knew I was right.

Makina stared at me. "How do you know that?"

"Doug wanted adventure, excitement. That isn't motive for murder. But he stumbled into some financial fraud. He talked to Walt. He talked to Ilena. Then Erik ended up dead. He must have panicked when he heard. He ran," I said.

"I'm with you so far. So why don't you think he's the vic in the Oak Park house?"

"Because Doug went back there. He's a careful guy. He's never been on the run before, so he needed help from people, from Walt and Vera. But he's not stupid enough to go back to his own house unless he felt it was safe. He would have just sent Vera to get his passport. He went himself because he was sure nothing would happen to him. Maybe because he knew Erik's killer was already dead."

Makina looked impressed. "It was Roman Papadakis. One shot to the back of the head, execution style."

"Did Doug kill him?"

"You can ask him yourself."

"Is he under arrest?" I asked Makina.

"Not yet. He's guilty of something, but I can't figure out yet if it's murder. I'm going to let him sit in interrogation until he lawyers up or figures out he's free to go."

"Can I talk to him?"

"Are you going to tell him I can't hold him without cause?"

"As far as I'm concerned, you can keep him here indefinitely," I said. "Just promise I can get it on tape if he does something stupid."

"Just as long as I don't have to get back on camera, you can have anything you like." He smiled. It looked as if he was out of practice, but it was definitely a smile. He pointed toward interrogation, and I moved quickly before he changed his mind.

Makina led me to a small, stuffy room with a wooden table and four chairs. Doug was sitting alone at the corner. He looked up at me, then burst into tears. I sat opposite Doug. Makina stayed near the door, watching. I knew Makina was giving me leeway, something that could be revoked at any minute, but I also knew he was using me, hoping I could pry something out of Doug that he couldn't.

Doug was a pathetic figure. He looked tired, he was unshaven, his clothes were wrinkled. If he'd been trying to fake the look of a man frightened for his life, this would be it. But I didn't think he was faking. His hands were trembling and his skin was pale.

"You didn't kill Erik," I said.

Doug shook his head.

"But you set Vera up to take the fall. You made sure she had a gun. You made sure she was at the restaurant."

"I . . . I—" More sobbing.

"Let me try and guess, and you tell me if I'm right," I said.

Doug nodded.

"You got involved in the restaurant. You helped get investors. Were Ilena and Roman secretly selling off their shares?"

"No," Doug said. Then more tears.

"Okay, so these other investors, the ones you got with Ilena, they were extra. You were selling shares that didn't exist. Maybe a hundred and fifty, two hundred percent of the restaurant." Doug nodded, so I continued. "That's why you didn't go to the police after Erik was killed. You knew that his killer was after you, but if you told the police what you knew, you could go to prison."

My guess was five years in Dugan wasn't on Doug's bucket list.

"This wasn't your idea, Doug," I said. "But you let yourself get talked into it. One small lie, but it kept getting bigger, kept getting worse."

"You don't know what that's like," he said.

"I know exactly what that's like."

Makina stepped forward. "Who killed Erik?"

"Roman," Doug said.

"And you killed Roman?" Makina asked. "Was it self-defense?"

"I didn't kill Roman. I found him like that. And then I ran." Doug took a halting breath. "When Erik stormed off after he fought with Vera, Roman told me he'd buy out my shares. He'd buy out Vera. He insisted on it. Roman's a dangerous guy."

"So you wanted to have a gun to protect yourself," I said. "Why not get one yourself? Why get Vera to buy it?"

Doug looked away. A little of the helplessness was gone. "It was just in case something went wrong. I didn't think I'd need it, but if I did, I didn't want it traced back to me," he said. I couldn't picture Doug going up against Roman, but it was his fantasy. "I'd planned everything out. I was supposed to meet Roman at the restaurant. I told Vera to come about twenty minutes after I was supposed to meet Roman. I told her to park around the corner so she wouldn't be seen. That way Roman wouldn't know she was there until I knew it was safe. I didn't want Vera to get hurt."

"Chivalrous," I said. He was fine with her being a murder suspect, just not a murder victim. If Doug represented the available dating pool, then I was going to be single for a long time.

"If it was safe, then we'd sign some papers," Doug continued. "We'd get our money back. But when I got there, Erik was dead. I knew it had to be Roman, so I ran."

"Leaving Vera to look like she'd killed Erik," I said. "And worse, leaving her to face Roman alone."

"I was scared," he said. "I had to save myself. It's not like we were in love."

"That's your defense?" I nearly jumped over the table to throttle him. "What about the roses? What about number forty-two on the bucket list?"

Doug looked at me but said nothing. Makina grabbed my elbow and escorted me from the room. "Why don't you get some air? Two homicides is enough," he said into my car.

\\\

Vera was waiting at Makina's desk. "Doug is here," she said. "I got a call from my lawyer. He looked into it for me and found that Doug hadn't been killed." She seemed hopeful. I hated to ruin it for her, but there was no choice.

"He's not a good guy," I said. Vera looked past me toward interrogation. I was half-afraid she'd run back there, looking for him. "Just trust me, Vera."

She looked at me for a long time. If I'd had a camera, I would have shot the play of emotions across her face in slow motion. Eventually she just looked resigned. "Okay." She didn't look back at interrogation again.

We walked out of the station together. Despite the five hundred bucks, my car wouldn't start. I left it in the parking lot and Vera offered me a ride. She didn't ask any questions, even when I made several phone calls and asked her to drive me to Club Car instead of bringing me home.

Sixty-two

It took an hour to get everything arranged. Andres and Victor moved boxes around, placing the camera nearby but keeping it completely out of sight.

"There," Andres instructed me as he pointed toward the oven. "Don't block the shot; don't move from that spot."

"Got it."

"We'll be right outside. We have a monitor plugged into the camera, so we'll see everything, but monitors don't have sound, so I won't be able to hear."

"I know."

Andres took one last look and me, then shook his head. Victor was arranging Vera's wireless mic so it was hidden. "This is nuts. It's a damn cable business show."

"I'm not really doing this for the show," I said for the tenth time. "I'm doing it so Makina will have proof of the real killer." I smiled. "But it will make a nice ending to the piece."

Andres and Victor left out the back door of the kitchen into an alley that was probably crawling with rats. I knew they'd be crouched in a corner, watching, in case I needed them. I was a lucky producer. Some camera crews gripe about just doing overtime.

I made a call and explained that I wanted to talk and would be at the restaurant in twenty minutes. Then Vera and I took a walk around the block to make it seem as though we were just arriving. By the time we got back, Ilena was in the kitchen, sitting on a stool and carefully arranging and rearranging the knives. She was, once again, dressed impeccably, in a brown tweed skirt, beige crewneck sweater, and a Hermès scarf tied around her neck, nearly hiding a pearl necklace.

I stood by the oven as I was supposed to, and positioned Vera next to me. With Ilena in front, the three of us formed a tight triangle. Perfect for the shot, but odd-looking given the size of the kitchen. Ilena didn't seem to notice.

"Was the restaurant always a scam?" I asked.

"What are you talking about?" She held a paring knife. It glistened.

"This was your chance at freedom," I said. "But, as my sister pointed out, Roman took that away from you by getting so involved. I just found out from Doug that Roman was trying to buy off the few shares that he didn't already have."

"And this is what? Blackmail?" She laughed. "How adorably sinister." She looked toward Vera. "Do you really need the money?"

"I'm tired of being treated like a ditzy heiress," Vera said, exactly as we'd planned. "Doug dragged me into this mess, conned me out of my money, set me up to be Erik's killer; he even cheated on me with you."

"You didn't lose much," Ilena said. "He's very dull."

"That's not really the point," I said. "Look, Ilena, you got screwed over by the man you loved. So did I. And now it looks like Vera's joined the club. We're not here to blackmail you. We're here to help you. You're going to need to get out of the country fast, before the police find you. You won't be able to access funds until you're somewhere safe. Vera has money, and I know people. I've done stories on faking an identity."

Ilena studied my face. I looked sincere, like a friend ready to help. Just like I always do when I'm interviewing someone. "What's in it for you?" she asked.

I knew I couldn't pretend altruism, so I went for a lie that, coming from me, would sound self-serving enough to be true. "I'm going to give you a camcorder. When you get settled, I want you to record your version of events and send it to me. No return address. You get away and I get an ending to my story that will get me noticed."

She smiled, if you could call it that. There was no joy in it, but there was approval. "Roman hated you," she said. "He couldn't intimidate you, and he hated it when he couldn't scare people. Especially women."

"Then the bastard got what he deserved," Vera improvised. I knew she was just playing along, but maybe somewhere there was a self-preserving bitch buried deep. I was a little proud, like a teacher watching a student cross the platform on graduation day.

"I need to know what happened," I said to Ilena. "If I'm going to put together a story, I'll need your side of things."

Ilena's shoulders relaxed a little. "I intended it to be real," she said.

"I met Erik at Shoulders, where he was working as the manager. He had vision. We were going to do something amazing." She blinked away a tear. "Roman promised me he would put up some money but stay out of it. He wasn't even listed as an official owner. I really thought . . ." Her voice trailed off, then got strong again. "I lined up Doug to get investors. And he brought me that silly woman who asked all those questions." She pointed to Vera, who, to her credit, didn't seem to care about the insult.

"And you thought threats would put an end to them?" I asked.

"She seemed less formidable than she turned out to be," she said. "She even had you wrapped around her little finger."

That made me smile. Vera was, in her own way, more strong willed than I. "When did it change from being a real restaurant to being a way to get money?"

"You saw it," she said. She was so calm, almost distracted. "Roman took over. Made every decision. Hounded everyone. Insisted on Walt. Canceled the uniforms Erik and I had chosen. Then Walt started playing silly games the way all chefs do, angling for more money. Roman gave him three of my points." She looked at me, anger and fear mixed with a determination that frightened me. "It was supposed to be my business, and Roman was handing it out to a prima donna fry cook. He and Walt started teaming up against me. They wanted it to be their restaurant. Little by little, they were pushing me out."

"So if you couldn't have the restaurant, then you'd have the money," I said.

She nodded. "I asked Doug to get me more investors. We found ten people, civilians, to give two hundred and fifty thousand each, in exchange for ten percent of the restaurant. I had set up an account offshore a few years ago, trying to hide what money I could from Roman. We sent money there. I halted construction. I made up stories about wanting the very best of this and that, hoping I could delay by pretending I was waiting for a shipment from some exotic place."

"And with a TV crew doing interviews, it would distract the others and keep you involved."

"That was the plan."

"But if you wanted to get away from Roman, why kill Erik?" Vera asked.

She looked at the spot where Erik had died. "He found out the restaurant wasn't really going to happen. When Roman canceled the uniforms, Erik went back and reordered them. The check bounced. Erik started checking into things. He went to Doug because Doug had been in charge of getting the money. He wanted to know how much money had been raised. And of course, Doug came to me."

"But then Doug made different plans with Roman," I said.

"It was all falling apart. If Erik talked to him, then Roman would figure out that the money was missing, and my last chance at freedom would be gone. I just needed a few days. Just a few more days. I told Erik that," she said. "There would be other restaurants for him. All I needed was to get away. I just needed to get the last of the investors' money. I'd earned it after twenty years of hell."

"But this was Erik's dream. And you were taking it away from him," I said.

"Why couldn't you do it together?" Vera asked. "You and Roman?"

Ilena laughed. "You are a romantic, aren't you?"

She started to move, so I stepped next to her, keeping her in the shot. I scratched my head, the signal Andres and I had worked out for when it was time to call Makina.

"Roman killed his cousin when they were involved in some legal mess," I said. "He slashed his throat, set his house on fire." I laughed a little. "That was the reference, right? 'Next to be slashed.'"

"I thought you would be more curious," she said. "I thought journalists hunted down stories and you would look into the fire and . . ." She rolled her eyes. "I even told Roman that you were asking questions about his cousin's fire. That pissed him off. I figured he'd do something to you and then you would have to make the connection."

"I'm not really a journalist. I'm a TV producer."

It sounded feeble. I could see Ilena losing energy with each minute that went by. Every ounce of that energy had gone into hating Roman. Now she had nothing left to feed her, and she seemed weak and tired. As we talked, I heard a noise from the front of the restaurant. Makina and his men entering, I assumed. Vera heard it too. Her eyes widened and she looked, for a moment, panicked. But Ilena didn't move. Either she didn't notice, or after everything, she didn't care anymore.

"You provided Roman's alibi for his cousin's murder in exchange for a wedding ring and access to his money," I said. "You figured it was a ticket to an easy life."

"It turned out to be a life sentence," she said. "Roman wanted absolute control over me. Over everything. After Erik's murder, he had the restaurant he wanted, but he still didn't let up. He found out the money was missing. I had no choice. I told him Doug had hacked into Roman's computer and put all of Roman's account numbers on a thumb drive."

"That could have gotten Doug killed," Vera said.

"He deserved it, after agreeing to sell his shares to Roman." She shrugged. "Besides, Roman persuaded me to tell him." She removed the expensive scarf to expose bruises on her neck. "I managed to break a vase over his arm and get away," she said. "But I knew it wasn't over. He planned to have me killed on the opening night of the restaurant. Even the idea that I wanted something separate from him was a betrayal."

Ilena was the "package" Tim had mentioned. He'd been telling the truth about that. I wish people could be made simple—the bitch, the bad boy—the way they are on TV reality shows. That way I wouldn't have to feel sorry for people I disliked, the way I had, temporarily, for Tim. And the way I did now, for Ilena.

"I told him where Doug lived," she continued. "I knew he couldn't stay away, and when he got there, I shot him. I called Doug and got him there too. I told him Roman was dead. I just didn't tell him he was dead in Doug's kitchen."

"You figured you'd have the victim and killer in one neat package," I said.

"It just didn't work out that way. Things never work out the way I plan them." She didn't say anything, but underneath that artificially smooth face she seemed to be crying.

Sixty-three

I walked outside the restaurant. The air was still cold enough to see every exhalation, but it felt good to be outside. Andres had made sure to get footage of Ilena being led away in handcuffs, and Makina was nice enough to let Andres get it from several angles. He made an apology of sorts for having been wrong about Vera. She, of course, didn't hold a grudge. I half-expected her to confess to the lies we'd told, but luckily for me she stopped short of that. There probably wasn't anything Makina could charge us with, but I wasn't willing to take the chance.

After Ilena had been driven off in the back of a squad car, Andres went back inside to check the tape, and Vera and Victor went in search of coffee. Only Makina joined me on the sidewalk.

"Don't you have a suspect to question?" I asked.

"She can wait. I have everything I need on tape." He smiled again, more relaxed this time.

"A copy of the tape," I reminded him.

He lit a cigarette and I watched the smoke drift into the breeze. "How did you know?"

"She was the only one desperate enough to strip away all the bullshit and live by her instincts," I said.

"You never suspected Ms. Bingham?" Makina asked. "Not even for a minute?"

I thought about it. "No. She's the only truly authentic person I've ever met."

I watched Walt park his car in front of the restaurant, get out, and come toward me, smiling. "I'm sorry about Ilena and Roman," he said. "But I'm glad you realize I was innocent, Kate. Maybe now we can actually have a meal where you don't interrogate me."

"Not innocent, Walt," I said. "Just not guilty of murder."

Walt stepped back. "I don't know what you're talking about."

"You knew Roman was going to burn down your old restaurant to free you up for Club Car. Maybe you planned it together."

"That's crazy."

I shook my head. "Your recipe book. You kept it here; you cooked from it here. Your kitchen at home isn't set up for lots of experimentation. If you used it here, then you used it at the old restaurant. The only reason you still have it is because you took it that night, the night of the fire. And the only reason you would do that was to preserve years of collecting."

"You have proof?" Makina asked.

"No," I admitted. "Just gut instinct. But I know he and Roman were partners. I guess Walt's job was to romance me, while Roman tried intimidation."

Walt bit his lip. "If that's all you have, I have a plane to catch. There's a restaurant opening in Seattle. A start-up. I wasn't sure if I should take it, but I think I could use a change of scenery. I'm just here to get my stuff."

Some people never recover from the loss of their dreams, I thought, and some people don't even skip a beat.

Makina dropped his cigarette on the ground and crushed it beneath his shoe. "I got a call the other day from a Tim Campbell. You know him?" he asked.

"He's an inmate at Dugan. One of the guys I'm interviewing. Murdered his wife," I said with emphasis. "Why would he call you?"

"He said he had some information on you. On your involvement in this Erik Price business."

"What information could he have?"

"He said you were covering up for Ms. Bingham. He said you admitted it to him."

That stopped me. I could have asked why, but it took only a second to realize that I didn't have to. Tim knew I'd find out he was lying about his wife's murder. He needed a backup plan. "What does he get out of telling you that?" I asked.

"Transfer out of Dugan. He wanted to go downstate, closer to home," Makina said. "Is it true? Because even if Ms. Bingham didn't commit the homicides, there's still the matter of filing a false police report."

I didn't answer. "You said Tim wanted to go downstate. Past tense. Has he changed his mind?"

There was, just for a moment, the hope that he'd decided to be the good guy he pretended to be. That part of me that was a sucker for a happy ending would not lose easily.

"He's dead," Makina said, his voice flat and a little bored. Just another dead killer. "A couple of days ago he was stabbed by another inmate in a stairway on his block. The camera was broken, so . . ." Makina rolled his eyes. "I guess that means you don't have to answer my question."

My stomach tightened, afraid of the answer to the question I had to ask. "What other inmate?"

"I don't know," Makina said. "But those guys are always sticking each other. It's hard enough out here to solve homicides, but when you got a thousand convicts as suspects? Good as you were with this, even you couldn't find that guy's killer."

Sixty-four

The wind had picked up. There was another storm coming, but I was hoping it would wait until I finished up the shoot. Dugan, on a good day, was isolated. Today, with snow swirling around me and the cold stabbing at my cheeks, it felt like the other side of nowhere.

"You're getting to be a regular," the guard at the desk said when I walked in. "Your crew got here before you. They're already setting up."

"I had a delay," I said. My car, once again, had refused to start. A jump from my neighbor had gotten it going, but I'd spent the whole drive watching a flashing engine light and praying.

The guard buzzed me through the security gate, and Russell greeted me on the other side, leading me back to the same small room where the lawyers meet their clients. The room where I'd first met Tim and Brick.

"I didn't think Joanie would let you guys back in," Russell said. "You must know people."

"The power of television." That, and a promise to the warden that Tim's death would be seen not as a failure of prison security, but as a tragic end for a man who had gone looking for trouble.

"You heard about Tim?" Russell said. I nodded. "Don't quite know what to feel," he said. "It's something I ought to be used to by now, but somehow I just didn't see this coming."

I did. At least it felt like I should have. If I'd been paying more attention, maybe I could have stopped it. Or maybe I was wrong. I got some small comfort from that.

\\\

Andres looked up at me as I walked into the room. "We're all set up," he said. "Ready whenever you are."

"I'll get your man," Russell said, and left the three of us to stare at each other.

"How's Vera?" Andres asked.

"Fine," I said. "Better now that she's not a murder suspect. She just needs some rest and a few distractions."

"We can provide that," Victor said. "Tomorrow night. Don't bail on me, Kate."

"I'm coming to your show, Victor. Promise. Ten o'clock. Andres, Vera, and me, front row."

"I'll be the one with the earplugs," Andres said.

"I'll be the one with the fabulous new hairdo," I told them. "My sister made another appointment tomorrow afternoon with her stylist. And then she and I are having dinner at my mom's."

"Couldn't get out of it?" Andres asked.

"Dinner was my idea. Ellen's trying to be helpful. And she hasn't been entirely wrong," I admitted.

Andres laughed. "Mark this on your calendar, Victor. Kate said she was wrong about something."

"And get this," I said. "Ralph at the Business Channel went crazy for the footage we brought. We're going to get a lot of business from him."

"Wow, more shows about pretentious idiots opening restaurants." Victor rolled his eyes. "Makes being a murder suspect worth all the trouble."

I laughed.

"You guys are having a time." Brick walked in the room with Russell. He was cuffed, legs and hands.

"Is that necessary?" I asked Russell.

"Just a precaution we're taking with every inmate while we investigate Tim's death," Russell said. "I can remove them for the interview."

"You don't know who did it?" I was asking Russell, but I was looking at Brick.

"Probably never will," Russell said. "But we go through the motions."

Brick sat in the chair facing mine, waited for Russell to remove the cuffs, and then relaxed. "You got the killer," he said.

"Channel Nine news?"

"That's right. They said the police nabbed the lady, but I knew it was you figured it out."

"I'm smart that way. But sometimes I'm a little late."

There was a slight smile, but it quickly disappeared. "I was sorry about Tim," he said. "But from what I heard, he messed up with some people on the inside. Messed with people's food—you know what I'm talking about. The guards found shit in his cell that makes people sick."

"So that's the reason."

"You think there was another reason?"

I took a deep breath and looked at Brick. There was no emotion in his eyes, no warmth. It was as if a window had opened for a brief time and now it was closed. "Caring about people is a slippery slope," I said. "But I couldn't live with the idea—"

"You don't have to." His voice was firm. The subject was over. "Do me a favor, Kate," he said.

"You want more books?"

"Don't come back to Dugan. Don't be thinkin' about me or Tim or anything about this place. Just walk outta here and keep going."

Most of my interview subjects ask me to keep in touch. Some of them just shake my hand and say good-bye. No one had ever asked me never to contact them again.

"Okay, Brick." I asked him for one last statement about the death of his fellow inmate, something I could use on the show.

"Someone told me that when Tim was confronted," he said, "he didn't fight. He just opened up his arms and smiled. I think maybe he was happy to be done with all this."

"Maybe."

"I don't think deep down he was all bad. I think he had regrets," Brick continued. "His mistake was not dealing with his present situation. Not facin' the reality of it. You want to survive, you have to let go of the past. Let go of what coulda been."

Andres turned off the camera. Brick got up and I did too. I shook his hand and held it for just a second longer than necessary. "I hope . . ." I left the sentence unfinished.

Russell handcuffed Brick and they left. Andres, Victor, and I just stood for a moment.

"It will be a good show," Andres said. "You got some great bites."

"And Tim's death adds a nice finish to it," I said, trying to sound like a producer. "So I guess we got lucky."

"I wasn't going to say that."

"I know," I said, "but someone will."

\\\

We packed up the lights and camera. The guys loaded everything into the van in the parking lot. The wind was picking up and the temperatures were dropping.

"I don't think we'll make it home before the storm," I said.

"I'll drive behind you," Andres said. "If that car breaks down again you're going to need someone to take you home."

I looked at my ten-year-old dented blue Toyota, the car Frank had said would last until our twentieth wedding anniversary. "Actually, you can follow me to the dealership near my house," I said. "It's time for something new."

THE KATE CONWAY MYSTERY SERIES
FROM CLARE O'DONOHUE

Kate Conway's divorce might have been killing her, but it certainly didn't make her kill her husband—so how can she convince the police?

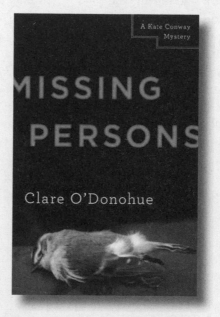

ISBN 978-0-452-29706-7

Available wherever books are sold.

VISIT WWW.CLAREODONOHUE.COM

Plume
A member of Penguin Group (USA) Inc.
www.penguin.com

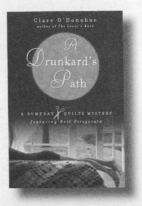